THE UNSEELIE KING AND I

FAE-TED KINGS
BOOK 2

MILANA JACKS

INTRODUCTION

The events in this book happen between the last chapter and the epilogue of the The Royal Obsession, book 1 in the Fae-ted Kings series.

1

AUGUSTA

Cecile flips her red hair and leans over the railing of the upper ballroom floor, positioning her body so that her breasts lift to attract a male's gaze.

Particularly one male's.

The commander of the Summer fae armies, the same male whose attention I'm trying to garner.

Not that it matters to him. While Cecile has had some luck with the commander, the most I ever got from him was that one time he took a lock of my hair and sniffed it.

I interpreted it as a gesture indicating interest, and I followed my eldest sister June from our boring farm in the mountains down to the Summer Court, where she enchanted none other than our heart-stopping king. Me? I went on rejecting suitors, keeping myself available for the commander in case he became interested.

But as the summer nears its end and I grow more desperate, so does Cecile. In fact, most singles at the party tonight will try to hook up with someone. Tonight's event precedes a series of events that will take place right before the royal wedding, and I'm out of time to snag the commander's affections for this mating season.

Too bad he's the only male in the world who can resist the charms of fae females in heat. Maybe he likes males. "Oh!" I say out loud.

My middle sister, Julie, flips her brown curls over her shoulder. "Oh ho ho." She rubs her hands together. "Did you have a vision?"

"I had a thought."

Julie's eyes sparkle from a few glasses of champagne. "Do tell."

"The commander like males."

Cecile shakes her head. "He does not."

"How do you know?" The moment I ask, I regret it. Although I can't see into the future, meaning I can't see what she'll tell me, Cecile is so mean, she might be an Unseelie fae who got swapped at birth and deposited next door to my parents' house for all I know.

"Because"—Cecile plays with the end of her braid—"he visits Klen's Brothel."

"He does?" Julie and I screech, then cover our mouths as people who were whispering in various parts of the upper floor above the massive foyer start moving toward us.

Cecile, loving the attention and knowing she has the ear of pretty much every fae within reach, leans in conspiratorially. "Monique said that Lady Grech and her sister said they saw our dear commander leaving Klen's just this morning."

"How did you already hear about it?"

She scoffs. "I pay to stay informed."

Julie and I stare.

"What? I like staying in the know."

"Where did you get the coin?" We're poor, as in my father piled up debt on his back just to dress us for the court this summer. Cecile is our next-door neighbor, who's no better off than my family.

She shrugs. "Here and there. But the point is, it's not the commander. The seer serves the crown, Augusta. Maybe he was interested in you before, but now that you're the royal seer, he can't touch you."

"Why not?"

"Because..." My sister clears her throat. "June slipped and told me the king forbade anyone from so much as looking at you."

I expel a breath, and all my hopes deflate. No wonder the commander is uninterested in me. Not only am I almost nineteen, I'm also inexperienced and those fae at Klen's ride him three ways from sundown, now I'm also forbidden. And while forbidden fruit sounds delicious to me, the commander would never disobey his king. He's the most loyal, most honorable male I've ever met. It's part of what makes him so appealing.

Sulking in my newfound self-pity, I prop my chin on my palm and my elbow on the railing.

"Ladies don't sulk or slouch," comes from behind me. I startle and spin to see El'jah, the Summer prince. He's wearing a one-piece golden suit with black boots that reach midthigh and a black blazer with two tapered tails reaching just past the back of his knees. He winks at me, and his blue eyes twinkle, setting my heart and every heart in the vicinity aflutter.

Few are immune to El'jah's charm. "One..." He lifts a finger. "The commander isn't into males. Trust me, I know these things."

Dramatically, I drop my shoulders even more, as if moping.

"Awww," El'jah says as he pats my head. "You poor thing.

Look up, I have number two." He lifts the second finger. "Don't be the dog who spends the last summer cycle of heat we have left barking up the wrong tree. A male worthy of all this"—he eyes me in that way of his that makes me feel both attractive and wanted—"virginal hotness will come for you."

"You think so?"

"You tell me." He pokes my forehead. "You're the seer."

Eh. The seer. On one occasion, I shared a terrible vision of my sister June that happened to randomly arise in my brain, and now the king thinks I'm a seer. Since foresight is one of the, if not the most, coveted forms of magic in the world, the king proclaimed me the royal seer.

Although I tried to tell him I'd love to have magical powers I could use to predict the future, but I simply don't have enough magic to do what he needs of me and what is expected of the royal seer, King Et'enne's title for me stands. There's no chance he'll change his mind.

El'jah takes Julie's and Cecile's hands and walks backward, dragging them away. "I'm taking you single ladies to a party. Yes?"

"Yes, sir," they answer.

"And you, my sweet, virginal seer, must stay, I'm afraid."

Julie blows me a kiss. "Don't wait up for us."

By the time they return, I'll be sleeping. Bored and alone, I head toward the gardens at the back of the Golden Palace.

Fae of all shapes and sizes dressed in bright, stand-out colors, heads crowned with elaborate hairdos adorned with expensive shiny jewels, linger on the winding staircase, sipping champagne from flutes and laughing while sharing gossip of other people's misfortunes.

At the bottom of the stairs, the commander awkwardly holds a champagne flute between his large, gloved fingers.

He doesn't drink while on duty, and knowing him, he's always on duty.

My heart does a nervous flutter as I walk up to him and casually greet him. I bat my eyelashes at his handsome face. "Good evening, Commander."

"Seer."

I used to be Augusta. Now I'm *seer*. The way he says it, though, is special. Crisp. Cold. And with a finality that cuts off further conversation. It's too bad for him I'm not easily scared or shoved away.

"I didn't think you drank on duty."

"He doesn't," a musical voice says, and a female joins us, plucking the flute from his hand. "Thank you." She smiles up at him and flutters her eyelashes. As I watch Fleur, the princess, and take in her beauty, it becomes obvious to me why the commander won't give me or any other female the time of span. It's not only because he's sated at Klen's, but because beautiful fae royalty surrounds him all span long, and in comparison, my appearance is average.

With his looks and station and, I bet, magical power, he can have any female he wants. He just hasn't had any. Not in the court, at least.

"Are you alone?" Fleur asks.

I nod.

"Where is Julie?"

"With your brother."

Fleur smiles knowingly. "Ah. I'm on my way to meet the Unseelie delegation if you would care to join me?"

"Um, no."

She giggles, and the commander chuckles. "Not a fan of the Unseelie?" he asks.

Holy Fates, he's talking to me.

I open my mouth to answer, but I'm too awestruck that

he initiated an exchange of words with me that I manage only to blink up at him. The commander frowns, likely wondering what sort of stupid he's chatting with.

"No," I answer after an awkward silence. Both he and Fleur nod, gazes everywhere but on me. The royals and high officers of the Summer Court are polite and hospitable, so neither of these two people will point out what they must perceive to be a lack of social skills. All conversation in the court should flow naturally, not stall. That's the expectation during parties.

We all aim to have a grand time.

Tongue-tied and feeling as if I'm intruding, I see my sister welcoming a long line of guests. Next to her stands our Summer king, arguably the handsomest male in all the fae lands. Out of all the opulence in the palace, I catch him looking at June.

"That is one love, history will write about," Fleur says quietly, privately to me.

"If I ever marry, I would want my king to look at me the way King Et'enne looks at June. But since I can't even answer the male I like who finally spoke to me, kings are not charted in my future. Perhaps I shall remain the virginal Summer seer for the rest of my life. It sure would make King Et'enne happy."

Fleur sips her flute.

The commander stands there in his usual silent manner.

"May I be excused?" I ask politely, not really waiting for anyone to excuse me.

The commander nods, and Fleur smiles. "Of course. I'll see you at the dinner table. We're sitting together." She leaves, and the commander's eyes stray after her retreating figure. It's brief, but I caught it, and it solidifies my fate.

Gah, I want to be more like Fleur in the sense she has all

the freedom that comes from being a female fae of beauty and power. But I can never be like Fleur.

I'm not a princess, and also, a little over a cycle ago, I was working on my family's farm, picking apples for our pig Millie. Now I'm having dinner with Fleur in the Summer Court, which is lorded over by the male who is to marry my oldest sister. There's so much the fates have already blessed me with, and I shan't want for more.

For a little longer, I linger to give the commander a chance to ask where I'm going, or to ask if he could escort me there (in the gardens, where he can kiss me in private), but the commander watches the entrance like one of his birds of prey. Always on duty.

Instead of occupying myself with "the wrong tree," perhaps I should take lessons from the commander and get on with my duty. The seer is supposed to remain alone and chaste so that her powers may grow vast. The Summer king wants to see me develop my powers and not mingle with males. Trouble is, I was born with only a little magic, so the suffering seems unfair.

Turning from the entrance, I walk toward the back of the palace and duck as a flock of pixies rushes out of the back service areas. The kitchens are in chaos, so nobody notices as I walk along the wall all the way to the back. I lift my skirts so I don't step on any porridge that missed the gutters and round the corner, then climb several steps to arrive at the back gardens, my favorite place in the palace.

The décor extends into the gardens as the party will move here after dinner, but for now, only the band is setting up the stage. Right before the gardens, I sit on the same wooden bench that King Et'enne likes to sit on. He says it's because the bench is positioned at a perfect angle that affords him a view of the back of the palace while also allowing him to watch the street before the bridge connecting the Golden Palace to the city.

A convoy of carriages is crossing the bridge. It's the Unseelie delegation arriving, an event everyone is eagerly waiting for.

It will mark the first time in over two centuries that Unseelie delegates have been invited to a party in the Summer Court. It's even more significant because it's our mating season, thus there's a possibility of Seelie and Unseelie coupling.

Not that we would ever couple with them.

"Waiting for someone?" a smooth male voice asks from behind me.

2

AUGUSTA

Magnificent long-maned horses gallop past the bench and distract me from turning around. The horses' hooves are kicking back both fine gravel and a mist of shadows that are said to be constant companions of the Unseelie fae.

I huff out an annoyed breath.

"Something the matter?" the male voice asks.

"Leave it to the Unseelie not to follow our reception protocol."

"What is the formal reception protocol?"

I turn toward the voice, but can't see anyone. "They're supposed to come from the front and not the back." I lean in further to try to make him out.

"They chose their own route."

"I expected them to come from over there, not here, and now I missed seeing the riders."

"Are you waiting on someone?" the male repeats.

"No one in particular."

"Are you sure?" The voice sounds closer, so I turn again.

In the path between the bushes, nothing but darkness registers, and yet I can feel him approaching. The moment I realize I might be chatting with an Unseelie fae, the shadows of the bushes converge, grow thicker and take on the shape of a male.

Standing two heads taller than me, the male has abundant midnight-blue hair that drapes over shoulders as wide as the door to the bedroom I shared with my sisters in our home in the village. The metal-covered neckline on the silver-stitched black-on-black uniform gives an impression of armor, and the silver stars embroidered on the elaborate collar that falls all the way to his navel tell me he's a decorated soldier, perhaps even the Unseelie version of our commander.

The shadows swirling around his leather boots make my breath catch in my throat. With a gasp, I pick up my skirts, prepared to sprint back to the palace.

"I will not harm you," he states, and I swear on all the fates, it sounds like an order for me to stay. Some males just make everything sound like an order. The commander is one of them, which makes me think this might be an Unseelie soldier.

As if approaching a frightened lamb, he walks slowly toward me, and if I didn't know better, he even averts his gaze, trying to appear less threatening as he rounds the bench.

Once at the bench, he pinches the bridge of his nose and winces.

"Are you well?" I ask.

"It's been a while since I've traveled a long distance in the shadows. Do you mind if I sit down?"

The Unseelie manipulate and scheme, are often cruel

and calculating, and I shouldn't invite the male to sit with me, but he's unwell, and my good manners get the best of me. "Yes, of course. Please have a seat."

A smile tugs his lips. It seems genuine and not sinister, but I'm wary of him and don't smile back, but instead scoot to the left edge of the bench.

The male's long black coat flares before he sits, making the seat groan under his weight. One of his knees stays bent, the other is stretched out as he leans back, though he doesn't slouch. Not a soldier. He carries himself like the commander.

"Are you an officer in the Unseelie army?" I press a gloved hand over my lips. "Sorry. My curiosity makes me appear rude. I only want to stop guessing about your station."

He turns toward me slightly, only a brief shift of his body, and locks eyes with mine, giving me his full attention. The pitch-blackness of his eyes freezes everything in me, except for my heart. Under the weight of his gaze, my heart starts thudding in my chest, the sound of it so loud in my ears, I'm mortified that he can hear it.

"You've guessed correctly." His gaze lingers for a bit longer before he shifts away from me again and watches the palace entrance. But I'm still staring at him.

His profile reveals a jagged scar over the left side of his neck. The four claw lines make me think an animal mauled him. Or a lycan. His nose curves down a bit. I find this feature masculine and attractive. In addition, a girl could almost cut her finger on the edges of his strong raised cheekbones and jawline.

"I take it"—his laryngeal prominence bobs as he speaks —"you've never sat with a Winter fae before."

Was I staring? I fold my hands in my lap. "I have. The queen mother comes from the Winter Court."

He raises a thick eyebrow. "Since you know the queen mother, you must be a courtier."

"My name is Augusta." I introduce myself more for my protection than for the sake of small talk. I'm not stupid. We're alone. He's an Unseelie fae who could destroy me with a flick of his claw, and just in case he has sinister intentions, I add, "The royal seer."

"You're the seer?" The male snaps his head toward me, interested now.

That's right. "You look surprised." As if my being a seer is hard to believe. Granted, I'm a seer with extremely weak magic, but if King Et'enne says I'm his seer, then the people choose not to argue with him.

"Not surprised. Only wondering about something."

When he doesn't elaborate, I lean in. "About what?"

He gives me the side-eye before turning toward me. "When you saw me, you seemed surprised. For a seer, that is surprising to me."

Unable to help it, I lean in more and sniff, curious about his scent, but all I get is the fragrance of the gardenia bushes behind us. "Why is it surprising?" I ask breathlessly.

"I expected a seer to foresee my arrival, especially when I've ambushed her in the gardens. Not by design, I assure you, but seemingly by fate."

"Maybe." I swallow as I lean in more. In the back of my mind, I register that I'm encroaching on his space, and yet I scoot even closer.

Our lips are almost touching, and I tilt my head.

He doesn't. His eyes stay on me, his eyebrows lifting slowly.

He has plush red lips, and I can smell him. It's the scent of leather and male.

"Maybe I'm not a very good seer." I close the distance and kiss the Unseelie stranger.

3

AUGUSTA

I've kissed boys before. Twice, in fact. Once when I was fifteen and Cecile dared me to, and once recently, just last turn during the Applelane, an annual celebration of harvest. Both times, I initiated the kiss, and the second time, I even tried to tongue kiss the boy. He didn't know what I was trying to do, so we ended up slobbering all over each other while he groped my breast until Father found us out.

This kiss doesn't feel like either of those.

This time, I kissed an older fae male who smells like fresh-cut evergreen and peppermint with a touch of cinnamon laid over a new leather jacket. It's as if he arrived in the garden straight from the winter-covered forest and all the outdoor scents are still lingering on his skin. The smell of him is masculine, strong, and foreign. I've never inhaled a male scent like this before, and it makes me curious about him.

His lips are soft, plush, expertly moving with mine, but not taking over the kiss. My eyes flutter closed, and when I tilt my head so I can deepen the kiss, he groans, a sound that makes me throw my hands up and grab his face to pull him into me. I open my mouth.

His fingers close over my throat and squeeze, and the lack of air wakes me up from some sort of spell.

I jump away. "You spelled me."

Standing, he uses his thumb to dab the corner of his mouth, then approaches me so I have to look up to meet his eyes as he hovers over me.

"If you mean to intimidate me with all your tall might, I shall have you know I'm not easily rattled."

A smile tugs his lips. Even the corners of his eyes lift. "I am beginning to see that, milady."

I step back.

The male stays in place. "What will you tell your king, I wonder?" He tilts his head, and I swear he's excited at the prospect of my getting in trouble with the king. And rightfully so. I know better than to mingle with strangers in the gardens, let alone Unseelie fae of the Winter Court.

I pretend I don't know what he's talking about. "Tell him about what?"

"Our interesting encounter."

"I will say nothing of it, for it warrants no examination."

He chuckles. "I doubt that very much."

"My king would be furious for sure. Not with me so much as with you. You didn't even pay him respects before you spelled his seer."

"Only because his seer attacked me."

"Attacked?"

"You threw yourself at me."

I gasp. "Liar. You used magic on me."

"Through no fault of my own, you kissed me."

"I did not!" I did, but I'm arguing this one to my deathbed.

The Unseelie laughs.

I scoff and gather up my dress. I'm making haste toward the palace when I hear boots hitting gravel behind me. I turn. "Stop following me."

He lifts his gloved hands. "I am simply trying to ensure your safe return."

"I didn't realize I was in danger."

"A soothsayer is always in danger."

I pause, my heart thudding in my ears. "Are you going to hurt me?"

The male runs a claw over my cheek, sending shivers down my belly and lower still.

"I will make you a deal. If you allow me to escort you back inside, your attack on the Winter Court fae who was simply trying to rest after a long journey will stay a secret. Shall we?"

When he offers his elbow, I rest my hand on it. "This is coercion."

The Unseelie male seems amused. "You're lucky I don't demand your hand in marriage."

We stroll back to the palace at the same time as the last of the Unseelie delegates makes his way inside.

"The king wouldn't agree to give you my hand in marriage."

"And why not?" he asks.

"Because I'm his seer, a servant of the Crown." As people love to remind me.

The Unseelie mumbles something under his breath.

"What was that?"

"We're just in time."

Taliant, a male with curly dark hair and a beautiful round face, wearing a tight white suit with royal-blue lapels that reach past the knees, spots the male next to me and looks away, then whips his head back to us. His hazel eyes widen like large plates. Taliant snaps his fingers in rapid succession. His seven assistants come rushing in and circle him briefly, then disperse in a flash of skirts and pants.

I try to remove my hand from the male's arm so it doesn't appear as if we're a couple walking in together, but the male slaps his hand over mine, pinning it. "The deal was that you let me escort you inside."

A deal made with the Unseelie fae is one most people must honor or else suffer great pains or even death. The Unseelie delegation has already arrived and everyone is practically waiting for us, heads turning, people wondering what's going on and why we stopped.

Farther ahead in the foyer, his people freeze and gape when they see us, while their prince, a male wearing a crown, walks toward our royal table, which is located past the foyer and in the dining hall. June and Et'enne stand to greet him.

"Shall we?" he repeats.

I nod, dreading having to answer my Summer king about the Unseelie escort, but the king invited them, invited him, and it's polite and in line with our Summer hospitality for a lady to escort a lone Unseelie male she might have found in the gardens. I'm sure it's perfectly fine. Except for the part where I kissed him, but the Unseelie won't bring it up. We made a deal, and all is well.

I square my shoulders, plaster on a radiant smile, and let the Unseelie walk us into the palace, where Taliant stands to announce him.

"King Et'enne welcomes Aamako, the commander of the Winter Court armies, creator of the Fallen Court, and the king of all the Unseelie." Taliant pauses. "And the Summer Court's royal seer."

4

AAMAKO

The Golden Palace houses the finest jewels and treasures collected from all around the world. The lights reflect from diamond chandeliers dropping from the ceilings and highlight the painted canvases hanging in golden frames attached to golden hooks on the pillars.

Between the pillars, one can hear waves stroking the shore while enjoying the gentle summer breeze that carries the scent of seashells, ocean, and heavily scented oils extracted from various plants around the court. But that's not all. The breeze carries something else as well. The Summer fae mating scents that stir desire inside me.

I ignore the temptations.

The opulence, though overdone, isn't unpleasant, and the people falling silent as I walk in make me feel quite at home. I live alone, only sometimes tolerating visits from the few friends I have left in the world. My nephew, the prince, not being one of them.

He's up ahead greeting the Summer king now, and he turns slowly, quickly masking his shock at seeing me. If he were to show shock at my attendance, it would seem as if he had no idea I was attending the Summer king's celebrations, which would openly reveal the existence of division in our court. We are Unseelie of the same court, and although we are enemies, we can never appear divided in front of the Seelie fae. They would exploit the opportunity.

I take a step toward the royals, but the seer doesn't. She tugs her hand away. My magic wraps around the bracelet she wears and lifts it. With her hand positioned back on top of my elbow, I whisper, "Do you need a moment?"

While my nephew is an expert at hiding his emotions, including surprise, the young seer is flushed from head to toe, her heart hammering like a rabbit's. However, she is collecting herself and gripping my arm, digging her little claws into my armguards. Before she breaks her claws, I slide her hand down mine and lace our fingers together.

She tries to tug away, but I hold firm and start walking. So as not to appear as if I'm dragging her along, she walks with me, albeit still trying to hurt me by closing her claws over my knuckles.

She might draw blood.

I genuinely did not expect a seer not to foresee my coming here, but it seems nobody was prepared. That poor event master at the door hadn't a clue. Later, I must remember to commend him for even knowing who I am. I guess the rumors about summerlings hiring the best staff are true after all. Perhaps I'll steal him.

With that said, the unreadiness of the Summer Court thrills me. I could've invaded, and they'd never see me coming. Perhaps I could add another fae court under my rule.

I shove the happy thoughts of destroying my longtime enemy away lest I forget I came here for a bride and not for the pleasure of maiming any of my southern neighbors. Particularly not the Summer king. It would rob the fae people of a beautiful face, and, if rumors are to be trusted (often they are), of a *voca* bloodline.

Seeing as how he's a mind manipulator, I clear my thoughts and conjure an image of myself swinging from a pink swing. A pair of unicorns appears on the meadow in my mind, and the male mounts the female at about the same time as I arrive at the royal table.

Born of a Seelie male and an Unseelie female, the Summer king inherited the best of both our peoples. He's got a sun-kissed complexion with straight dark hair pulled back into a tight bun, and pitch-black eyes. Those eyes lock with mine in what I'm certain is his best intimidating glare. If he walked into my court with my seer, I'd glare at him too.

A hand slips into his, and the king's gaze loses some of its edge.

The hand belongs to a young fate wearing a tiny, tight, pearl-colored dress and a black veil that stops at her jaw. Her physique is appealing, and her scent is gentle and arousing.

Powerful magic pounds me and creates pressure in my ears, while a void flashes before my eyes. That'd be a warning from the Summer king. I better hurry along and show his lady some respect, so I flare out my coat and bow deeply, allowing my hair to sweep the floor, before straightening and not looking at the fate again.

The Summer king returns the bow with a slight nod. "King Aamako, what a pleasure to finally meet you. We were unsure if you could make it due to your condition." The invitation came. Of course it came. I read all the invitations. It's just that normally, they become fuel for the fire. This invitation I kept.

Since he attacked me with his magic, and his seer attacked me outside (these Seelies are proving very violent), I show him mine. My magic grabs a spoon and gives it life. The soup spoon jumps in the air, and its eyes flutter open, long eyelashes batting at the Summer king. "Which condition do you speak of, my handsome king?"

Some of my people chuckle, and once the spoon loses life and thumps back onto the table, returning to nothing more than a piece of metal, the Summer king smiles. "What condition indeed." He flicks two fingers, and the event master appears next to him, a bead of sweat on his left brow.

The king whispers something to the male. From the corner of my eye, I see a table is being added, chairs are being moved, plates and settings arranged, and in a few moments, the king offers me a seat next to him.

Huh. I guess he likes to keep his enemies closer than I do. Nevertheless, it's a grand gesture.

"Augusta," he says, "won't you let the Unseelie king dine with us now?"

As a final parting shot, the little seer squeezes my hand again, digging her tiny claws into the leather of my gloves one last time trying to bleed me. I lift her hand and kiss it.

5

AUGUSTA

The whisper of his kiss lingers on top of my hand. I cover it with my other palm as I fold my hands in front of me, now having no clue where I'm sitting anymore. During these types of events, someone always guides us to the tables, and as the royal seer, I sit wherever Taliant puts me, often at the royal table.

The seating placement matters. Taliant agonizes over it for spans, cycles probably and when, at the last moment, an important guest arrives, it changes the entire event. But at the Summer Court, hospitality is of utmost importance, and every guest is made as comfortable as possible, their every whim attended to.

The Unseelie king now sits with the Seelie king. The show of unity or power or whatever the kings are projecting will be written about in history books. The Unseelie king should be sitting with his delegation over at the table right in front of the royal table.

"Augusta," a male calls.

I turn and swallow under the commander's furious gaze. "A word." He offers me his elbow, and much like the

Unseelie king, he expects me to place my hand there the moment he offers it. In fact, he's already starting to walking away.

I grip his forearm lest he figure out my hands are shaking.

Regardless, he feels it, and he steadies my wrist as we disappear behind the last pillar, where two layers of royal guards create a wall of privacy.

The commander stops and stands, holding his hands behind his back. "Augusta," he says, and the tone he uses to say my name immediately annoys me. My mother says my name the same way right before she chastises me. He's not my elder or my parent or anything, and I dislike his tone.

I return it. "D'Artaron."

His dark eyes narrow.

I narrow mine.

He huffs and shakes his head. "You think this is a game."

"Which this?"

"Showing up with the Unseelie king."

"The way you say 'show up' makes me feel like you're saying I was with the male. King Et'enne invited the Unseelies. I escorted their king inside."

"And what of the message you're sending? The Summer Court's royal seer can't walk into the hall on the arm of another king!"

I step back. "You're being dramatic."

The commander breathes deeply. Several times.

"Do breathing exercises really help?" I ask. "I've tried them a few times for my own anger issues, and nothing."

"They do not."

"You want to bite someone? The Unseelie king, maybe? I hear that works."

"This is not a game," he declares through clenched teeth. "You are consorting with an enemy."

I pat the armor of his chest. His hard chest. It occurs to me that the commander and I are finally having a conversation. It's the most attention I've gotten from the commander since I met him. Had I known all I had to do was attend events with other males, I would have done it sooner. I'd never have made myself available almost the entire summer so that he could ask to court me.

That's neither here nor there now. The Unseelie king's arrival seems to have rattled everyone, and I have no idea why. "If he's the enemy, then why bring him here?"

"Nobody expected him to come."

"Not even you?"

The commander shakes his head and looks out at the ocean. The moon illuminates his face as he assumes one of his pensive-asshole expressions. "I would never have guessed Aamako would show up."

"Excuse me, I'm not privy to the invitation list, but I'm certain that if we invited the Unseelie prince, surely we invited their king."

"The prince serves as the king. The Unseelie king hasn't made an appearance at his own court for over five decades. Maybe more. This is the first time anyone has seen him in a while."

"He looks well." I slap a hand over my mouth and speak under my fingertips. "I have no idea why I said that. Total lapse of judgment. Temporary madness, I assure you." The one time the commander has an adult conversation with me, I tell him how I find another male, our enemy, looking well.

D'Artaron stares me down. "Aamako is not a male any

female should toy with. He's dangerous, insane, and, if provoked, a ruthless warlord."

"I would not toy with him."

"Allow me to rephrase. Aamako is a dangerous, mad male with powerful magic. He is not someone our king would wish to be around the royal seer. It is possible he has come here to steal you."

"Steal me?" I chuckle. "That's ridiculous."

The commander grabs my shoulders. "Listen to me, Augusta. You have foresight. It's the most coveted magic in the realm."

Our bodies are closer than they've ever been. "I know it's coveted. I covet it as well since I don't have it. The brief glimpses of the future that happen once in a blue moon hardly make me a seer."

"You just need practice."

Even as he says it, his words hold no conviction. A fae is born with a finite capacity for magic that no amount of practice can increase. Sure, I can use what little magic I was born with, but it's so minute that it requires great effort, making the forecasting of the future frustrating, and when nothing comes to me, it makes me feel like a loser. I've been practicing foresight for over a cycle now with no results.

"Tell me what you want from me, Commander." I rise on my toes and sniff. Like the Unseelie king, he smells like leather and male. I guess military males are my thing. Wait, am I saying the Unseelie king is my thing?

"I want to know how you came to be with the Destroyer."

"Is that what they call him?"

The commander nods. "Tell me."

I tell him of the garden encounter, sans the kiss.

The commander taps my nose, and his eyes soften. "You wouldn't lie to me, would you?"

"No, Commander." His proximity and the gentle touch on my nose should make me melt. And yet I stand indifferent, wondering why I'm indifferent and dreading the reason why before I even know it. Even the least powerful seer gets the annoying sides served with foresight magic, such as unexplained feelings of dread.

"Okay, get on with the night with no more incidents, and stay away from the Unseelie king."

"Yes, sir."

"Good girl." D'Artaron smiles a gentle smile I've never seen him give me, and over the course of the summer, I've seen him smile...a few times. The way he says "girl" should turn me on, but instead it makes me realize he thinks of me as a young fae he's duty bound to protect and sometimes parent. For what it's worth, his praise makes me perk up and feel ready to get back into the dining hall.

D'Artaron's sister, who guards June, walks up, but stops when she sees us. "A word when you're finished."

Instead of saying we're done and moving on with his duties as I expected him to, as I have seen him do countless times, the commander offers me his elbow and escorts me back into the hall, where the music and conversation flow have renewed.

The Unseelie king sits to the left of the Summer king, and the empty space next to him makes me think I'll be sitting there. One needs no foresight for that.

The commander stops, and I can tell he's coming to the same conclusion. He could seat me wherever he pleases, but King Et'enne looks up and nods, a tiny movement of his head.

The commander is escorting me toward the empty seat.

Some folks murmur as I pass, and I try to hear the gossip, but the dancers and the drummers enter the hall, drowning out the murmurs.

The Unseelie king rises and walks toward us.

Oh no.

Oh, he wouldn't.

He wouldn't ask the commander for my hand, would he? He would wait for me to sit, and that is all.

But no. The Unseelie king meets us at the end of the long royal table and extends his palm, not even his elbow. "I will take her from here, Commander."

"Allow me," the commander grits out, his teeth so clenched, I think they might break. He and the king engage in a stare off, barely contained magic seeping out of their very pores. I do what I think my king would wish me to do, which is to prevent mayhem at a public event.

While we love dramatics, violence at a public event discourages people's attendance in the future, and we want everyone invited to attend the royal wedding. The Summer Court is the center of the world. We must all behave.

I accept the Unseelie king's hand, and he leads me away.

6

AAMAKO

Summerlings make a lot of noise.

Since I've lived in seclusion for the better part of the century, it's rather refreshing to see colors other than shades of gray, smell the alluring scents of the Summer fae, and hear music other than the kind I can make by banging spoons on pots.

Hmm. If I needed entertainment back home, I could play a military song called "The Song of Shield and Maiden," a somber Unseelie patriotic tune I whistled while I conquered the other Unseelie court.

Eh, the good ol' spans of war and fun.

"Reminiscing are we, dear king?" a pleasant female voice asks, and for a moment, I forget where I am and stand knee-deep in mud, sinking farther and farther. How did I get here? Before I can lift my leg to try to step out of the mud, I'm back at the table, my head spinning.

I pinch the bridge of my nose. "Message received," I tell the fate who invaded my memories and who is threatening to send me into the past by triggering memories of my last conquest, the one I had right before I went into seclusion. The horrors of my past haunt me still.

Next to me, the little seer raises her hand and calls over a pixie. When a male pixie wearing a yellow jumpsuit, pointed golden shoes, and a long yellow hat bats his purple wings over to us, she says, "The Unseelie king needs service."

"We are retrieving his drink. Pardon the wait, milady."

The seer looks at me. "What did he say?"

"He's getting it." Augusta doesn't speak pixie. Most royals and courtiers speak the language, seeing as the pixies work in the Summer and Spring Courts. I presumed fluency in pixie tongue is required education here.

A pixie with breasts each as large as her head flutters in front of me carrying a white porcelain bottle of *ianke* I gave the Summer queen a century ago. Another pixie, this one with short hair and breasts just as large, stops at eye level and offers me a matching cup. Without a word, I accept, and she flies away faster than she arrived. The other pixie pours me *ianke* and leaves the bottle on the table.

They fear me, or else one of them would be refilling my drink as I enjoy it throughout the night. Pixies provide top-of-the-line service for the fae courts. Well, the Seelie courts. Unseelie not so much, since the suffering the pixies endured during the fae wars haunts them to this very span.

The lady next to me gets a champagne flute, and when I raise my small cup to toast with her, she grabs my wrist and brings my hand closer to peer inside. She sniffs the drink. "What is it?"

"It's alcohol made from rice," I answer, hiding my shock. She is rather bold for touching me in such a familiar manner.

"Rice?" she asks, wiggling her nose.

Bold and cute.

"Mmhm. Not grapes. Can I offer you a taste?" I move it closer to her lips, and she sips, then pulls back. Her lips part, her tongue swiping a drop sliding over the bottom lip. The scent of her pleasure reaches my nose and reminds me the Summer fairies are in mating season. She smells of...innocence.

Lazily, I drag my gaze up from her lips. "Do you like it?" I already know she does.

"It's served warm."

Not an answer, but I pour her another cup and she drinks it while motioning to the pixies for another cup. I guess she's keeping mine. It occurs to me, the Summer king on my right hasn't said a word to me. That's likely because I turned toward the seer, practically giving him my back.

I sit up straight in my chair.

Next to me, the king snorts, and I swear the annoying headache coming and going since my arrival at the hall vanishes. I conclude that the *voca* was indeed probing me occasionally.

The dancers start retreating, and the noise of the orchestra settles into a few stringed instruments pleasing to the ear. Clearly, something is changing. A flock of pixies rushes out of the kitchens carrying dishes. Each pixie settles behind a guest, and it occurs to me that each of us gets personalized service here in the Summer Court.

A chime rings, and the pixies serve the starter. My pixie's wings flutter past my ear before she uncovers my plate. Escargot. I lean in to inhale the vapor, my mouth watering instantly. I pick up the tiny utensil and dig into the snail. The flavor of butter and ocean flesh sparkled with herbs explodes in my mouth, and I moan, making the king next to me smile.

"I take it the appetizer is to your liking," he says.

"Everything is to my liking." Granted, when it comes to food and entertainment, I'm easily pleased, but he doesn't need to know that.

"It has been centuries since our two Courts gathered for anything other than bloodshed."

"Indeed." I finish my plate, wipe my mouth, and lick the butter off my teeth. Mmm. "I might steal your cook."

The Summer king chuckles.

But I don't know if I'm joking or not. I'll decide after the main course. The cook makes a better escargot than I do, so kidnapping him or her is an option.

A head pops up behind the king's body, her gauzy veil shielding her face, though showing her white teeth, telling me the fate is smiling. "If you steal our cook, you must send us yours."

"I don't employ one, sweet fate."

"Milady will do," she corrects me.

"You will continue calling her 'fate,'" the king says.

"Queen might settle it," I suggest.

Although they're not yet married and the fate has not had her coronation ceremony, the Summer king nods. "It is settled, then."

My pixie isn't refilling my drink, so I serve the seer and myself more *ianke*. The future queen leans in over the king again. "I'm curious, if you don't employ a cook, do you prepare your own meals?"

"In a way, yes."

"In which way?" the Summer king asks, while my pixie replaces my plate with a red tomato soup rich in vegetables. No steam rises from it, so it's a cold soup that smells spicy. I don't think I'm going to enjoy this, but everyone gawking over it makes me think I'm missing out on an extraordinary taste. I only like chicken soup with twirly egg noodles. Also, I don't have "fear of missing out." At the risk of appearing rude by not tasting the soup, I let it sit there.

"Would you like something else?" the Summer king asks almost immediately, making his pixie fly over to join mine. Several other pixies start gathering, looking terrified, as if I'm going to hurt them for bringing me the red soup, which I most certainly will not.

"I shall await the main course."

My soup disappears, and the main course arrives on a long silver plate, piled with several whole domestic animals roasted to perfection, their skins fried to a crisp. The pixies place the course on the table, but not in the middle so as not to block the view people have of their king.

Dipping sauces along with animal fat are served in small bowls surrounding the main dishes.

While the party folk enjoy the soup, I take the liberty of continuing the conversation with the future queen. "My magic, or rather what you might consider madness, prepares my food."

The queen pushes her soup away. "I don't know what you mean."

"The Unseelie king commands objects," King Et'enne says.

I smile and wrap magic around his spoon again so it can wink at the queen.

The queen giggles, her laughter stroking parts of me below the waist.

"How very amusing," she says.

"Very," the Summer king says, annoyance lacing his tone.

"Do you do your own housekeeping, gardening, everything?" she asks.

"Yes, dear queen. I am my own humble servant." It's unfortunate she is a fae fate, for I find her pleasant and charming.

Next to me, the young seer leans in so she can see the fate. "His magic is called *animato*."

She doesn't speak pixie, and her magic classification is inaccurate. I get the impression the seer lacks the basic education available to all the courtiers. I would not expect a courtier or a royal seer to mistake me for an *animato*. Yet, I don't correct her, for I have not had a pleasant conversation with a member of the opposite sex since... Seems like a lifetime ago. I wish to remain in the company of the two ladies and the very annoyed Summer king.

I'm enjoying myself.

Having finished his soup, the Summer king leans back and dabs his mouth with a napkin. "The Unseelie king commands objects rather than simply bringing them to life." He levels his seer with a look that I interpret as a warning. "He is an *armatuno,* meaning an army of one."

The poor pixie tasked with serving me yelps as if struck and disappears in a flutter of falling dust and frantic batting wings. The seer swallows, and the future queen just says, "Oh."

In conclusion, the Summer king is a twat who ruined the mood. On purpose, no doubt. I dislike it and will retaliate tonight.

7

AUGUSTA

The Summer king calling the Unseelie king an army of one ceases the conversation. Like chastised children, June and I return to our plates. Our king is warning me about the Unseelie king, not that the Unseelie need a warning at all, their king least of all.

King Aamako goes to pour another drink for the two of us, but King Et'enne tsks.

Now, when my king tsks, we, his people, put a stop to whatever it is that he's annoyed with. King Aamako doesn't even flinch, so Et'enne covers my cup with his hand. Instead of stopping, King Aamako tilts the bottle and pours hot *ianke* over King Et'enne's hand, spilling it on the table. Calmly, he puts the bottle down and offers me his cup instead of the one my king is guarding.

I have a choice now.

To refuse his attention or not.

My king is glaring daggers at me, and I avert my gaze. Across the room, the commander is watching, his fists clenched, his eyes narrowed. It occurs to me that he is a parental figure indeed. Moreover, King Et'enne has been parenting me, treating me like a kid ever since I met him. I'm young, but I'm an adult, and if I want to drink, I will.

I could take the cup from King Aamako's hand, but I lean in and let him serve me his *ianke*. It's just a few sips, but in that moment, I catch a foreign masculine scent. It's the arousal of the Unseelie fae, and it kindles mating fires inside me.

I finish the drink and swipe my tongue over my lips, knowing he'll follow the movement and interpret it as flirting. My behavior will piss off both the commander and King Et'enne, which is my intention tonight. I'll reconvene with my sanity tomorrow.

King Aamako brings the cup to his lips. He sticks out the tip of his black serpentine-like tongue and flicks it over the place my mouth touched, reminding me that I kissed him.

"Do you dance?" I ask him.

"Often alone."

"Would you dance with a partner?"

"Are you asking?"

"No."

"Shall I ask you?"

"If you wish."

King Aamako's plate lifts, and I follow it to where the largest butcher knife I've ever seen and the carving fork are arguing over the food. The knife hovers above the meat, a sliced piece of meat stuck to the blade while the fork is dancing around the knife, trying to steal the meat, it seems. The utensils are debating if they should serve me food before serving their king.

The fork has an accent.

I look around the table to see that everyone is averting their gaze, and I realize this is the madness we're not supposed to notice or, at the very least, bring up, but I am fascinated by this magic and how he can have a conversation with me while conjuring the conversations of two other made-up personalities. Who are, in fact, utensils.

"I'm mad, you know," he says.

Something about that warms my heart. I offer him my plate. "They're soon going to call me crazy too. No seer makes it to her thirties without losing her mind."

"Or sight." Before taking the plate away, his magic brushes across my fingertip, leaving frostbite. I suppress a yelp, but quickly jerk my hand away. Ouch. It was an accident, and so I play it off as if nothing happened, while tucking my finger under my bottom to warm it back up.

"What would you like?" he asks.

"To settle the argument and take the piece of pork the knife sliced off."

The Unseelie smiles, and the knife lets the fork serve me the sliced meat before serving him too and dropping back into their places afterward. The other utensils take up personalities because the vegetables, gravy, and bread need serving too. The silence that falls over the table is deafening. Mercifully, the madness is short-lived, lasting only long enough to serve me and the Unseelie king.

Since our guest is completely oblivious to his madness and it's not threatening anyone, at the royal table we simply exchange looks and carry on.

"Augusta," King Aamako says toward the end of the main course, "it seems to me you arrived recently at court. Where did you come from?"

I'm trying to gauge if he's genuinely curious or if he's poking fun at me. The courtiers mention my upbringing often, especially when discussing the end of our mating season. They concluded powerful males wouldn't court me because I'm lowborn with hardly any magic, no matter that my sister is the fate and the next queen. Magic is power, and most powerful males seek powerful females to make more powerful children. Except for King Et'enne, may the good fates smile upon him for loving my sister so.

"My family are farmers," I offer by way of explanation.

"Even farmers have access to the Catalogue of Magic."

"They do, but they haven't time to peruse it when the farm needs tending." Having finished my meal, I push the plate away, then remember that a lady at court, once done eating, simply leans back and folds her hands in her lap. It is a signal for a pixie to retrieve the plate.

The Unseelie king takes notice of my poor manners and surprises me by pushing away his plate and offering me his hand. "Shall we dance now?"

I look around the room. A quiet background tune plays while people are still eating.

"Do you not want to try dessert?" I ask.

"Surely a dance with you is better than dessert."

I'm sitting, and as he stands, my corset tightens and my underpants lift me up. Gasping, I jump as if struck and feel the cold bite of his magic across my belly, releasing my corset, but not fixing the underpants he ruffled.

Oh my...

8

AAMAKO

Telling the Summer seer a dance with her would be better than dessert fits well with our mutual flirting this evening. Lifting her by her underpants is more than just flirting, and since her eyes widened as she stood up, I realized she might find it offensive. I wish not to offend her. She is pleasant, adventurous, and I like her, so I explain, "Lifting you by the seat of your underpants was simply the easiest way to make you stand."

She blushes prettily. "Apology accepted."

Oh, but I'm not sorry. Nevertheless, I let her think I've apologized.

She's eyeing the dance floor that's now clearing of pixies and the other service folk running around the dining hall. It's as if they know we will take to the floor. I must admit, the ease with which the staff rolled with the changes my arrival caused and how smoothly they're running the event is commendable.

Because my family and my court are full of vindictive cutthroat fae, we rarely get together for events as large as this one. I guess a royal Unseelie wedding would warrant a large event, but I don't plan to take a wife, and so we shall wait on my nephew, who, judging by the way he sleeps around, might marry all the available (and some of the unavailable) ladies in my court.

The Summer king rises, and people instantly fall silent. "Our esteemed guest King Aamako is quite a busy male, and it is with great regret I must announce that he will be departing early." He pauses and looks at me, smiling, daring me to contradict him.

I wonder if I should. I could slice him up in tiny little pieces before anyone so much as moves to save his life.

The pressure I've been experiencing off and on in this court returns in my head. Before, it was an annoying headache, but now, it's a heavy pounding causing pain.

Suddenly, Augusta grabs a napkin with one hand and my jaw with the other and turns my head away from the crowds. "Your nose is bleeding," she whispers, then dabs at it. I growl for her to stop.

She snatches her hand away and drops the napkin. A pixie picks it up and flutters away.

"Dear King," I say in my head, knowing he's in there somewhere, *"I just wanted to dance with your lovely seer. You attacked me. Again. I will enjoy destroying your court. You can ask your queen who sees all that's come to pass for details on how that will go, or you can watch me dance with the pretty seer and I promise to be on my way."*

While I speak at him, he's talking to the room, and it occurs to me I'm not the only king who's challenged to mentally carry on several conversations at once. Granted, he knows I'm mad, while I don't know if he is. Surely the power of a *voca* would drive a fae to madness eventually.

Finally, I swear I hear an exhausted sigh in my head, and the pressure is released.

Upstairs, the band stops playing the current tune, and several members of the band step forward, carrying the kind of instruments often found in Unseelie music ensembles.

"Request any song," the king says. Under his breath, he whispers in an old fae tongue spoken when the unicorns and stags roamed our lands, "This is not over. I demand answers."

"To what?" I return in the same tongue.

"We will start with your intentions."

"I have no agenda." I take the seer's hand and kiss it. "Besides dancing with the seer."

"The seer is mine," he hisses.

"You are marrying a fate," I remind him.

He grits his teeth. "You know what I mean."

"People are watching," the seer says.

The king smiles as if we're having the most pleasant of conversations and motions with his hand, gesturing to the now-cleared floor. The lights are now dimmed, the band has arrived downstairs, and everything seems...more like a dinner in my own court.

I nod, pleasantly surprised that although the Summer king hates me, he will show me how his court treats guests. Like they're at their own homes.

Briefly, I consider offering the seer my elbow, but change my mind and do the most inappropriate thing yet again and interlace our fingers as I move toward the dance floor. Since the hall's lights dimmed, thereby creating a space with more shadows, I gather the darkness to me. The shadows leave the corners, slip from under the curtains, wriggle between the table legs, and scurry over the pristine marble floors to collect at my feet.

The discomfort in the room is palpable. The Seelie fear shadows.

A gentle hand lands on my shoulder, and I lift our entwined hands that shouldn't be joined in this way. It signals intimacy far beyond our kiss.

But the seer doesn't seem uncomfortable.

She is bold and unafraid of me, which is very naive. Or she is a formidable seer who fears nothing because she knows everything will eventually turn out in her favor.

The drums strike, the piano keys follow, and I twirl the seer around the dance floor, her luxurious golden gown sweeping away at my shadows. She's with me every step as if she's done this a million times, as if we have done this a million times. But this dance was lost to the fae people long ago. It's a dance my mother taught me when I was a young boy and there is no way in seven hells that this seer with no formal education could possibly know it.

But she does know it. Hells, she could even lead the dance.

She's laughing as we twirl around the room.

This is what happiness looks like. I wish not to ruin it while it lasts.

Thus, I gather up the shadows, step back from the seer, and leave.

The shadows take me straight to my chambers, where I wait until my stomach settles before sitting on my reading chair by the fireplace and lifting my foot.

The ottoman's eyes open, and it yawns. "Good fates, why am I awake?" It wabbles to the window to peer at the moon, then spins around and blinks. "My king, what are you doing at this unforsaken time?"

I smile.

The ottoman gasps. "And you're smiling. Did we finally kill our carpenter?"

"Guess again."

The ottoman shakes, excited. "We're going to war again."

"I met a girl."

The fire poker stands up and jabs the leftover firewood, then whistles, waking up the wood cart. The old cart that's been broken twice before groans. "Who wants anything at this time?"

"The king met a girl, and we need more wood."

"Coming, coming." The door opens, and the cart rushes outside.

In flies the kitchen chair, which whispers conspiratorially to the fire poker. "We heard the king met a girl."

The poker bends at the top a few times in a manner of nodding.

"Where did you meet her?" another chair asks from the door.

"At a party."

Collective gasp. "You went to a party?"

I recite the events as my staff helps me prepare for bed. When I lie down under the covers, I reach for my sac before stroking myself and thinking about the pretty seer. At the Summer Court, where their king practices his *voca* magic, I hid my intentions for the seer.

The truth is, I know exactly what I'll do with her.

9

AUGUSTA

Before dawn, my sister Julie returns from Prince El'jah's gathering and crawls into my bed. We have our own rooms, but we often still sleep together like we used to at home in the village nestled in the mountains above the city.

Dark circles of charcoal surround her light brown eyes, and she yawns, looking tired and worn out.

"You're back early," I say.

"Because my sister was abandoned on the dance floor by the Unseelie king. It's not something every girl gets to brag about. Or feel awful about. How do you feel about it?"

"Gah, you heard already. Everyone watched it happen. It'll be the talk of the court tomorrow."

Julie smiles. "Try tonight and several nights thereafter. People were leaving El'jah's gathering for Et'enne's party."

I roll my eyes. "You're kidding."

She shakes her head and yawns again. "No joke. Of course, El'jah was shocked someone would attend the king's boring parties over his island fuckery, but once he found out the Unseelie king had arrived, he collected us all and we rushed back."

"But the Unseelie king had already left."

"Much to our disappointment. You should've seen Cecile."

I giggle. "I'm sure she cried." She would have loved to try to steal King Aamako from me. Besides, Cecile fears she'll miss out on just about anything, and missing out on seeing or meeting the Unseelie kings might make her cry.

"How was he?" Julie asks.

"He was... " Sexy. "Different."

"Is that all?"

I nod.

"Be careful."

"He left." In the pit of my belly, something tells me he'll be back. Call it intuition. Call it precognition. It's a knowing all the same.

Banging at the door awakens me. Before I can even tell whoever it is to go away, he's already inside and leaning over me, his scent giving him away. With his dark hair combed and left loose to curtain his face, along with the scent of leather, it takes my morning brain a moment to deduce it is not the Unseelie king.

"Rise and answer the call of your king," the commander says. "You do remember you have a king named Et'enne, no?"

I cover my head with the fluffy feather duvet just as Julie says, "Go away."

"Rise, Augusta," the commander says in a warning tone.

"Is it even noon yet?"

"It is well into the brunch time now, and the king is expecting you."

"Tell him I'm sleeping."

"He's expecting you at the terrace immediately. It is a matter of duty."

"I don't know what that means."

The commander snorts. "I'm aware you have no sense of duty, but unfortunately for you, when our king calls, we answer. No exceptions."

Fine. Fine. I sit up and rub my eyes. "I need to dress."

The commander sits on my bed.

Wooo. Wide awake now, I pull my knees toward my chest.

Julie does the same.

We stare at him as he clears his throat. "The events of last night, namely the arrival of the Unseelie king, have stirred unrest in the Winter Court."

"But why?" Julie asks.

"It is a long story that our king and your sister hope to tell you over brunch. Please get dressed and come with me."

I've never seen the commander so distressed and informal, and he appears tired and worn out, as if he just returned from El'jah's party himself. I crawl to him and pat his back. The moment I touch him, he jumps off the bed and marches out of the room.

"Damn, sister," Julie says, "it's like he's allergic to your touch."

"Thank you, Julie, that's very kind of you to say."

She scoots back under the covers.

I gape. "Aren't you coming?"

"Where?"

"To brunch."

"With the king? Nah, I'll pass."

"I'm sure I could use your support."

"June will be there."

"I'm afraid she won't, and I'll end up eating with the king alone."

Julie groans. "All right, all right, but you owe me."

She crawls out of bed and we put on the clothes picked out for us by the designers.

Our dresses match. They're the same style, but different colors. Mine is baby pink and hers is baby blue. June wore a similar champagne one only a few spans ago.

The dressmaking and wearing is deliberate. It has everything to do with the sale of the style and the dress. Whatever June wears (and its designer chosen for her as it's done for us), we also wear within a few spans of her wearing it so that courtiers will start buying it, and then it looks like the Summer queen is setting trends for the court, meaning the rest of the world.

News of royal blue, the color of our mating season that June chose on her own, appearing on the Stenan princess reached our gossip mills. Fashion is our court's currency, and we love looking good.

Outside, I notice that the number of guards has doubled, and they carry additional weapons over their chest armor, as well as red ribbons tied to the hilts of their swords.

Julie tucks her hand under my elbow and whispers, "Something's happening."

"I hope it's not the Unseelie king."

"I hope it is so I can meet him. I can't believe I missed out on the second biggest event of the season." The biggest being June mating our king. We didn't miss out on any of that. It has been the best summer of my life so far. If only I could snag a male, I would be fully satisfied with my life.

The commander flicks a wrist and opens a portal I didn't

know existed in the tower. He motions with his gloved hand. "After you."

The portals have become an ordinary sight now, but before two cycles ago, my family and I hardly ever saw one, and we hadn't used them at all until we arrived at the Golden Palace.

We step through the purple shimmer and appear in the long hallway leading to the king's chambers. The guards line the entire hallway on both sides, and these are not faces I recognize from court. The scent of alcohol, sex, and leather permeates the hallway. These guards wear royal blue capes over black-on-black uniforms. They're older males, appearing gruff and moody as if someone dragged them here from the fields and taverns.

"You changed the guards?" I ask.

The commander mumbles a yes.

The pair of males stationed at the large wooden door open it. The commander leads us inside to a seating area with plush chairs and rich tapestry. I so want to linger and admire the art on the walls and the sculptures adorning the corner spaces but I hurry along with the commander, who leads Julie and me onto a terrace.

The moment I step outside, I know I should greet my king with more than a quick bend of the knee, but that's all I can manage before I rush to the railing and take in the view. The entire city can be seen from here: beaches full of people, packed streets, carriages coming and going from the main square, and lines of folk walking up and down the bridge connecting the city to the Golden Palace.

"We are on top of the world," Julie says.

"Mmhm," says our king, reminding us that he's here and our backs are to him.

Julie tugs my hand, and we curtsey, "Good morning, King Et'enne," we say in unison.

June is with him and not wearing a fate's veil. A hickey marks the side of her neck, and red bruises surround both her wrists. Those are the king's markings. Our king is an extremely possessive lover who demands June wear evidence of his desire for her all around the court.

I think it's hot, and I imagine my lover's bruises would be worn somewhere on my bottom instead of the wrist. Suddenly, my forefinger stings where the Unseelie king's magic brushed it last night. It feels like frostbite, and I rub my finger to warm it up. The pain passes quickly and makes me think I've conjured it up. But I haven't. The Unseelie king's magic touched me there last night and might've done something to me. Which is concerning, I admit, even if it seems harmless.

"Hi, June," Julie says, stroking her neck in the same place where June wears her hickey. Our sister ignores the teasing and grabs the serving spoon, but the king tsks.

June corrects herself, and instead of serving us, she raises a hand. "Service, please."

June is the eldest of three and has always taken on more responsibility than both Julie and me combined. She worked with our parents, and some spans, when Father would take ill and Mother couldn't handle the chores, June would work the entire farm on her own. Sometimes I think she might've raised me instead of my mother, particularly because I came late and was likely unwanted in a home already struggling for coin.

Once, I overheard my mother saying they didn't need three mouths to feed.

Since we stay up late (or early), at this time of span, the staff arrives and serves breakfast, turning up the breeze on the terrace. Although we're in the shade, it's well past midspan in the hottest month of the turn, and the elves our king hires for their magic of air manipulation are summoned to create even colder winds.

Everyone seems starving and eats with great gusto, especially when consuming the bacon. It's tasty and crunchy.

"Now that we're all here," Julie says, "I have an announcement to make. I've decided to return home." When June gasps, Julie continues. "I'll attend your wedding, of course. It's just that I want to return with Cecile. I want to be there for her."

"Has something happened?" I ask.

"Her parents had an accident and have been bedbound. Nobody is tending the farm."

"She will hate farming."

"I know," Julie says. "We hate her for hating the domestic chores, but I think we just hate her for saying the things we all know we hate. She exposes our truths." Julie shrugs. "She needs me, whereas you guys have each other."

King Et'enne sips his tea. He's not wearing a shirt. I must say it's distracting, and the effort it takes for me to keep my eyes above the neckline is great even if he is June's. Our king is handsome, and I'm a virgin with excellent eyesight.

"June, will you dismiss her?" he asks.

"Of course I will. Julie is my sister. She may do as she wills."

"Not at the expense of your happiness. If you want her to remain in court, surely she will oblige. Won't you, Julie?"

"Yes, my king."

I whip my head around to stare. "No! Julie would not like to stay out of duty. She prefers hanging out with Cecile at our home in the village anyway."

The king turns those pitch-black eyes on me, and I avert my gaze. "Pardon me for raising my voice."

He grunts. "The reason I summoned you is not Julie, so Julie, you may be excused and return to your home whenever you wish. And take your friend with you. This afternoon, in fact."

Julie tries to say goodbye to June and me, but we promise to see her before she departs, so she finishes her meal and leaves. The staff replace a seating next to me with a new plate and a setting.

"Are we expecting someone?" I pop a blueberry into my mouth.

"The Unseelie king."

The fruit gets stuck in my throat, and I try coughing as ladylike as possible, but when that doesn't free up my airway, I bend over and hack. Bright red in the face, I'm trying to expel the fruit when a giant hand lands on my back. The berry shoots out of my mouth, and I inhale a desperate breath, look up at the commander, who bends at the knees.

Eye level with me, he asks, "Are you okay?"

Nodding, I clear my throat.

He stands and assumes his position by the king, who stares at me.

"Sorry about that," I tell the king. "You were saying?"

"The Unseelie king has returned to our shores. This time, he requested brunch with you."

Oh no.

"It will be a supervised visit," the commander adds. It's so out of the norm for him to interrupt the king that all three of us look up at him. He simply gazes down his nose at us. "I spoke out of order. Big deal."

King Et'enne shakes his head.

"If King Aamako is coming, why didn't we wait for him to eat?" I ask.

"Because we are rude and unwelcoming when people play with our toys without our permission," June says.

King Et'enne narrows his eyes. "That's not why, June."

"It is, my dearest," she says. "You think my sister is your property."

The king clears his throat. "I do not."

"Yeah, yeah you do," I confirm.

He flicks his wrist. "Fine. I take care of what's mine, and I will not allow another male access to my royal seer. Augusta..." The king leans in and beckons my attention. "If you're looking for a male for the season, I will find you one. Surely one of my officers will do?" He looks at me pointedly.

Is he offering the officer on the terrace?

I look up at the commander, who is glaring daggers at the king. But the king is unaffected, waiting for my answer. Are we all really at the king's disposal? I think we might be, or at the very least, he thinks we are, and that's as sure as actually being at his disposal.

"He's here," the commander says and opens the door.

There stands the Unseelie king. In a black beach suit that clings to his skin and outlines all the large parts of his glorious body. I find him even more distracting than both the commander and our king. Uh-oh.

10

AUGUSTA

The Unseelie king is large and muscular, with multiple scars on his chest, arms, and thighs that a skilled healer could've healed, but didn't, probably because the king chose to keep them. The most prominent of the scars is the clear slice of a clawed hand over the right pectoral. It matches the scar on his neck.

A tattoo of a red serpent coils around his body.

Since the king seems to have enjoyed our beach this morning, the sun has kissed his scars, making them redder than before. It also tanned his body and has given it a silvery glow.

Oddly, he's wearing his boots. They're unlaced.

The commander disappears inside and returns with a robe which he tosses at the Unseelie.

The king slings on the robe, covering his tight black swimsuit, which outlines the biggest penis I've ever seen. I glance at my sister to see that she dropped her gaze already.

His powerful muscles ripple across his body as he swaggers toward the table.

Bending, he puts one hand on the back of my chair and

the other near my plate so he can lean in and sniff the top of my head. "You are real, then. Good for me, for I thought you might've been a beautiful dream." He sits and picks up a napkin, flares it out, and puts it over his lap. Looking up at our Summer king, the Unseelie says, "You look more surprised now than you did last night."

"You're wearing my beach pants."

Oh, those are Et'enne's! My imagination is running wild right now, and oh no, my king cuts me a look that says I need to quit thinking altogether. I should stop thinking about males, and I will when I finally have a male of own. The mating season is still in full swing.

"And?" King Aamako asks.

"Where did you get my pants?"

"From the laundry room."

Our king glances at the commander, and the other male disappears, leaving the three of us on the terrace.

"Do you want them back?" the Unseelie king asks.

King Et'enne sighs. "No, no, you can keep them."

"Thank you. They're rather comfortable." He pulls back the elastic waistline and releases it with a pop. "And stretchy."

"I will have more delivered to the Dakkuyasu if you wish."

"No need for any there."

June smiles. "Are you hungry?"

The king shakes his head.

Our king puts his elbows on the table, a clue to his foul mood, and leans in, "What do you want, Aamako?"

The Unseelie throws an arm over the back of my chair. "I thought that was obvious."

A vision of a female running down a hallway with black-

and-silver tapestry flashes before my eyes. "A bride," I say. "He wants a bride."

"Okay," King Et'enne says. "There are many potential brides in my court. Is there someone in particular who has caught your eye?"

"Not really, but it seems I caught hers," King Aamako says. "Your seer will do."

"Will do?" June asks. The old magic of the fates flares, threatening to suffocate us. Once she realizes she's lost control of the magic, she pulls it back. Old June would apologize for almost choking us, but new June shall be the most powerful Summer queen who has ever lived, so she simply pinches her lips.

"Will do," the male repeats, seemingly not threatened. He swipes an apple from a bowl. Mouth wide open, he pulls back his upper lip, briefly showing us his sharp fangs before biting into the fruit and ripping out a chunk of it. Moaning, he throws back his head and chews, prominent throat protrusion moving, the outline of his strong jawbones showing clearly.

I dare to glance at June, who's also staring at his features. He's devastatingly handsome in a raw masculine way.

"Your leaving her at the dance floor in front of everyone will not do," King Et'enne says, "when you want her for a bride."

"I would think that pleased you," the Unseelie says.

"It did. But now you're back asking for my seer."

"I'm not asking."

Magic ripples in the air. If this goes on, they'll start a war by ripping into each other. There's no love lost between the Summer and Winter Courts, not even by marriage or children. Our king is part Unseelie, but it seems to me that's only made more enemies in the Winter Court than friends.

"My sister shall marry whomever she pleases," June says, easing some of the tension.

"This arrangement will please her as it will please you."

"How so?" I ask.

"I offer freedom for you and the extradition of the queen mother, who is hiding in my court, for your king."

"Explain," King Et'enne demands.

King Aamako smirks. "I don't do well when others are ordering me. Address me again, summerling."

"Do explain, King Aamako," Et'enne says, adjusting his bossy, irritable tone, not by much, but enough for the other male to reply.

"Not to mention closer relations between our two nations as an obvious benefit, I will allow your dragons, even the lycans you send after your mother to roam my lands, and once they find her, I will extradite her. She won't find safe haven in the Winter Court." He turns to me, "My nephew seeks to take the crown from me, and I can only secure it by taking a bride."

"You can only secure it by having an heir," King Et'enne says.

"A bride will do," the Unseelie king says, and it makes me think this *will do* is what he meant when he said *will do* earlier. He meant no offense to me personally. It's not his problem we took it as such.

"Until I can make other arrangements. It will be temporary. A turn, maybe two. During our engagement, you will stay with me, and I will ensure that you're comfortable and well cared for."

"And what of her protection?" my king asks.

"You aren't considering this, are you?" my sister asks.

Me? An Unseelie bride? That's ridiculous.

King Aamako sips my apple juice. "I assure you nobody

in my court would dare steal my beach suit, let alone my bride."

King Et'enne laughs. "You were making a point. My security against the shadow travelers needs improvement."

"It does."

"Point taken."

"The seer?" King Aamako asks.

The Summer king pauses and seems reluctant, as if debating something, and then he looks at my sister and says, "I will consider the offer."

I stand in protest. "You can't." But he can.

June stands with me. "Et'enne, please. She's my sister."

"I said I will consider it."

"I will return for the seer tonight."

"He said he would consider it," June and I screech at the same time.

"Kings say stuff like that all the time. It's a yes." King Aamako eats his apple.

He might be right.

11

AAMAKO

Taunting the Summer king by stealing his beach suit from the laundry sends a message. It tells him I can and will take his seer should he refuse my fair request. Fair because I'm not asking for her hand in a marriage forever. Simply put, I wish he would loan me his seer.

Due to too much bad blood in the past, he and I both know an alliance between our two courts will never happen, but a truce with a fair exchange is welcome. For my engagement to his seer, he'll get his mother back. From what I heard, he will punish her severely, and that pleases me.

"May I be excused?" the seer grits out, then leaves before her king excuses her.

Her sister, the fate, a pretty, kind-looking fae with a genuine, gentle smile, follows her. Not allowing the guards to do their jobs and close the terrace doors, the fate slams them behind her. Maybe not such a gentle female, hm?

Finished with my apple, I wipe my hands on a linen napkin and examine the embroidery along the edges. "All fine work," I compliment the Summer king.

"The finest." He flicks his wrist, and the guards depart. "On account of your madness, I've allowed you more freedom than I normally would a guest, but I draw the line at you sneaking around my palace."

"You're upset about the beach suit."

"Fuck the suit."

"You've lost your temper."

King Et'enne smirks. "When I lose my temper, Aamako, you will sing my national anthem for the rest of your life."

I place a fist over my heart. "I sincerely hope you're threatening me, for I need an excuse to use the ropes from the thousands of boats docked on your shores to tie them around everyone's necks and let them dangle in the air. A skyline of dangling bodies, like loose lanterns at the solstice."

Et'enne grinds his teeth, and I can tell he's struggling with his temper. He can't hold it back and snaps, "Try it."

Standing, I strip off his beach suit. "I would rather make love, not war."

Et'enne doesn't bat an eye at my nudity while we engage in serious conversation.

"With my seer, I presume?"

"I won't touch her."

"Of course you won't. You'll use her foresight."

I snort. "Isn't that what you're doing?" Standing nude at the terrace with the gentle summer breeze cooling my sweaty balls is pleasant. No wonder the Summer king wears nothing but a linen kilt. The breeze enters under the loose fabric and cools his package. Should've stolen his kilt. Maybe I will on my way out. Oh wait, he's talking.

"...while you violate my sister-in-law."

I missed half of what he said. Oh, well. "She will stay at Dakkuyasu with me and won't spend most of her time at the

Unseelie court. Once the matter of my crown, namely me keeping it on my head, is settled, she will return to your court. That will look like a separation, and eventually, we will dissolve the engagement."

"So this was your plan all along."

"I'm actually planning on the fly."

"I don't believe you."

"Read my mind, then."

His fight to resist the invitation and give himself away as a *voca* Seelie is remarkable. He's red in the face from the mental struggle, looking more and more like a constipated rabbit. I laugh at the simile.

"Something funny?"

"Yes, actually, but I won't share. Though if you like, you can invade my brain and pick up on the joke yourself."

King Et'enne slams his hands on the table. "If you seek a fight with me, I recommend you also not seek the hand of my seer, because I will not hand her over."

I sigh. "You will hand her over because you want your mother back to make her answer for her crimes against your bride. I must say, if June were my bride..." My brain stalls, no words come out, and I can no longer even remember how to speak.

Et'enne approaches me. "Go on, you were saying?"

My magic rebels against his intrusion, and the screws that hold up the terrace railing pop out so I can use the strong metal. The railing groans as I start ripping it and crafting shapes of steel soldiers. As Et'enne watches, I feel him invading my mind and compartmentalize him away while building a group of six sculpted steel soldiers.

They each hold various kinds of sharp objects left over from the terrace. I have them line up behind me.

The terrace doors bust open, and the seer rushes out. "I

will go with you!" She stands beside me and laces her hand with mine. The touch of our bare skin is so unexpected that my brain scrambles and the soldiers behind me wobble, almost falling like useless metal. At the last moment, I get ahold of myself, and the soldiers hit their chests.

Augusta looks up at me in question, while Et'enne contemplates my counterthreat to his mental invasion.

"I agree," she says. "I will go to the Unseelie court as his bride."

12

AUGUSTA

June and I stayed in the living space next to the terrace and witnessed the entire exchange between the two kings. Judging by the flare of Et'enne's magic, which tends to create pressure in my ears, he hit the Unseelie king and the other one retaliated. June balled her hands into fists and I feared that if she used her magic too, things would get out of control, so I reacted and practically flew out onto the terrace to accept the Unseelie king's...offer of fake marriage.

King Et'enne withdraws his magic, and the pressure in my ears eases. My skin's crawling with Unseelie magic. The metal soldiers standing on my left creep me out. They look alive, even blinking with the holes made for eyes they don't have.

"You may not call my June by her first name. Ever. It is too familiar, and I will strike. Is that clear?"

"Jealous and possessive, are you?" the Unseelie king asks.

"I am. Even of my seer."

I'm not really his.

"We have that in common."

Holy fate. What's the Unseelie mean by that? He lifts my hand and kisses it before walking around me.

"Would you like to put on pants before you leave?" my king asks, amusement coloring his voice.

The Unseelie king looks down at his body as if surprised he's nude with only a robe over his shoulders.

"I still have your robe, thank you."

"Did you want to take your soldiers with you on your way out?" my king asks, but it sounds like a suggestion.

The Unseelie king makes the soldiers hold hands, then reattaches the hands of the two soldiers at each end to the walls, in a way returning the terrace rail to its place.

"Keep them. I only want the seer." The Unseelie king walks through the sitting room and bids June goodbye before the guards escort him out.

I stay by the door when Et'enne walks past me and stops in the middle of the room. Fuck!" He starts pacing. "Fuck! Fuck!"

When I said I missed my sister, I meant that I missed joking with her, sharing baths with her, and even doing chores with her. I didn't mean arguing with her about my short-lived future as the Unseelie king's bride while my pissed-off king is pacing along the windows like a lion.

Finally, he settles. "June," the king says, "I will not give her up."

My sister's all but melting on the sofa. "Thank you, Et'enne."

"With that said, his proposal changes everything. I mean everything. We must consider how a refusal will be taken and what it will mean for our people. For the peace.

Aamako is too dangerous to be allowed to live when I refuse to give him my seer, so I will have to make him disappear. Outright killing the Unseelie king will send us into another fae conflict." He bares his teeth. "That motherfucker!"

My sister rises and walks to her betrothed. She takes him by the hand and guides him to the sofa, where he sits and spreads his arms, knowing she will sit on his lap. June kisses the king on the cheek. "We cannot go to war again. The price of fae wars is too great. And I can't let him have my sister."

"I accepted the offer. The deal with the Unseelie king can't be broken now."

"You don't know what you're saying," my king snaps.

I pull back my shoulders and lie, "I do know."

The king raises his eyebrow. "You can't lie even if your life depends on it. You won't last a span in the Unseelie court."

"The Unseelie king will make sure I last."

"How do you know he won't smother you the moment he gets his hands on you?" June asks.

"Because I see the future. Duh."

June huffs. "Get serious, Augusta. This is a matter of life and death. These are the crossroads of our lives where we make choices and those choices affect our future."

The Summer king doesn't want me to go.

I don't want to go.

June is near tears, so nobody is really arguing in favor of my leaving.

"What's the future hold?" King Et'enne asks.

I shrug. "I wish I knew."

The commander bursts into the room, making me almost jump off the sofa.

He marches in, going straight to our king. "You can't possibly consider his proposal."

"I'm not considering it."

"No," he says and squeezes next to me. He throws an arm over my shoulders and brings me flush against his body. "I will hide her."

I gape at him.

June's fate magic blankets the room, making the roots of my hair tingle. I'm unsure what she's seeing in the past, but whatever it is makes the commander whine in the back of his throat.

However, he doesn't back down. "If the seer is seeking refuge, I will hide her. You can trust me, my king. We are both chaste and have vowed to remain chaste forever. I will care for her as if she were my daughter."

We are chaste? And vowed to remain chaste for the rest of our lives? Hell no. "We are not chaste. Maybe you're chaste, but I'm not. Technically, I am, but not by choice." I blush as I recall pining after someone who thinks of me as his daughter. His offer upsets me. "I'm not desperate for your attention, so please don't offer anything to me out of pity."

"I am greatly fond of you." The commander looks down at me with kindness, not love, in his eyes. Still, the commander is *greatly fond of me*. I've waited what seems like forever for this moment and for him to declare his fondness for me, but this isn't the fondness I want.

This male would never love me the way I need him to. Besides, I want sex. I want to go into heats. I want a partner who will ravage me and let me experience all the different emotions in life. I want to orgasm so hard, I see three moons out of one, but most importantly, I want to choose the direction of my life.

"The Summer Court is not in my future," I blurt.

June leans in after a brief glance at the commander. "What do you mean, Augusta?"

"I once had a vision of a bride. Her white dress was sweeping a red floor."

June's breath hitches.

I go on. "The decision to leave the Summer Court for a while feels right. Doesn't it, June?"

My sister gives nothing away. "I can't say, because I don't know."

"You must know," I tell her. "You know everything."

"That's come to pass," she says, her gaze sliding to the commander. "Which is how I know Augusta is not your charge."

Eerie magic, heavy and dreadful, blankets the room, and the commander fixes his uniform. He stands then bows and turns on his boot as if to leave.

"You are a male of honor," June says.

The commander pauses at the door. "I am at your service, future queen." The commander departs.

King Et'enne kisses June's shoulder, lingers there, his mating scent stirring. The Summer king loves my sister fiercely, and since I've seen what fierce love looks like, I want this kind of devotion too. But if I do accept less, if I accept a deal with a male who won't love me, let it be the craziest thing I've ever done. Let it be a fake engagement to the Unseelie king.

13

AAMAKO

Stepping out of the ceramic tub onto the cold floor makes my leg hairs stand on end, and the rugs know it, so why I can't get a rug to land beneath my feet is beyond me. I glance across the room at five rugs arguing over which one will grace my floor.

This has never been an issue before.

One of the five rugs has always been there.

Only now that I've announced a female is arriving this evening, the rugs are arguing, the chandelier is shouting at everyone working to tidy up the ground floor, while the painting crew redecorates the spare chamber directly across from mine.

I pose my foot above the floor, water dripping off my skin, wetting the hardwood. "One of you better get in here," I warn the rugs.

A pastel pink-and-gray rug slides under my foot, and I step on it and welcome the warm towel wrapping around my shoulders, and another around my waist and yet another drying my hair. The one on my hair tightens into several knots and rubs my scalp, giving me a massage.

The towel on my shoulders does the same, and I groan, crack my neck, and pad over to the wardrobe, which directs me straight to the mirror because the hangers are hovering near it, my clothes for the evening picked out. My uniform, the one I wore when I paraded the head of the Fallen Court's king though the streets of his court sure looks old-fashioned.

"Not that," I tell the wardrobe.

"But it's the nicest piece we own," she says in her rough voice, which sounds as if she smoked pipes all her life. She hasn't. She's an object, but like all my tools, she appears sentient.

"It's outdated."

"You're outdated," the wardrobe fires back, sounding offended.

The hanger sweeps in and puts the uniform back. "I've seen what they wear in the Summer Court. This old coat won't impress anyone."

"We need to impress someone?"

"No," I snap.

Hidden laughter sweeps the house. I dismiss the crazy objects. "I need new clothes made in the newest fashions. The fashion now is unicolor collar and tightly woven breathable textures."

"We don't have anything like that," the wardrobe says.

"I'm coming, I'm coming," says a voice I don't recognize. Who the fuck is that? All I need is more voices in the house.

Giant scissors and a basket full of tailoring equipment rush into my chambers and start fussing around me, taking measurements, pinning fabric, and making general mayhem.

"Settle down." As soon as I say that, what I think might be items from a local tailor shop in the village below fall to the floor. I'd love to use them, but I don't know how to make clothes, so I command them to return to the poor fae who's likely already packing up to run as far as possible after I made his equipment come alive. But in case the fae remained at the shop, I send a purse of coins and a commission for clothes with his scissors. If he doesn't faint at the sight of talking scissors, I'll have new clothes by the evening. The yellow tape takes my measurements, and the tailor shop tools leave the castle.

The chair appears just before I land my ass on it.

"Why don't you take a nap, my king?" the wardrobe says, then offers me a nice warm blanket.

I rise, walk to the bed, and fall facedown, my eyes closing almost instantly. Who knew renovating a chamber would knock me out?

~

Augusta

The full moon shines on the mini square in the heart of the Summer Court's gardens, while those lycans who've remained in the court after their alpha departed circle around, looking for any foul play perpetrated by the Unseelie prince's delegation. In order for the Unseelie king's ploy to work, Et'enne said his people have to witness the handling over of the royal seer. Apparently, it's a ceremony.

The seer bride wears a little white dress, and in front of witnesses, the Summer king walks her to the Winter king. The handover signifies the passage of time and the seasons. The blood of the seer, once spilled, alerts the fates, and they turn their attention to the transpiring moment in time. Since my sister is in attendance, the blood isn't necessary. Actually, since it's a fake engagement, I don't think any of this is necessary.

Yet I stand in the middle of the circle in a little white dress as in one of those myths about sacrificial virgins the villagers would sacrifice to pay their dragon protector. In the stories, the dragon would swoop in and steal the virgin.

I double-check the skies. All clear.

In the shadows surrounding the gardens, nothing's amiss. The Unseelie king is late. Maybe he forgot. Or died. Either would work for me.

The Summer king stands with his brother and sister and June while the commander hovers around the Unseelie delegation like a hawk. The Unseelie prince brought his two female companions who double as spies, and an attractive male who keeps stealing glances at the Summer prince.

We're all facing the shrubbery, anticipating King Aamako's arrival, but he takes his time. Just as most people are getting antsy and my feet start hurting from standing too long in one place, our shadows extend and pull away from us. They slither over the ground and collect in front of a shrub. The Unseelie king is creating his portal from the other side.

My sister June and the Summer king approach and stand on either side of me.

June slides her hand into mine and squeezes. I didn't realize how nervous I was until her dry hand touched my sweaty one. "Give him hell," she says.

She is wearing the fate's dark veil, so I can't read her face. I wish I could, but I also know that the Unseelie love power, and June is showing the delegation and the incoming king the power of the fate.

Et'enne leans in and kisses the top of my head. "You can still change your mind. I will protect you."

"At what cost, my king?"

The shadows are dense now and forming into a tall person wearing a black uniform with wide shoulder guards that lift and broaden his already large frame. Thick red-and-white embroidery adorns the left shoulder guard, and the sleeve under it is also red instead of black, making the outfit unusual. Many different fabrics are layered over what appears to be a single suit.

His black hair is neatly combed and pulled back, likely into a braid, and he's clean-shaven so the hard edges of his facial structure are highlighted. From his neck by a thick platinum chain hangs the Unseelie seal, an image of a sharp mountain carved into a platinum medallion, identifying him as the Winter Court's king.

Another seal hangs from his neck. This one bears an image of a leaf carved into a round bronze plaque and identifies him as the Fall Court's king, ruler over what is now proclaimed the Fallen Kingdom. Hence, the king of all the Unseelie has arrived to claim his bride.

Now, even though I've little to no seer magic, I'm the kind of person who enjoys casting out visions and projecting events and possibilities. This is the biggest event of my life, and today as I bathed, trying to relax and failing to do so, one thousand and one scenarios of this moment ran though my head. The Unseelie king would wait in the shadows while I said goodbye to my sister, and then my king, Et'enne, would walk me to the Unseelie, handing me over as tradition requires.

Or perhaps the Unseelie king would chat with King Et'enne and June before we depart.

Or perhaps even the commander would step in and slay

the Unseelie king. Those were my top three choices among the scenarios, however likely or unlikely.

None of what I envisioned actually happens. The moment the Unseelie king fully materializes and he sees me, his eyes flare silver with magic, and he strides right up to me. The back of his black cloak flares out, making the shadows dance all around his feet. I'm frozen because there's a menacing Unseelie coming at me. My lips part.

The Unseelie king grabs the back of my head and the small of my back and yanks me to him. His mouth comes down on top of mine, and since my lips are parted in shock, he must think it's an invitation to kiss me. He pushes his tongue into my mouth and swirls it, seeking a response from me.

The moment our tongues touch, visions assault me.

Magic buzzes through my body, creating visions at speeds I'm unaccustomed to, but I welcome it because the magic feels glorious, energizing and arousing. I moan into his mouth at the same time that I hear the commander shouting in the distance. I'm sure I should worry about the fact the commander is shouting, and that his voice is becoming faint as if one of us is moving away, but I can't summon a single caring fuck, too consumed with the way the Unseelie king is kissing me.

It's as if he's trying to imprint his taste into my mouth and sear the memory into my brain so when any other lovers who come after him kiss me, I will know they are lacking. Those two boys from my village whose names escape me now didn't kiss this way.

As the king slows his pace, taking me from highs to lows of both magical and sensual ecstasy, I sway on my feet, eyes opening slowly as I recover from the assault of at least a dozen visions. Dazed, I stare up into the dark eyes of the Unseelie king.

Silver stars dance around his pupils. It's quite beautiful. I could stay like this for a while longer, staring into his eyes, but he blinks and the stars vanish, leaving only darkness behind.

It's a good thing, because it reminds me I'm with an Unseelie fae. Their king, no less.

His hands are still around my waist, and I grip his fore-arms, trying to push them away.

He steps back.

It's awfully dim in here. Wait a moment, where are we? I look around and gasp. "Oh my fates." I keep turning and turning, taking in the dark place. "Ooooo."

Black-and-white paintings of fruit trees in bloom framed in white or red wooden frames hang on the black painted walls of a large house I don't recognize. "We left the Summer Court?"

"Welcome to Dakkuyasu. Your new home."

It happened. I left my fairy court, and I'm alone in the middle of fates know where with a ruthless and insane Unseelie king who will make me his bride.

The walls start closing in on me. "I'm feeling a little faint."

14

AAMAKO

S hadow travel isn't for everyone, and even some of the Unseelie fae (me) hate it for it causes nausea and vertigo. While some Seelie portals cause unwanted side effects, theirs are conjured of readily available light taken from the sun, light bugs, or fire, and aren't conjured out of gathering shadows. Most often, theirs just create some pressure in the ears that most people don't even notice.

Since I've used shadow travel for several spans now coming and going from the Summer Court, first as a reconnaissance, then for the party, and now to fetch my bride, I've grown accustomed to it again. Somewhat. My head still pounds, but lightly, whereas the seer's unsteady on her feet.

And yet she separates from me and clearly won't let me help her.

Fine. I won't let harm come to her, but if she wants to wobble around the house and throw up here and there, that's fine by me. The house staff is on alert, mop in the closet at the ready.

I sit by the fireplace. Keeping an eye on her, I note the moment her head lolls and rush to

scoop her up and sit down with her on my lap, immediately noticing the room has only one chair. Sure, there're chairs around, but I need only one large plush chair by the fireplace.

I spent the afternoon and the better part of the evening preparing the house for her arrival, but many things she will have to find on her own, for I have no idea what she could possibly want. Not only is she a female, she is also far younger than I, and a Seelie fairy, meaning she's a member of a weaker faction of fae. Seelies are...more fragile.

She is also fairly light. I bet she watches her food intake.

Sitting up awkwardly I pat her head while the fire poker stokes the wood to create more warmth. Without commentary, the poker returns to its place. The chairs around the dining table beside me sigh, seemingly going to sleep, and I don't hear the kitchen staff either. Even the mop is just a mop.

The fire crackles.

Outside, the wolves howl.

This must be what peace sounds like. This must be what sanity sounds like. I look at the unconscious seer in my arms and lean back in the chair, moving only slightly to adjust my position so I can gaze down upon her without her knowing I'm staring.

Augusta has a pixie nose and dark hair, with rosy cheeks over a grayish appearance. It's rather unusual for a Summer fae, but perhaps some of her ancestors mixed with the Unseelie, particularly those from the Fallen Court.

The light material of her short white dress dips between her breasts, giving away their size. They would fit into her small hands. She has a flat belly and a toned muscular body, telling me she might be a swimmer. Most Summer fae enjoy the ocean and are excellent swimmers, maintaining their physique in such a way.

Since I scooped her up, her legs dangle over my arm, so that the dress is pulled away from her knees, revealing most of her thighs. Slowly so as not to rouse her, I rest her legs over the chair arm and free my hand so I can slip a claw under the hem of her dress and lift. White panties cover what I'm certain is a cute little pussy, one I might want to taste.

Seers must remain untouched.

It has also been said that seers are faithful. Their foresight almost always predicts events involving the people they're closest to. Overall, she's cute, and apparently, having her on my lap quiets my mind. I stroke her head as one would pet one's lap puppy. I love puppies. They're cute, and at first disobedient, but with training, grow into loyal companions.

Augusta slowly blinks open her eyes.

"There you are," I say gently, not wanting to startle her. "You fainted."

At first, she smiles, but then she takes a look around, and the moment she realizes she's not in the Summer Court anymore (again), her face turns more ashen than usual, and she starts scrambling off my lap while I'm holding her so she doesn't fall off.

"Let me go," she orders.

I lift my hands. Because she's still disoriented from the shadow travel and busy freaking out, she rolls off my lap and hits the floor, then stays there for a moment.

"I tried saving you the embarrassment," I say.

She whips her head around and growls at me.

A puppy comes to mind again. Cute.

Augusta rises and fixes her dress, her gaze on the windows. "Are we underground?"

I frown. "No."

"In a cave?"

"We are in my home." I stand and regard the windows, wondering what gives her the idea we're underground.

"Where is your home?"

"Hymasan Mountains in a village called Dokka."

"There're windows all around, but nothing to see outside."

"Ah, I understand now why you might think we're underground. The house is reinforced with steelnite shutters. They're dark as granite and tough as steel. They can't be penetrated."

She appears frightened. I'm confused. I just told her how I reinforced my home. It took me an entire span, and I passed out from exhaustion. The least she could do is acknowledge the safety I ensured for her.

"I assure you, this is the safest place in the world."

She pinches her lips. I can tell she dislikes my home, but Summer fairies are raised to be polite, and she says, "I don't doubt it." She eyes the spiral staircase and covers her yawn. "My room is on the first floor?"

I gesture toward the stairs. "After you."

My home has five stories, each floor spreading out from a single staircase that winds about a pillar made entirely of stacked weapons, mainly hundreds of thousands of steelnite arrows packed so tightly together that they appear blended as a single construct. My weapons are hiding in plain sight, my army always at the ready.

We step off the staircase onto the first floor. I'm disappointed it took her no time to climb the steps. Peeking up her skirt made me feel like a...a male again. It has been many turns since I coupled with a female, and I've certainly never brought one into my home.

"Where to?" she asks.

"This way." I walk toward the room on the right, which I designed for the seer. "I had it prepared for you. Thought that maybe all the dark walls and other gloom and doom that makes me chipper might bother you, so…"

She smiles. "That's unexpected and thoughtful of you."

Since I concentrated most of my efforts during the span on securing the shutters around the home, I'm curious what the house staff has done here. I commanded a remodel for a young bride. I open the door and step inside. The moment I see what happened in here, I want to step right outside again and close the room, but she's already following behind me.

I rest my fists on my hips and sigh.

"You remodeled this?" she asks, amusement in her voice.

"No, no, wasn't me. The house staff did it." They painted the room in pink and drew pale blue unicorns all over the walls.

"Will I meet the staff tomorrow?"

The fire poker in her room starts stirring and her wardrobe creaks open, but if everyone comes alive now, the seer might faint again.

"Yes, tomorrow."

Augusta walks around, then lies down on the bed. Her eyes go wide and her hand flies over her mouth. Her gray eyes regard me and then stare at the ceiling.

I'm almost frightened to look, but I sit beside her and lie the same way she is.

On her ceiling is a painting of me. Which would be awkward enough already, but not as awkward if I wasn't lying bare-chested in a bed made of silk and fur, with my hand tucked under a silk sheet and holding my package.

Last night, I recall jerking off to a vision of the seer. It's almost the exact image of me from last night.

"Dream well, little seer."

15

AUGUSTA

The loud howling of the winds outside wakes me from deep sleep. I pull the soft feather comforter up to my chin and blink open my eyes, then squint against the sunlight piercing the sheer white curtains, wishing the steelnite-reinforced shutters had stayed down and let me sleep in.

Nevertheless, the view is stunning.

The snow-covered landscape reminds me of my village home, and even though I love the beach and all the amenities living in the Golden Palace offered, there's nothing quite like waking up in a snow-covered home bundled under the covers, protected from the cold.

Yawning, I inhale fresh mountain air and stretch well before grabbing a warm red robe that was thrown over a white leather chair. I approach the window and spread the curtains then step back in awe, my heart filling with something that can only be described as love at first sight.

Directly across from my chamber's window is a snow-covered mountain peak, above which the sun has risen, brighter than I've ever seen it. Under the mountain is a narrow valley nestled between two large lakes. At least three different villages are set in the valley, with no more than a hundred homes between all three of them.

"Hello," a tiny voice says.

I scream, almost jumping out of my skin. Back plastered against the window, I look around the room for the person who spoke, but there's nobody here. Also, the chamber is large, much larger than I noticed last night, with two fireplaces: one near the bed, the other within the seating area. As I take in the space, it appears as if I have an entire floor all to myself.

"Hello," I answer, matching the tiny voice.

Something touches my left toe.

I leap onto the bed.

Under the window, a pair of fluffy red slippers shimmer and pad toward the bed. I lean over the mattress, and the slippers start talking. "Wear us and come downstairs."

Okay, it's the Unseelie king's magic, and like all magic, it's perfectly...strange and totally sane for him. I drop my bottom onto the bed, but hesitate, sliding my foot into the talking slippers.

"Wear us," the slippers say again, punctuating the words and losing their gentle girly voice, now sounding a bit more like the Unseelie king.

Hoping they don't bite my toes, I wear the slippers and open the door, then duck as paintbrushes and canisters and all manner of paint supplies fly past me and into the room. "Get rid of it all," the Unseelie king's voice booms via the largest paintbrush of the group.

The brush hovers in the air and turns to me.

"Any special requests?"

I look around the rest of the floor, noting dark walls with paintings.

"Dark walls are fine."

"And the ceiling? Shall we paint over it?"

I feel my face heat up. "I would want to know why it's there in the first place."

"Nobody knows."

"Not even the king?"

"Especially not the king."

I giggle. Either he's funny or truly as mad as they say he is. Unsure how to answer, I make a turn about the first floor, counting three more floors above it. A five-story house made entirely out of dark wood except, the central pillar that's made from the same dark metal as the shutters. I've never seen such dark wood or such metal used in construction or elsewhere.

I lean over the railing and spot the Unseelie king at the dining table near the large fireplace. He's wearing a heavy black-on-black uniform with white buttons closing diagonally over his torso. Gloved hands unroll a map and pin it with a few figurines in the corners. A rustling sounds all around me, and the ground starts shaking at the same time as I hear a flock of birds coming from somewhere. Books and maps tumble from an upper floor.

I duck before one hits my head.

When I think all the maps he'll ever need have flown down, I rise back up and peek over the railing again.

"Will you be standing there all span witnessing my madness, or will you join me?" He looks up, a smile tugging at his lips. "Not in madness. For breakfast."

I make it down the steps, and the king greets me by pulling out a chair for me to sit. I thank him, shocked he didn't just simply move it with his magic when he's doing everything else that way. The entire house seems to be alive, and his magic thickens the air I breathe.

The king returns to hover above his maps. "Eggs, bacon, grains?"

"Hm?"

"The breakfast, seer. What would you like?"

"Yes, that sounds lovely."

"All of it?"

"Yes, please."

"So then you do eat."

I nod. What kind of statement was that? Why would I not eat? Doesn't everyone eat? Wha...

In the kitchen, I hear pots and pans and voices as if there're other people. That must be his staff, but something tells me there's nobody here besides us. Just to be sure, I walk into the hallway next to the fireplace and find the kitchen busy preparing my breakfast.

Not a soul is here. The pans and pots and utensils are alive, and when I walk in, they all stop and turn toward me. I feel the weight of their eyeless stare as if I'm intruding on them.

I lift a hand. "Hi, all." I hook a thumb over my shoulder. "I'll just be over there."

Turning, I walk back to the table, where the king keeps studying the same map. "Did you meet the kitchen staff?"

"Yes, they are lovely." I sit down.

A red cloth napkin flies over and tucks itself between my breasts.

The king snaps his head my way and tsks. The napkin drops to my lap, and he goes on about studying his map.

What was that about? Did he touch my chest? Does this count as magical groping? Does he want to touch me and his subconscious is touching me? The questions might give me a headache. The cure, however, arrives on a tray. Boiled eggs, bacon, sausages, fresh veggies, grains, and a steaming red drink.

"May I please have tea?" Any tea will do.

The teacup wobbles and says, "I'm filled with kalia tea."

The spoon stands from the sugar bowl. "This is the morning brew in our parts of the world, Seelie."

Oh, so this one doesn't really care for my being a Seelie. I pick up the teacup and blow on the liquid before sipping. Bitter. I make a face. The spoon snorts and scoops up sugar three times. I grab it and add some more before I find it drinkable.

"You will get used to it," the king says.

Seeking utensils, I look around the table. "May I please have some utensils?"

"They're beside the plate."

A pair of white wooden sticks with red tips lies beside the plate. "These things?"

He nods.

I take one in my right hand and the other in my left, and start with the bacon while I figure out how I'll eat boiled eggs without digging inside them with the spoon. The bacon drops back on the plate. Awkwardly, I pick it up with one stick and kind of balance it as I bring it to my mouth. Just as I do, I catch sight of the king. He's staring, looking horrified.

I'm doing something wrong. I drop the sticks, the bacon, all of it, and fold my hands on my lap.

From the other end of the table, a chair moves back and glides over the floor to position itself behind my chair. The king rounds me and sits down, his thighs closing around my chair, his hands settling atop the table as he leans in.

His body surrounds me.

Without him releasing his mating scent deliberately, the

scent of leather and evergreens he wears makes me lean back and into him. I sniff near his jaw, and the urge to trail my nose down his neck is so great that I ball my hands into fists so my claws hurt me. My heart starts pounding in my ears, making my blood boil. My entire body comes alive as if I'm one of his objects.

"The commander of the Summer fae armies smells like you," I murmur. "Are you related?"

"We are not."

"Why do you smell almost the same?"

"Our magic is related."

"How so?"

"He can manipulate objects."

"I wish I could do that," I whisper seductively. "It would make using the sticks to put food into my mouth easier."

"I will teach you."

The finger his magic brushed before and caused frost-bite starts throbbing again just before King Aamako rests his hands atop mine. They're gloved, and the touch of the leather zips to my clitoris, makes my nipples harden. My heartbeat practically rings in my ears like some sort of bell. It's probably the bell heralding my doom.

This male's scent and proximity might send me into heat, while all he's trying to do is teach me how to use his utensils to get some food into my belly. *Good fates, please pour a bucket of ice over my head.*

The king uses his fingers to show me how to position the sticks between my own fingers, and while I'm watching him maneuver the twigs, all I can think about is those long, thick, leather-clad fingers stroking between my legs.

Try as I might not to think it or visualize it, the image of him and me on the chair by the fireplace comes to mind. He's fully dressed while I'm nude and draped over his lap, my legs spread and my head thrown back while he's stroking me between my legs.

A whimper escapes my lips as I feel wetness grow between my legs, and my mating scent starts escaping my control. I'm struggling to pull it back while the king talks about the history of the utensils, trying to teach me something useful. All I can think about is getting off.

"Augusta." His crisp voice cuts into my carnal visions. "Have you been paying attention?"

"Yes, sir."

He chuckles. It's one of those rumbles that males make from their chest that sound dangerously close to a purr.

"Good, because you will use the *lashi* for the duration of our time here so that when I present you to the Unseelie court, you will eat as if you were born with them in your hand."

I gulp, suddenly losing my appetite.

The king squeezes my hands and forces them to pick up the piece of bacon I kept dropping. Using his hand over mine, he maneuvers the bacon toward my mouth, and I feel like one of his objects. A doll, but instead of strings, he's using his hands to feed me. And do what he wills with me. He will take me to the Unseelie court.

He holds out the bacon, and the smell lures me in. My belly growls as I lean in and bite the edge of it, then some more, moaning at the taste. "This is some excellent bacon."

"Chew, swallow, and then speak."

He sounds like my sister June, and I obey. Once I have a good idea of what to do with the sticks (what did he call them?), the Unseelie king returns to his maps.

And that's when I see it.

The huge bulge in his pants.

He's aroused. By me.

After being turned down by the commander nearly all summer long, I started feeling like a reject, and frankly, watching June charm the king, and Prince El'jah going through males and females like morning teabags, and more than half of the ladies at court finding partners, I started to doubt my looks.

"Do you think I'm pretty?" flies out of my mouth.

16

AAMAKO

Her question reflects her boldness. Even if she covers her mouth and her eyes widen, telling me she's horrified she's asked, she asked anyway. I could say no, and for a young Summer fairy who is also a virgin (and I'm sure this one is, because she's a seer) it could crush her confidence. But that's not why I answer, "I do."

Considering the subject closed, I return to perusing the Winter Palace's current map. Grabbing rolls of several more maps from the past, I spread them out and peruse the layouts, seeking patterns in the designs. I tap my claw on the table.

The seer gets up and stands next to me, her mating scent now under control. When I tried teaching her how to eat with *lashi*, I didn't expect her to find my touch arousing and for her to release her scent. Most females release the scent in response to the male releasing his. It's a dance of a sort called courting, and my people love the dance as much as we love the act of sex itself.

I hadn't released my scent; thus she hasn't responded to my invitation. One of two things happened. Either she's inviting me to have her, or her mating scent escaped her control. Arousal is one thing. The release of a scent is another. Arousal is more out of our control than the mating scent. The mating scent invites my touch. It tells me she wants me, but I wonder if she truly does.

I lean in slightly and sniff. Her natural Summer fae scent comes back to me, light and breezy with a touch of ...something I'm sure I've smelled before but can't quite place.

"Augusta," I say, and note how her shoulders pull back as she goes on alert.

"Yes, King Aamako?"

"There's a peculiar scent about you that I can't place. It's as frustrating as the lack of patterns on the maps."

She leans in as if expecting me to continue, but that's all I had to say, so I continue with the maps.

"What you smell is my mating scent. It slipped."

It slipped. It was not deliberate, so she didn't invite my attention. "That's not the scent I was referring to." I wiggle my nose. "It's your natural scent. Has a touch of something—"

She interrupts. "Is it a bad smell? I shall bathe." She blushes profusely. "I'll go sit back down."

I catch her by the hip and pull her to stand between my body and the table. I press against her slightly, allowing her to feel my hardness. "You smell familiar. It is pleasing to me, and I am pleased you're losing control of your mating scent. It tells me your body recognizes the sensual dance between a male and a female. If you weren't attracted to me, you wouldn't have kissed me moments after we met, and if I were not attracted to you I wouldn't be aroused." I press closer yet. "And if you'd like to invite my advances..." I pause to listen to her heart. It's beating as fast as a rabbit's, telling me I'm the predator in the room.

"All you have to do is lie on top of the table and spread your legs."

I step back and wait.

The seer seems stricken, her expression one of utter shock.

"And there you are, surprised again. I'm starting to believe the little magic you do possess isn't foresight at all."

"I told you I'm not a very good seer."

"I don't need you to be."

"You just need me to play the role of your bride."

"That's right."

"And that *will do*."

I nod, wondering why she's emphasizing "will do" while she contemplates my offer. I'd rather she didn't have to think about it. I'd rather she responded with wild passion and invited me to lick her relentlessly.

The seer moves aside and points at the map. "What are you doing with these?"

I approach the table again, my shaft straining, suppressed arousal making my balls throb with a heartbeat of their own. "I'm studying the different layouts of the Winter Beauty."

"Isn't that the Unseelie court's palace?"

"The Winter Court's palace," I correct her.

"Are you redecorating or..." She leans over the table, reaching for the map on my right, and her scent intensifies. Sniffing, I release a rumble from my chest she can interpret any way she wants. Her scent is pleasant and makes me want to purr, and thus I shall purr.

I offered my affections, served them up as one would serve butter at the table. She declined and can keep declining for the duration of her stay with me.

As she straightens, her wrist brushes my erection. A

strained growl escapes my chest. Is this little summerling teasing me? She wouldn't dare, would she?

I give her a side-eye and raise my eyebrow.

Augusta steps away, her face the color of a radish. "Pardon me."

Clearing my throat, I say, "The reason I'm studying the maps is because we will host an engagement party in my court, and my nephew is an *architektus*."

"An engagement party in your court!" she shrieks.

Unaccustomed to screeching people in my house, I wince. "Our party, yes, and my nephew is an *architektus*." I repeat that bit and emphasize it because my nephew's magic is why I'm agonizing over studying the patterns in the maps.

Both hands fly to her mouth, and then she cups her cheeks. "An engagement party in your court."

"And my nephew is an *architektus*." Did she not hear this vital piece of information about going to the Winter Court when there's a plot to remove me from the throne by force if necessary? And it is necessary. I will not step down.

"Okay, okay." She stretches out her hands. "Stay calm, Augusta, stay calm."

She speaks to herself. We have that in common. How nice to know.

"When is the party?" she asks.

"Immediately after I've studied the court's layout as it currently stands. Because he's an *architektus*, we will have to respond instantly." I await the moment she realizes the significance of his magic with respect to me claiming a bride and him wanting the throne and us visiting the palace.

"And how long will it take you to study?"

"A night, two at most."

"You're saying our engagement party in the Winter Court could happen on the morrow?"

She seems fixated on the party. "Correct."

Augusta's breath catches in her throat. She really is the worst seer in the world, the position likely given to her only because she's the fate's little sister with a tiny bit of foresight. Not that I care. As I told her, her seer powers aren't the reason I picked her. I picked her because she kissed me, and I enjoy her company probably more than I should.

"A party in the Unseelie court," she says, though I think she's speaking with herself again. Also, blood is draining from her face, and she sits back down.

My magic picks up the teacup and lifts it to her mouth. Augusta sips, eyeing the maps now. She's coming to her senses, comprehending what I've been saying.

Excited that we're finally on the same page, I tap my claw on the most recent map spread out before us. "Once done here, I will visit the palace for reconnaissance and will be gone most of the night. Before you worry about staying alone, I assure you again, this house is well defended."

"Do you think we could return to the Summer Court for dresses? I don't have a gown befitting an engagement party. Or a gown for a party at all. In the...your court." She answers me in the same tone I answered her about my nephew's magic.

Clearly, she's gathered intelligence I haven't. "Do go on, dear."

She tilts her head. "You're announcing me as your bride."

"Correct. And?"

"I would prefer to have a nice gown, if it's not too much trouble for you."

"It isn't any trouble at all, but I left instructions with the Summer fae in the laundry to have your trunks delivered.

The staff in the village will alert me once they arrive. Your gowns should come any moment now."

Augusta swallows. "Dear king, no trunks will be arriving because I don't have any gowns."

Oh. Oh. Awww. She told me she lacked extensive education and that she's from a farm. Among the myriad things my mind handles at once, the information stayed filed in the back of my mind because her situation must've changed when the Summer king fell in love with her sister. I presumed this would mean the royal seer would have been provided with gowns. I'm shocked to find out she still has nothing.

"You were wearing a lovely gown when I met you."

"So lovely."

"Is there more where that gown came from?"

"Many more, but they all belong to my sister. At the court, she gets to pick from thousands of dresses presented to her practically each morning. Once she chooses"—Augusta smiles, and her eyes dart to the fireplace as if recalling a nice memory—"once King Et'enne picks out her clothes, the royal family gets second pick, and then the courtiers come in for theirs."

"This seems like protocol."

"It very much is."

Summerlings and their fashions. "I get it now. You're in urgent need of a dress."

"A nice gown feels like armor to me, and I will need armor."

"Hearing you think about your safety and the dress as armor pleases me." I'm debating whether I should return to the Summer Court and steal a dress or if I should commission one.

Augusta sips the tea and dabs her mouth. "Will you tell

me what *architektus* magic can do? It makes me think of construction and design."

Finally she asks about it. I guess we all have our priorities, don't we? "I'll tell you what, little seer, I will secure a lavish gown if you do something for me."

The seer positively lights up. "You want to make another deal?"

It's almost as if recklessness excites her. I'm the Unseelie king who's broken more fae with deals than any other living fae and possibly any fae in the history of my people. The fae kingdom died at my sword because they broke their deal with me. If the seer knew her history, she would never make deals with me. Everyone avoids and hates me, and for good reason. I wish to conquer them all.

Yet this young fae female gets up from her seat and faces me, craning her neck so she can lock her eyes with me. "Well, state your terms."

Her mouth forms an O as I dip my head. There it is, her arousal and that strange scent I've smelled before but can't quite identify with a place or a person.

"In exchange for my securing your gown—"

She interrupts. "A lavish gown."

I tilt my head, my lips atop hers. "A lavish gown," I purr. "You will study the marked pages of these books." While I speak with her, my magic sorts through the books in my library. On the third floor, the library door bursts open, books rush out, and fall in a dramatic fashion. One of them starts screaming, "Look out, look out!"

Augusta startles and takes hold of my biceps as the books thump on the table, dust exploding from them.

I wave off the dust and wait for it to settle.

The seer stares at the historical tomes as if they're baby fire dragons that are going to burn her.

"What's the matter?" I ask.

Augusta picks up a book and weighs it in her hand. "Thick."

"Mmhm," I purr, my perversion seemingly knowing no bounds.

She counts the marked chapters of the book she's holding, then the others from the stack I want her to read. "Fifty-four chapters?"

"Correct." At the very least.

"It'll take me a turn to read all this."

"You have a span or two."

"But I can't possibly read all this in that time."

"You can and you will because your life depends on it. If you go to my court without knowing who will be there and what they can do, you will fear the unknown, and they can smell and sense fear."

Augusta snorts. "Even if I read all the books in the world, I will still fear the Unseelie fae."

I tuck my claw under her chin and lift it so she looks at me. "They will fear you because you're mine."

What little control she's held over her mating scent seems to disappear, and the aroma blossoms in the room, invading my senses. She's drowning me in her mating scent, but the horror on her face when she realizes her mating scent is spreading all over the house tells me she's not quite ready for my affections.

"They will fear you because you're mine and for as long as you're mine. And because I like you, little seer, I shall impart to you a secret, a law of power, if you will."

She nods, so I lean in and sniff around her neck. Good fates, she's perfect. What was I saying? Oh yes, one of the laws of power. "They will fear you indefinitely if they think you're the next fate."

17

AUGUSTA

At King Aamako's declaration that I am his, the dam holding back my mating scent from flooding me with need bursts. I release months' worth of the pent-up sexual energy the commander rejected. While I tried flirting with the commander, I never had this happen to me in his presence. I never lost control of my mating scent in such a violent way.

King Aamako speaks without reservation, and the brutal way he expresses his affection for me makes me want to kiss him again. I mean, he's even offered to eat me out, and while the phrase "will do" that he keeps using regarding me as his bride bothers me, even if in our fake arrangement, it's not supposed to, the Unseelie king treats me kindly.

I recall our arrangement. In order to gain favor with the powerful courtiers, he must convince them he'll take a bride, thereby promising an heir and the continuation of his bloodline. The same bloodline that carries his extremely unique and powerful Unseelie magic.

During the time we spent downstairs, the king's magic kept the house moving. I heard the things in the home he calls "staff" painting and chatting in my chambers. Then there's the kitchen staff arguing over what they'll serve for lunch and dinner. There's also someone (or no one, actually) chopping wood outside, as well as the fire poker down here obsessively stoking the logs in the fireplace, trying to create something only it considers perfect.

All this is going on while King Aamako converses with me effortlessly, never once making me feel like he's doing anything else or that I'm secondary to whatever he's perusing, even the maps. It seems he's truly interested in my troubles, however girly and stupid they might seem compared to whatever goals kings chase, whatever burdens they carry.

He will fetch me a dress so that I might look as powerful as he thinks I should, even though every fae can sense I possess very little magic. And me being in line to become the next fate is as likely as snow falling on the roof of the Golden Palace. "You have me mixed up with my sister. She's the fate."

"There are three fates. One of them sees all that will come to pass."

"Yes, but she's an Unseelie. They say the future fate is an Unseelie."

The king frowns. "Who says that?"

"I don't know their names exactly. They're 'they,' the people."

He laughs. "You're talking out of your ass."

"A lady doesn't talk out of her bum."

"Seers talk out of their bums more often than kings, and that's saying something."

I gasp. "We do not."

He winks and taps the books. "Read."

I stand and salute him.

Before he leaves, we share a moment where we look at

each other. A black jacket with a high collar obscures his neck and hugs his body, and his hair is pulled back and tightly braided, then coiled to make a tower high at the back of his head. His eyes are so dark in the morning light, they're almost indigo, and the sharpness of his cheekbones makes him seem more regal somehow, more dangerous, like a beautiful serpent luring his prey. I wish for the serpent's kiss again. Good thing he doesn't grant me my wish. Instead, he lets the shadows swallow him whole.

It's dinnertime, and I'm still downstairs at the table, content to spend the span span-dreaming while staring at the view of the snow-covered landscape and not getting much of my required reading done. My belly rumbles so loudly, I fear the sound might wake up the entire kitchen staff from their nonmagical slumber. When the king leaves, the objects he commands take up their normal positions and behave as, well, nonliving things.

Hence, I made lunch myself.

It appears I'll be making dinner too.

In the kitchen, I consider starting a fire for cooking, then decide that'll take forever. Luckily, when I snoop around, I find a heavy marble door to what I'm pretty sure is a cellar. Using my shoulder, I shove it open, and the icy cold that escapes the room makes me close the door immediately. Cellar in the Winter Court indeed.

Returning to the living space, I shrug on the robe from the morning before I descend the steps into the freezing cellar, where different types of alcohol are stored inside large barrels placed throughout the open space, which stretches the entire length of the castle. From what I gather, it's divided into sections and filled with all the reserves one would need for a family of ten to survive over the span of a decade, not just a single male living out here in the middle of nowhere. But to each his own.

Rich folks love collecting stuff they'll never need.

I pass barrels of what I know by smell is wine, then ale, then *ianke*, and come to the dry storage section. Inside, various meats hang from the ceiling, and there are barrels full of aged dairy. Father would love this. Mother would too.

In the village, preparing for winter was an event all families celebrated, and since my father is a pig farmer, people would gather at our farm and help my father prepare our livestock for their tables in the winter. Most of the meat was preserved in the same way as it is here, by drying and hanging it in attics or cellars for cold storage.

I locate a table with a large butcher knife on it and pick it up to slice a piece of dry meat already there. Tasting it tells me it's not pork. I don't know what kind of meat it is, but I slice a few more pieces and look around for a ladder. There's already one against the barrel, so I climb it to grab some cheese. Holy fates.

The cheese!

It's packed into round balls of different sizes and smells delicious. I grab the biggest piece I can carry and climb down.

A glass of wine would be nice.

There are a bunch of leather flasks hanging from the hooks on the walls. I grab one along with a basket that I stuff with meat and cheese as if I'm going on a picnic. Or to Grandma's house in the forest. On the way out, I sling the ladder over my shoulder. When I reach the wine barrels at the front of the cellar, I climb the ladder and siphon red wine into the leather flask, then head for the door.

Or rather the place where I think the door leading to the stairway was. Except it's just a stone wall now. I turn and take stock of the room. Yes, I'm certain this is where I came from.

Turning back to the wall, I tap around it. Of course, there's no door, so I walk along the wall searching for an exit. I circle the entire cellar twice, slowing down the third time, but knowing if I stop, I'll fall asleep and never wake up.

The frost has already accumulated on my lashes, and I'm shivering violently. The sound of the only thing keeping me alive, the wobbly steps I'm taking, bounce off the walls when I can no longer hold myself up.

As I near the fourth round of circling the cellar—and I can count the rounds I'm making because of the flask I dropped off by the barrel right across from what I know used to be the entrance—I start doubting myself.

Have I lost my mind?

I have not.

Maybe I have, though. Maybe it's in the air. They call King Aamako "the Destroyer." And maybe the Destroyer changed his mind about me once he got to know me. Maybe I'm not likable at all. In addition, I'm scared of going to the Unseelie court. I know what he's doing with the books too. He's making me read books about magic because he knows I lack a proper education and thus also lack the prestige to move in his circles.

Everyone will figure out I'm a fake.

No amount of education or books can make up for the lack of my magic or the ability to fake anything. I'm honest to a fault. And he seems to be a forward type of person as well.

Faking anything isn't in the cards for either of us.

He will lose his crown, and his family will end me.

I stumble and hold myself up against the wall, my teeth no longer even chattering, my fingers so cramped, I can't move them, my legs unfeeling. I'm so bloody tired. I'll take a nap.

I lie down, cheek on the frozen ground, and catch sight of the shadows retreating under the barrels.

18

AAMAKO

A royal seer from the Summer Court walking into the Unseelie court on the arm of a king who is intent on keeping his crown must wear a garment that sends a powerful message. And while I believe a nude Augusta would send a clearer message, I will enjoy her nude body in private.

I wince at my disturbing thoughts.

The seers are chaste. Heck, I'm chaste by fae standards, having not enjoyed the company of a female in over half a century. It's no wonder my brother's widow is considered the Winter queen and her son is considered the king, even though I'm still alive and he's by all accounts a prince regent.

Since I'll never make children, the Winter crown passes to my nephew, and by default, the Fallen Kingdom crown as well, making him the next Unseelie king. But not while I'm alive. I like my crown and the two courts, one of which I conquered and paid for in blood, the other I inherited for being the eldest son.

My nephew, while powerful, is vain and cruel, as well as

a poor strategist, having allied himself with the losing party in the short-lasting conflict for the Kilseleian crown.

Had it been up to me, and it would have had I been the one directing the Winter Court, I would have sent aid to the savage hordes.

Anyone carrying ancient magic is a dangerous creature, one I want an alliance with. The Summer king swiped that alliance right out from under my nephew's nose.

The Summer king intended to keep the seer as well. The moment I realized she was a seer who is a sister to the fate who sees all that's come to pass, I had to have her. Moreover, Augusta kissed me as if I was hers to kiss. That alone made me want her in a way I shouldn't.

Yet, here I am, materializing in the royal family part of the Winter Court's palace, seeking old friends and even older garments, troubled that I haven't stayed on the frozen lake outside the court and picked up the garments from the wardrobe inside.

I don't need to pick out her garments in person. I could use my magic. I could, but instead, I'm walking down the dark halls I once ran through with my brother when we were kids.

Judging by the spiderwebs and the mice scurrying across the hardwood floors as I make my way down the hall toward my sister's old chambers, nobody's frequented the family parts of the palace since I left the court. It feels like a century has passed since I went into seclusion, but it's only been... I pause. Almost a century. Perhaps about eighty turns, give or take a few. In seclusion, I lost track of time.

I enter the chambers of my dear sister and inhale, seeking her familiar scent. In return, dust and mold fly up my nostrils, and I cough before wrapping a black scarf over the bottom of my face.

It reeks in here.

Of course it does.

My nephew left this part of the palace rotting, perhaps to show how my family abandoned the Winter Court and lost interest in governance. In a way, it is what my sister and I did. She because her call to duty couldn't be ignored, and me because the stupids who thought they could steal my crown and the stupids who thought I would give them the Fall Court's throne started fighting, threatening the stability of the populace.

Every good ruler knows that stability in the kingdom is the key to prosperity for the kingdom, and that happy folks who thrive and prosper will celebrate their monarch. If the various noble houses started sensing a division in the crown, meaning if they sensed my little family started cooking up plans of dominion, the nobles would form alliances around whichever male they believed would keep the crown or around whichever male promised them more power in terms of land or marriage or some such.

My nephew is blessed with good looks and ladies love him, so he's used his body as a way to garner support. I simply beheaded traitors, until I recognized that if I kept it up, I would have harmed the powers of the Unseelie fae and my people. Hence, I proclaimed my brother's widow a regent, and once my nephew came of age, he took on the majority of the responsibility of ruling the court.

After I removed myself from governance, things settled. Or so I thought. Now I see I only delayed the inevitable. My nephew and his mother covet my crown, and since I heard he's making an attempt on my life, I came out in the open.

Kings fear no one, least of all little princes.

Several torches hang on the walls, and I pick one up, wondering if it's still oiled. I see fine in the dark, but I could see the dress better in the light. There's nothing I can use to ignite the oils with, and I'm too lazy to start the fire from scratch, so I rely on my magic to seek the nearest fireplace.

Behind me, the old door creaks. I wrap the shadows around me, hiding until I know which guard is roaming this part of the palace. I don't know if it's a friend or a foe. Foe, likely, since guards are younger males, and I don't know them.

The guards get selected for duty right after their military training, which starts at age five and ends at eighteen. Depending on how well the training goes for them and how much magic they wield and what kind of magic they carry, they get assigned posts.

Some guard kings. Others roam abandoned parts of the Unseelie court.

Shadows slither inside the room, and if it weren't for the old unkept door that creaked only slightly as it slid open, I would likely be dead by now. By the way the Unseelie maneuvers the shadows, I recognize the guard as a shadow crawler, a fae trained as a spy and assassin.

Shadows climb the walls, but before they reach my shadows, I materialize in the flesh.

The male does the same and swings his sword.

I carried no weapons.

Often, I have no need to carry weapons.

I also happen to think combat is fun, so I bend backward, the tip of his sharp sword slicing a button off my coat. Whew, that was close. I dance around him, my feet moving quickly.

The male lifts his left knee and kicks out, hitting me right in the chest, instantly knocking the breath out of me. In pain and struggling to inhale, I bend forward as he skips away to materialize on my left, sword lifted, ready to slice off my head.

My magic takes his sword and holds it in place. The male tugs his sword, and when he realizes magic is in play, he lifts his knee into my nose. Blood soaks the cloth I wrapped around my face, and I rip it off with a growl.

Instead of his traditional guard uniform, the shadow crawler wears thick, wide-legged, black pants and a long. black cotton tunic cut at the sides to allow easier movement of the legs. His long hair is bunched up at the top of his head, and there's some sort of clay mask on his forehead.

At first, he lifts his bare foot to strike again, then pauses midstrike, awkwardly holding his body in balance while his brain (likely) is piecing together the information his eyes are sending in the dark room, the only light that of a waxing moon.

I wipe my face with a sleeve and flinch. "You broke my nose. It tells me you haven't lost your deadly touch. Well done, Kense."

The crawler's still unsure of me and steps back, but doesn't lower his guard, eyes darting at the sword poised above him. I breathe life into his sword to reassure him it's really me.

The sword gains eyes and lips and says, "Take me into your hand, lover boy."

Kense drops to his knees, forehead on the floor. "Pardon me, Your Majesty. I did not recognize you."

Another crawler rushes inside and joins him in kneeling, a female I recognize as Kense's wife, Tima.

"What are you two still doing here?" I clearly remember disbanding the crawlers and sending them off with handsome rewards.

They're still on the floor and turning their heads to look

at each other. Arguing in their native tongue commences, and Tima answers, "We hide here."

"No, you don't."

"We do too," she says.

It warms my heart to hear defiance in her voice. It makes me think of the seer. I enjoy fiery females. That should not be mistaken for enjoying disobedient ones, however. I dislike disobedience, no matter if it's in females, males, or things.

"Get up," I order, then dab my bloody nose.

"Serves you right," Tima mumbles.

I grip the bridge of my nose and set the cartilage right. It cracks, and my eyes water. Fuck, that hurt like frostbite in the brain. Stars play over my eyes, and the pair of people becomes a blur of obsidian cloaks.

"I disbanded my staff and gave you land. What did you do?"

Kense answers. "We farmed as you wished, but the prince regent called the crawlers back to duty."

"For?"

"The coup, my king," Tima says. "He didn't announce it in exactly those words, but there was a secret meeting and Hosen was sent after the ones who didn't answer the prince's call."

"I presume you two didn't answer."

Tima juts her chin. "We serve the mad king." She winks at me.

"And?"

"And," Kense says, "we hid everywhere, then grew tired of running and decided to take on the life of shadows most of the time." He looks around. "These halls are familiar, and the house stays dark."

"Hmm, I'm surprised my nephew isn't staying here."

"They say your brother haunts this house."

"Oh, how fun. Does he?"

The couple shake their heads.

"Good. Now that that's settled, you will continue lurking in the shadows and slowly spread out to the court, to be my eyes and ears."

"Like in the old spans." Kense's eyes twinkle.

"Just like that. Are there other crawlers still loyal to me?"

"Possibly, but the ones already here can't be trusted."

Tima nudges her husband. Gently, he elbows her back. They're so cute together, one would never think these are coldhearted killers loyal exclusively to me.

"At ease."

"What are you doing here?" Tima asks, leaning in eagerly.

"I'm looking for a dress for my engagement party."

The wardrobe comes to life with a long sigh. "Finally, someone remembered me." She spreads her doors. "Welcome, handsome."

I approach and cross my arms over my chest as the wardrobe shuffles through the various dresses, spitting out some on hangers, then putting them back. My sister's fine dresses seem to have aged with the wardrobe, but they haven't lost their flirty charm. Emishi chose her clothes carefully, always ensuring she never blended in with the rest of the courtier. If something was trendy, she would commission the designers to make her the complete opposite of the trend.

Because she stood out, her dresses became famous and thus memorable.

"You're getting engaged?" Tima comes to stand next to me.

"Mmhm."

"Oh, my king, that's wonderful news!" she squeaks, then covers her mouth.

I contemplate if I will mention the engagement is a short-lived phase and that I will release the seer from the deal as soon as she's served her purpose in my court, but I don't. While I trust the pair of shadow crawlers with my life, I trust only myself with Augusta's life. Besides, if they believe her to be a true bride of mine, they will guard her better than if they thought I cared very little about her.

I do care about her, and while she's in my care, I will ensure her safety. I also would enjoy dressing her in a gown of my choosing if only I could find *the one*. The most famous one, the one most painters like to paint my sister in, the one nobody in the court will mistake for another, the one that sends the loudest message: *I'm your future queen*.

19

AAMAKO

Sneaking around my own home so that the seer downstairs doesn't see the dress before the party tomorrow makes me feel like I'm in my twenties again. Whatever that felt like, I'm sure it was energetic and fun.

Using the shadows, I arrive in my chambers and fling the dress through the air. The sword catches it on its hilt and returns to the other swords displayed on the wall. I throw the matching cloak over the sword hanging next to the dress and start humming the army's marching song.

The shadow crawlers have informed me my nephew has been gathering forces for many turns, slowly but surely, guided by his intelligent mother, once a queen regent who never forgave me for not marrying her.

She would see me dead, or my people turned against me. It's how I ended up eliminating an entire court of the Unseelie who conspired with her after my brother's death. She collected an army, which then started marching on me. I met her army at their court, and the rest is the very history

I tasked the seer with reading about, a pastime I hope she enjoys as much as I do.

Since Kense broke my nose, I check the mirror before going downstairs. There's a smear of dirt on my cheek. I lick my thumb and wipe it off, but the blood on my chin and chest, I'll have to wash off. I strip off my top while the buckets downstairs start filling with water. The rest of the staff assists with the bath setup and a late supper.

Still humming because my nephew might attempt to kill me tomorrow, I descend the steps two at a time, and when I can't arrive at the bottom fast enough, I hop on the banister and slide down.

In the main living space, the staff's picking back up where they left off with their duties when I was around. Augusta isn't where I left her. I expected to find her at the table reading, bleary-eyed and tired from all the knowledge she consumed.

Displeased, I ask the fire poker in her room if she's there. She isn't.

"Augusta," I call out. I check the stack of books, which are exactly the way I left them, apart from one. Bending, I sift through the page markers. They haven't been moved. While it's possible that after reading, she returned everything to the way I left it, I highly doubt that.

She would leave the books in wild disarray.

She would disobey.

Oh yes, she would. I bet she read a page, got bored, and left. Left? Escaped?! I rush outside and shout, "Augusta!"

She doesn't answer.

New snow's been falling all span on top of the snow already here. There's nowhere to escape to, and the villages are too far. She would freeze. Augusta doesn't strike me as daft enough to leave the confines of a warm home.

The arrows stacked on the wide pillar running through the center of the house start stirring. My magic's reaching out into the village. Doors are opening, windows too, beds are turning, tables are talking, asking where the fuck is the little seer?

Inside the house, one by one, the arrows start drifting outside and arranging themselves behind me.

"Hear me," I whisper via every object I can reach as far as I can reach. "I am King Aamako, and I seek the Seelie seer. She has long dark hair, gray eyes, and wears a male's red robe. Anyone?"

The objects talk back to me, most of them telling me what their owners in their homes are telling them, and most are saying they haven't seen such a female.

"If you're providing her safe haven, I will kill you no matter who you are." This includes that commander of the Summer Court's army, as well as the pretty Summer king, in case either of those two would dare steal my seer.

More arrows fill in behind me, like in the ol' spans when I used to march on the various enemies in their courts. Now, I march back inside my house and listen to the staff chatting among themselves.

At the entrance, I catch a voice that says, "Shhh, don't say anything. He'll come and break us."

"Who is this?" The arrows filling in the living space part so I can pass. The front door slams closed behind me, startling the chairs. They scurry and hide behind the curtains.

"Who speaks?" I whisper, barely containing the magic. Control is power, and power is everything to me.

"It's the hammer," a small voice says from far away.

"Where are you?" I ask on my way to the kitchen. Most of the kitchen staff are all tucked neatly in the drawers, and any that are out have twisted into angry-looking weapons. I'll have to craft new kitchen staff.

"The cellar," the hammer says.

Dread coils in my belly as I descend the steps into the cellar and kick open the door. "Augusta." I barge inside and look around, my magic lifting everything, seeking everywhere at once.

"Here," the hammer's voice says. I follow the voice to find the little seer on the ground, unmoving, her color so gray and blue that immediately, I know she's frozen.

When I scoop her up, I shiver.

20

AAMAKO

"Fire!" I shout as I climb the steps three at a time. "Fire, blankets, furs. Now."

My magic brings the chair closer to the fireplace, and I sit down with the seer in my lap, trying to thaw her body.

Her shiny, dark curls are dull and drape over my arm like a heavy curtain. The blood has disappeared from her cheeks, making her appear lifeless. Frost colors her dark eyelashes and turns her eyebrows white, and she's clutching the hammer as if her life depends on it.

That's how I notice that one of her ten fingers, the right forefinger, has retained its normal color while the rest of them are gray.

"Augusta, can you hear me?" I press my lips over her temple, and a whine escapes me when my lips grow chilly from her low temperature. The Summer fae run colder than the Winter fae and she's more sensitive to winters, thus the reason why the cellar isn't a place I'd send her to. What the heck was she doing down there?

"Augusta, open your eyes."

She can't. Of course she can't, and I don't think there's enough fire or warmth in the house to revive her. If I don't do something quickly, the seer will remain this way forever. One of my objects. A statue I could place by the fireplace and gaze upon for the duration of my life.

My heart thuds loudly, my thoughts jumbled as the fire poker stabs the logs in the fireplace. The kitchen staff start banging on the walls, and the thousands of swords clash against one another.

I'm losing control.

I clutch the seer closer as if that will help her. I need to think clearly, but I am unable to, and I don't understand why.

"Fuck!" I rise and begin pacing, her forefinger drawing my attention once again. The idea hits me. Immediately, I send the fire poker through the shadows, and it materializes in the drawing room of a local notturno, a male the villagers call Vane the Vicious.

Vane wears a thick, black robe layered with silk. Barefoot and standing by his fireplace, he's holding a long, elegant sword, his teeth bared. "How dare you barge into my home?" he speaks to my fire poker.

Shadows wrap around his feet, and Vane slashes down with his sword, though he can't hurt me until the shadows draw him in, and spit him out inside my house. Vane's in full battle mode by now, his long, sharp fangs extended, making his jaw larger to accommodate all his now-larger teeth, which are made for ripping into flesh and drinking the blood of his enemies. Rage is pulsing off him in waves as he steps toward me.

My army of thousands of weapons all point their sharp ends at him.

Vane takes only a moment before he drops his sword. "To what do I owe this inconvenience and displeasure?"

"Give her your blood."

He blinks. "Excuse me?"

I don't have time for an argument. I must act quickly. Notturnos are known for speed, and the old ones like Vane can move at a speed even my keen eye can't see. My magic grabs his robe and yanks him toward me. One of my swords slices his palm. I wrap his sleeve tightly around his wrist and force his hand over the seer's lips. It lasts only a moment.

Vane frees himself and appears behind me, his sword digging into my throat.

I growl, but keep my gaze on Vane's blood smeared over Augusta's lips. I managed to feed her some.

"Who the fuck is she?" he asks.

"She's a seer."

"The one from the Summer Court?"

Word that I have the Summer seer is spreading. There aren't too many seers, so even a weak seer is coveted by the powers in the world. I know what Vane will want. We all want something. A deal will be made tonight, hopefully not one I will regret.

Vane lowers the sword from my throat and walks around the chair. He bends as if to take a closer look at the seer, and I bare my teeth, my horns poking from the top of my head.

Vane raises an eyebrow and clenches his fist above her lips. As his blood drips, I press my thumb against her teeth to open her mouth.

"She's not swallowing," I say.

"The dead don't swallow."

I suck in a breath, my gaze falling on her one healthy finger. "She's not dead."

"You better hope not, because I will want payment. Blood for blood."

Already aware of what Vane will ask for and that I owe him a blood debt, I nod and turn my head away. "Make it quick and don't linger, and don't take too much. I swear if you—"

"Done."

I snap my head back and catch him licking his lips. A tiny drop of her blood wells up from where he pricked her finger. I swipe it and taste. It's warm. I frown. It doesn't make sense that she's frozen and yet her blood is warm and flows so well out of the tip of her finger.

"Shall I seal the wound?" Vane asks, knowing I'll refuse. Sealing the wound means he's offering to lick her, and there's no way that's happening. Ever.

"Leave it." The small cut will close on its own when Augusta wakes.

He chuckles. "I didn't think you liked females. Or males. Or anyone."

"I don't."

"You sure like her."

"She's a seer. Don't tell me you wouldn't be protective of a seer if you happened to have one."

"I would be, yes, but I wouldn't want to fuck her."

My horns grow more, and I can barely hold back my battle form from expanding my muscles and pumping my body full of the adrenaline I could use to fight Vane. "She is under my protection, and I promised her she would be well. She is unwell. That is all." My voice sounds like I'm hailing from the bottom of the well.

"How did she become catatonic?"

"I found her in the cellar."

"Oh." Vane makes a noise as if he's tasting something

delicious. I bet it's the aftertaste of Augusta's blood. "I can tell she consumed wine, so she might've gotten drunk and passed out. I would get drunk too, if I had to spend my spans with you."

Now he's just annoying me. "Did you get anything from her blood?" I watch Vane carefully for signs that he received a vision. That's why notturnos hunt our seers. They can drink their blood and bask in visions of the future. It's like a drug for them.

"A brief and blurry montage of images I'll have to decipher. Her magic seems weak."

"Mmhm. Of no use to anyone."

He tilts his head. "Except you."

"I don't need her for the magic."

Vane snorts. "Right." He doesn't believe me. "For any reason, don't ever barge into my home again." He starts walking away. "But if you want to come over, bring me your seer for dinner." He runs off before I have a chance to stab him.

And now I wait.

21

AUGUSTA

The fire crackles, and the heat of my body makes me push off the comforter. It's coarse under my grip. Is it fur? Odd. My comforter is fluffy and soft. Slowly I peel open my heavy eyelids to see the roaring fire in the fireplace downstairs. I roll my head to the left.

The Unseelie king is sleeping, his head thrown back in the chair, his corded, thick neck exposed, prominent protrusion poking out from the middle. Um, what is going on and where am I? I raise my head and look around.

I'm sleeping in the lap of the Unseelie king, who is sitting by the fireplace on the ground level near the dining room. Surrounding us is a wall that reaches from the floor all the way to the roof. It's blocking the view of the rest of house. I scrub my eyes and blink them a few times. Finally, on the wall, I make out shapes of arrows, swords, and a few megaflails with long, thin spikes.

An army of one.

The weapons are standing upright, even though the magic wielder is sleeping, telling me he's subconsciously on alert and probably not sleeping very deeply.

"King Aamako," I whisper.

He snaps his head down, making me jump. I nearly fall off his lap.

"Oh." I hold my head. "Ooooo, my head."

The king props me up on his lap and removes my hand from my forehead. He cups my face and brings it closer to his, his eyes wide, wild, and completely silver, the color of his magic. Whatever he sees must satisfy him, because he releases me and grabs my hands, seemingly to feel them. He grunts, also pleased.

"Hi," I say shyly, sitting on his lap while he's bare-chested and sweaty. "The house feels like a furnace. Are you cold?"

He shakes his head no, and I take it the king isn't in the mood for conversation.

A tray piled with the food I gathered from the cellar appears on my left. The king says, "You will eat."

Now, had I never met the Summer king and dined with him when he was in one of his primal moods, I wouldn't recognize the curt command that brooks no argument. June once told me everyone wants to be king, but only a few can carry the burden of such duty and the power it entails. A great big power thickens the air, almost palpable. I can taste it in the back of my throat.

King Aamako is in a strange mood, riding the fine edge of his madness, and I will do what he asks. Now is not the time for teasing him. I can sense it, and I can definitely confirm it because when I reach for the cheese, he tsks.

I jerk back my hand as if he slapped it.

The king takes a piece of cheese and offers it to me. I stare at the food and then at him, not knowing if I can (or should) accept the offer. I am a Summer fairy in mating season, and males feed females as a means of courting them. Is he offering me just food, or is he offering me his body? Between his legs, the king is very much hard, and I've done well enough ignoring it, knowing that males get aroused often and can't help themselves. He's not hard for me. Right?

The king forces the cheese into my mouth.

I chew as politely as possible before he pushes the dry meat into my mouth next, in a fashion that a lady shouldn't find arousing. He's brutal, savage, wants to feed me...and of course, because I favor danger, I find that sexy, especially his thumb, which I trap between my teeth when he pushes more cheese into my mouth.

At first, I think biting him is flirtatious, but when the weapons start realigning, metal clinking against metal, I release his thumb. He examines it. There are tooth marks on his flesh. When he looks up, his eyes blaze silver, his magic flaring. The weapons as one slam against the floor, again and again, creating a crescendo beat, music that makes my heart thump faster.

"I'm sorry," I tell him. "I got carried away."

That seems to make him smile, a tiny tug of his lips before the tray squeezes into the space between us and we eat. Once we're done, the platter flies away, leaving us alone.

I'm starting to understand why others consider the king mad. The objects, when his magic works them, are in fact alive and feel alive even more than a houseplant. A house-plant can't speak. The tray was mumbling the entire time we ate.

I couldn't tell what it was saying because it spoke a foreign tongue. Maybe some form of pixie language, but it kept us company and dispelled the tension between us.

Now that the tray is gone, the tension is back, though the magic in the air is thinning, no longer feeling like a heavy blanket pressing against my lungs. The king's eyes are dark as they should be when his gaze lands on my lips. I can't stop myself from leaning toward him. I even rest my hand on his chest. Oh, his chest is made of rock, and I wish he would move in and take my virginity by plundering me on the hardwood floor.

Hardwood.

Hard. Wood.

I can see the act clearly as if it's happening already. I moan as I press my lips against his. Again. Oh no!

I pull back. "I'm sorry. Again. If a male kept kissing me uninvited, it would upset me greatly. I am terribly sorry. I will fix this...urge as soon as the summer comes to an end. Not too long now, and then, maybe, you'll be the one kissing me." He's staring, and I'm rambling. "Because after summer comes fall and winter, both your seasons for mating. Get it?"

"You will bathe."

"I smell?" I sniff my armpit. No. No smell. He must be in a foul mood because I snooped in his cellar. Or is it because I didn't read much of what he assigned? I have no idea what's gotten him into this mood, but clearly, he's ill-disposed after he found me in the cellar asleep from the cold. "I think you saved my life," I say, too embarrassed to admit I got lost. "I think if you hadn't come, I would have frozen down there. I have a giant headache. Is it morning yet? But it feels like it's night. I'm tired. Good cheese, by the way. Tastes sharp and hearty, just how I like it."

The furs and blankets he's piled on us fall off as the king scoops me up and rises with me in his arms. The weapons part, opening a path for him when he heads up the stairs, where the weapon clusters are particularly dense, so dense that I tuck my feet in so one of the axes doesn't nick me. The king snorts.

"Something funny?" I ask.

He won't indulge me in a conversation, even though I hear chatter in the kitchen, something freaking out over being bent like a pretzel. A ladle, I believe, judging by the way the others are addressing the speaker.

The door opens wide, and the king and I walk into my already warm chambers. He sets me on my feet, and in one fast slash of his claws, rips off my clothes.

I cover my breasts, my middle, my breasts again, not knowing which to cover or how. "What are you doing?" I shriek.

The king points at the steaming bath. "You will bathe."

"You drew me a bath?" I curl a lock of my hair around my finger.

He narrows his eyes.

"Thank you." *Oh, for the love of fate, Augusta, stop swooning.* I drop the lock of hair. "You didn't have to rip my clothes, seeing as the little white dress and the robe you gave me are all I have to wear. But the robe is yours, so whatever." I step into the bath, terribly aware I'm in the chamber alone with the Unseelie king, one of the most powerful males in the world. He's also handsome and hard as wood. I can tell. His pants can't hide his erection.

He did tell me all I have to do is spread my legs.

As I enter the bath one foot at a time, I stay standing and spread my legs. Not obviously or too wide because I still fear rejection, but wide enough. Before the summer I spent flirting and failing over at the Summer Court's palace, I used to be a lot bolder with males. Granted, none of the males were kings. None were Aamako, who broods with the best of them tonight.

I like it when he broods.

When he's moody.

When he's quiet.

I can't predict what he'll do, what he's thinking. Nothing is given away, and that's dangerous. I like danger, especially this kind. The moody, sexy kind.

From above the fireplace, the silver chalice stirs and travels slowly through the air. It scoops up water, then dumps it over my head. The doors open to admit a caddy bearing soap, a sponge, towels, and bottles of oils.

The king approaches the tub. He wets the sponge and starts lathering my hair before moving the loofah down my shoulders and over my arms. And while he's doing all that, the stars that I saw playing in his eyes before return, twinkling as if they're excited or happy. I can't tell which or if it's either. Not quite.

"Breathe," he orders, and that's when I inhale, having no clue I'd been holding my breath. If not for the way he's pressed his lips together, I would probably have kissed him already. I seem to want to make out with him all the time.

The king crouches and starts washing my legs. Since I kept my legs slightly open, he guides his sponge between my thighs and lathers up my middle. I moan at his firm touch. I might even come from this small attention.

What was I thinking not taking him up on his offer earlier? I bet the king would get me off faster and better than I ever could with my fingers.

"Wash your hair," he says.

"What?"

"Your hair."

I blush. "I don't have hair down there."

"The hair on your head."

Someone please drown me now. My face is so hot, I think I might be feverish with embarrassment.

The magic works the chalice that washes my hair while

the king rises. He stands there watching me. As the water travels down my face, I lick it off my lips. The king's eyes grow hooded, and he mimics the movement of my tongue.

Our fingers intertwine in my hair. I want to take my hands away and let him massage my scalp (and body, bum, and clitoris) with those long, thick fingers of his that are almost always covered in leather gloves. Now they're bare, his claws combing through my hair, getting the kinks out of the large curls.

When I start moaning again, the king purrs, telling me he likes something. Maybe me? Entirely? As a whole person instead of just the bride I can fake being, perhaps? Wouldn't that be something crazier than what's already crazy, huh?

A white towel twists in my hair. Another towel drapes around my shoulders, and I hold it as I step out of the tub. The red slippers pad over the floor and stop in front of me. I put them on, and they start moving, forcing my feet to follow them to the bed, where I sit and they slide off.

On the mattress, I turn to see the king is already exiting with a last set of orders. "Now, you sleep."

22

AUGUSTA

Even though it's well into the night, I can't fall asleep. It has nothing to do with sleeping by the fire, on the king's lap, but everything to do with the way he touched me. No male has ever touched me that way, and while I did experiment some with village boys, they can't compare.

For one, he's the Unseelie king and I'm a Seelie fairy and we're alone out here in the middle of no-fae's-land where he can do whatever he wishes with me. Two, he's the Unseelie king who washed me and fed me and put me to bed.

Kings don't do such things, and I know this because Et'enne doesn't wash anyone besides himself and maybe my sister. Even when he washes himself or my sister, the Summer king has to use his hands, while King Aamako can command the sponge to do all the washing without him ever having to move a finger.

And yet the king did move a finger. Oh, yes, he did. He moved all his fingers freely, in my hair and elsewhere, and he massaged my scalp and purred...and my fingers work over my clit, seeking orgasm. Abruptly, I pause.

The painting tools from the morning painted over the portrait of the king on the ceiling.

"Hey," I call out, but nobody answers me. "Hey, painters." I see them in the corner of the room, so they're still here. I don't know why they're not answering. It's not as if the king isn't in the room with me if they're here.

Oh. I gasp. Does he know when I touch myself? So what if he does? There's no shame in getting off, especially after the bath he gave me. My fates, that was nice, and totally unexpected. I wonder what made him bathe me. He seemed different tonight. More...personal. Closer. Perhaps something happened when he visited his court. That's where he said he was going. Reconnaissance.

I hear music. I sit up in the bed and tilt my head in the same way our sheepdog Floki does when I make weird noises at him. The head tilt doesn't actually make me hear better, so I put my feet back into the slippers and head for the door. The slippers freeze my feet in place, and I trip and fall, sticking out my hands to prevent a busted nose just before I land with a thud.

"What the hell?" I mumble. I stand back up and try the slippers again. They're made of steel, it seems. Fine. Barefoot, I pad to the door and slowly, quietly, open it to hear a piano being played somewhere in the house. I think it's upstairs, the floor right above me.

I tiptoe outside and hear the footsteps behind me. Turning, I see the slippers walking up and a new white robe following behind. I put them on and climb the steps.

When I reach the upper floor, I spy the king at the piano set in the corner of the empty floor that appears to double as a ballroom. There's one door leading into what I presume is a small chamber, but mostly the room consists of an open space hosting the king and his piano.

His hair curtains his face as he watches the piano keys, which I believe he is actually playing with his fingers instead of his magic. For a while, I simply listen to the climbing intensity of the tune, the composition reminding me of a marching army. The thousands of arrows that have yet to clear the downstairs and the bottom staircase start tapping on the floor. My foot taps with them, and the rest of my body vibrates as their collective force makes the entire house dance.

The king is moving his fingers faster now, his body swaying. He throws back his head, his lips slightly parted as if in ecstasy. My brain flashes an image of what this male looks like when he's coming.

The image is followed by a full-blown vision of him poised above me, roaring in orgasmic victory, the muscles of his corded neck stretched to the maximum. He's pounding into me, and there's a black piece of cloth in my mouth. Is it a gag? I have gag fantasies. Who knew.

As my body heats up, I start sweating. I better get lost and finish myself off in bed before I do something I most definitely will *not* regret. Like have the Unseelie king be my first.

I won't ask him, of course. But I sure want him to be that male.

The king snaps his head toward me, and our eyes lock. His gaze spells danger. If I approach him, I think he might ravage me. My arousal churns in my belly, threatening to send me into heat. But I can't do that with a male who wouldn't welcome it.

We are not really betrothed.

And yet he fed me and bathed me. Was it because he found me lost in the cellar and felt bad? The way one would feel bad for a stray doe one brought from the woods to feed and bathe, then release into the wild again.

The king changes the song into something slow and decadent and takes a sip from a half-full bottle. He's staring somewhere outside, maybe at the mountain across the valley.

I debate whether I should go back to sleep or approach him. I can't sleep right now. No way. And this king is a magnet for me, my body simply moving toward him as if I have no control of it.

It's how I kissed him. I leaned in and did it as if he were mine to kiss, as if I'd known him for centuries, not mere moments.

I never kissed the commander, and I thought I liked him.

Clearly, I had no idea how liking someone really feels.

This is what it feels like.

I want to be near this male, especially when I'm aroused.

I start toward him, but once again, the slippers won't move. This time, I don't trip and fall. Thankfully, I can be a fast learner when I want to be. I walk toward him on bare feet, but just as I'm about to sit beside him on the padded leather bench, the king grabs my hips and drags me to stand between him and the piano.

He looks up, silver stars skipping in his eyes.

I cup his face.

At first, he lets me, but then he pulls away, standoffish and cold, and it makes me want to leave before he has a chance to reject me.

The stars in his eyes flash as the king leans in and starts unfastening the tie holding my white robe together. The cold top of his hand brushes against my belly, inciting goose bumps to scatter over my skin. With a palm at the small of my back, he pulls me toward him and kisses between my breasts, his trimmed beard prickling.

I run my hands through his beautiful silky hair. It's straight like his arrows, thick and shiny. Touching his hair makes me wet. My building arousal slips out and between my folds.

In response, the king starts purring. His mouth trails toward my left breast, and he blows on my nipple before drawing it into his mouth and sucking.

Moaning, I curve my back. His palm holding me up feels large and I feel small and dainty, and I want him to have me. The vision of him pounding into me returns, and I moan louder when the king switches to suck on my other breast. My hands fist his hair, and I pull him closer, wanting him to devour me.

A rope materializes and winds around my left wrist, then the right one. It brings my wrists together and ties itself at the small of my back.

I guess the king doesn't want to be touched.

He kisses below my left breast and then grips my bottom and squeezes. I think he's asking for me to spread my legs.

The king wants me.

And he will take me at his pace and leisure the way a king ought to. All I have to do is be a good doll.

I lean my elbows on the piano and spread my legs. The moment I do, I can feel my arousal leaking out, and I quickly try to close my legs.

The king snarls.

He actually snarls at me, and I can see his horns peeking out from under his mane of hair. Using two fingers, he swipes the arousal from between my legs and brings it to his nose. His nostrils flare as he sniffs, purring loudly now.

A grunt, and his hand is on my hip, turning me. A palm

between my shoulder blades pushes me down gently over the keyboard until my breasts touch the cold, polished wood.

With my left cheek on the wood, I'm facing his right, so I see the moment a little flask makes its way up the stairs.

The scent of cherries in blossom explodes in the room. Warm, slick liquid that I presume is cherry blossom oil touches the base of my spine and trickles between my butt cheeks and down more, between my folds. The king slaps my bottom.

I yelp at first, but pinch my lips as he lands a few more slaps that heat up my behind something fierce. They also heat up my channel, and my arousal starts leaking out of me again.

The coolness of his large palms feels wonderful as he places them on the spots he spanked. I sigh in pure ecstasy even before he spreads my butt cheeks. When he spreads them, he pauses for a moment. A long moment. Long enough for me to start feeling self-conscious.

I am tied up and at the mercy of a powerful king who has lived a long life and has had many females. What if I'm not what he expected? Or worse yet, what if he changed his mind?

Silence stretches.

I swallow.

The king swipes his tongue over my clit, my virginal entrance, and all the way up to my butthole, where he lingers, poking it with the tip of his tongue all while thumbing my clit.

I buck wildly, my clit sensitive and swollen. It takes me no time to come and scream out my orgasm. Just when I think it's over, the king growls and starts licking me, purring his lungs out, the vibrations creating more heat in my belly.

He licks me and kneads my butt, then he pushes his thumb into my butthole, and I gasp as he moves it in and out. It feels so good with his rough tongue flicking my clit that I come for the second time, screaming out his name.

Heaving breaths, I snap open the eyes I don't remember closing.

The sound of a bench scraping the floor makes me lift my cheek off the piano. My hands are suddenly rope-free, and the king is walking away, long, straight, black horns fully erect and jutting out of his head.

At the top of the stairs, he pauses, but doesn't turn.

"Augusta?"

"Hm?" I don't think I can speak.

"Did you enjoy that?"

"Yes, my king." My breath catches. I shouldn't call him *my* king. He is not my king.

At my outburst, the Unseelie king turns his head toward me so I can see him smirk.

23

AAMAKO

After I ordered Augusta to sleep, I wondered how long it would take her to disobey my orders. Not very long indeed, which makes me think the same thing happened with her yesterday after I left for my court.

I left presuming she would sit at the table or on the chair even and read the marked pages in the books I assigned to her. I was certain she would not disobey because the books hold important information on the people in my court.

I did not expect her to wander off into the house.

And then she wandered off again later at night while I played the piano.

She sought me out. Perhaps for the music, perhaps for company, but certainly not for fucking. And while I would not fuck her, her body calls me as the sirens of Escan call the lycan sailors.

Her arousal tastes better than the oysters of the finest summer seas, and her body responds to my touch, does exactly what I need and when I need it, coming at the mere stroke of my fingers. It feels wonderful and satisfying, and her submission, although not quiet and meek, is perfectly... arousing to me.

Still arousing.

I can't get my dick to go down.

This morning, my hand is tired, leaving my skin raw from stroking. I dressed and came downstairs to sit at the table and stare into space. I'm hard and annoyed at being hard, and also at still tasting her arousal in the back of my throat. I'm tempted to start breakfast without her, if only to replace the taste of her with bacon. Or cheese. Or anything at this point.

My balls contract, and semen leaks from the tip. Leaning back in my chair, I stare between my legs. "Are you kidding me?"

My shaft doesn't answer, but it might have taken on a life of its own, seeing as how I can't seem to get ahold of this arousal. I hate losing control, and lacking it when it comes to the seer is dangerous.

I grip my sac and squeeze so that the pain zaps my lower belly and makes me bend over. I don't let go. I squeeze harder, almost digging my claws into my balls until the excruciating pain makes me want to squeak like a little bitch.

I don't, though.

Kings don't squeak.

Once I get a headache, and the staff working around the house quiet, I let go with a groan. Leaning forward, I thump my head on the table, making a book fall. I extend a hand, and the book lands in it with a thud, slamming my knuckles against the wood.

"Hey, what was that for?" I ask.

"For hurting our crown jewels."

I snort and shift through the book, its thick cream pages

old but well preserved. "The crown jewels. Who talks like that?"

"The villagers. They're talking about your crown jewels."

"And I care what the villagers say about my dick because...?"

"Oh, don't be crude." The book slams closed over my fingers.

"Spread your thick pages, my sweet. You know you like it when I flick them."

"Stop it," the book says, sounding coy. After a pause, the book says, "The seer's dress will need fitting."

"We're ready, Your Majesty," the scissors and needles shout, flying out of the drawers.

"Quiet, you."

They start whispering. "Is it the new dress in the wardrobe?"

The wardrobe in my chambers wakes and starts walking toward the door, which swings open to bang against the wall. "Not in here!" the wardrobe shouts. "He hung it over the damn sword."

"Quiet," I shout back. "You'll wake up the seer."

There's a collective gasp.

"For fuck's sake. What?"

"Why do we care if we wake up the seer?"

"We don't," I announce. "She's late for breakfast. What time is it?" I glance out the window. The sun is making its way to the crest of the mountain, so it's midmorning.

I don't know if I'm annoyed that she's sleeping in because I want to ensure her wellness, or because I wish she would join me, or because I just hate lateness. Granted, I eat breakfast whenever I eat it and expecting her at a certain time is unreasonable. Nevertheless, we should dine together as much as possible.

The wardrobe in her chambers gives me a visual of Augusta. The seer is a bundle under the comforter, dark curls splayed over the pillow.

"Pretty curls," the wardrobe says.

"Shhh," I answer, and take away the magic from the object.

I tap my claw over the aged, brown leather book cover.

"Get a tailor from the village?" the book suggests.

"Mmhm," I mumble.

"He is a nice male with two daughters, both in the trade."

"Yes, I know."

"I know you know. You're the one who's talking."

Sighing, I purse my lips. "Fine, fine. What's the village talking about again?"

"The wedding."

"Whose?"

"Yours."

The sensation of a gentle breeze brushes over my chest. How very strange. "But I'm not getting married."

"They don't know that."

True. "I'll send the carriage for the tailors. Anything else?"

"A hairdresser," the book says. The book knows everything. So smart, this book. "And a makeup artist," it adds.

"Augusta will enjoy the pampering."

Silence falls in the house again. Not a peep from anyone, but if parts of my body could talk, I bet my dick would have plenty to say, but it can't, so I squeeze myself again and cause another wave of pain.

24

AUGUSTA

If last night's burning kernel of fire in the pit of my belly is any indication of what the mating heat feels like when a dominant fae male stokes it, it's no wonder my people flock to the court during the summer season. I have no idea what Unseelies do during their heats, but if their king is any indication, they perform dirty, devious acts that I want to learn more about.

Warm under the covers, I stare at the pictureless, white ceiling, then lift my head, snatch the pillow, and put it over my face. I scream into it, kicking my legs. Fates, how I wish June were here so I could tell her about last night. This is the first time I've been away from my family, the Summer Court as a whole, and I miss my sister. Both my sisters, even Cecile.

I wish all of them to hear about last night.

Flinging the pillow aside, I vault out of bed and walk to the window to open it. The freshness of winter sweeps inside, and I shiver from the cold, but not enough to deter me from what I feel like doing. My heart is full of joy, and I want to share it with my sister June. In her absence, the gorgeous mountain will have to do.

Double-checking there's nobody around, because we're on top of the world where nobody can reach us, and not caring if the king hears me, I shout, "Last night, the king ate me out!"

Oh, that felt amazing. I shout again.

I would shout at the mountain some more, but it's cold as fuck, so I'm done. I close the window and rub my shoulders, then look around for the white robe. I find the robe I wore last night thrown over the sofa. I sling it on and use my chamber pot, then think about the chamber pots I've been using.

No living soul works here, which means the magic empties my pot. I'm not sure how I feel about that or why I'm having gross morning thoughts after the glorious thoughts about last night, but sometimes my strange thoughts have thoughts about how strange it is to think what I'm thinking.

Finished with my business, I wash up, then tie my lucky robe I shall wear in the castle for the duration of my time with the king if it means he will administer such sexy attentions on my body when I wear it.

Thinking about the piano scene again makes me wet between my legs, and I whistle as I walk downstairs. I hear footsteps behind me. The slippers follow me down. I slide my feet into them, curling my toes at how good the fur inside feels compared to the cold wooden stairs. In the Summer Court, we often walk barefoot.

The new slippers take a bit of getting used to, and I'm careful not to fall, so I watch my step as I descend. Five steps from the bottom, I stop, then hop over the rest, landing on my feet. "Ta-da!" I announce, and finally look up.

There're people in the house. Several people. Five to be exact, plus the king.

I thought we were alone.

Horror.

The king ate me out. I screamed that at the top of my lungs on this lovely span of all spans, when the reclusive Unseelie king decided he'll host visitors. Or, rather, workers.

With his dark hair pulled up and away from his face, the king stands on a circular platform, his arms outstretched, legs shoulder-width apart as an older male with receding dark hair in a braid, wearing a black jacket and green pants, crouches beside him, sewing needle between his teeth.

A female, about my age, I suppose, holds out a tray for the male who is tailoring the king's leather pants made of what I think might be dragon skin. Real dragon skin, which has been outlawed in the Seelie courts since we formed an alliance with the Dragon Lords of Insetme.

Her shiny, straight, dark hair drapes over her back. She looks like a copy of the female standing across from her. They're identical twins who are barely holding back laughter, exchanging looks they think I can't decipher.

June and I communicated silently too.

Fates, how I miss June.

She would know what to do in my situation, namely how to handle the humiliation of shouting the king's and my private business. Heck, June would never shout about her king eating her out in the first place. After she spent a night with King Et'enne, who left a million marks on her body, I couldn't get any details about their night out of her at all.

Two more females sit at the table, each with sacks of what I presume are supplies next to their chairs. They're here for the fittings for when the king will announce his engagement to the Winter Court.

"Good morning, Augusta." The king's voice booms in the space, and everyone who wasn't standing now does so and curtsies. The tailor bows. They all hold their positions, and I curtsey as well before the Unseelie king, because I'm guessing that's what they do when he speaks. I really should've brushed up on Unseelie etiquette.

Read the books, the king had said. Instead of obeying him, I went into the cellar and then couldn't even find my way back and fell asleep there, almost died, got saved, and had my pussy eaten. Everyone knows about that last part.

"Augusta," he says.

I keep my head down, wondering how long I can hold this curtsey. I hope I don't wobble and fall on my face. My muscles strain, but they haven't started shaking, only because growing up running chores in the village made me fit. A female whines, silently asking for the king's release.

"Augusta," the king repeats in a tone that sounds like a slice of a blade.

I snap my head up and straighten like a soldier. "Yes, Your Majesty."

"Unless you've already assimilated some of the crueler practices of Unseelie royalty and now enjoy making your subjects suffer, do tell them to rise."

"Me?" I point a finger at my chest.

The king adopts this look I can't quite place. I think he might want to throttle me.

"You are my bride."

It is happening. Oh my fates. It is really happening. We're really doing this bride-and-groom thing, and I will have to fake it before the entire Unseelie court. I can barely command five workers without feeling like an imposter. It'll never work, but I must make it work, because King Aamako's got this mean look in his eye and he's not to be messed with.

"R...rise." I swallow and say it again. "Please."

The king shakes his head.

I dislike disappointing him, but I get over it quickly, because the twins rush up to me and curtsey again, this time with their hands extended, each presenting me with a short tree branch in her palm. There are fuzzy red buds on the branch. I've seen them all around the castle. I think it might be a winter magnolia, a native of the Winter Court. I take the gifts with a polite thank-you.

They jump up and down. "You will not regret this, milady."

Regret what? Oh crap. I did something. Not knowing what, I lock eyes with the king the way I would lock eyes with June, my gaze pleading for help. But the king is not June. Not even close. The slight narrowing of his eyes tell me he's mighty annoyed. No help there.

As trays, plates, and settings fly out of the kitchen, the two females near the table step away from it and look like they're going to flee. Before they leave, I walk toward them. Now they seem as if they want to flee even more.

"Have a seat." I say it gently, but they sit instantly, with their backs straight and their heads at attention as if I'm their military commander.

"The staff is bringing out brunch."

They exchange looks which I presume are because I used the word "staff" for the objects in the kitchen. I take it they've never been up here in the castle or around their king. If it wasn't for King Et'enne taking a fancy to my sister, I would never have been around kings either. They're common fae folk like me and probably just as terrified as I am.

Any king makes people nervous, but the Unseelie king also has unusual magic, one that puts folks even more on edge.

They will get used to it, and I can help. "I'm acclimating to the staff as well," I whisper.

They eye me warily.

A tray slams down on the other end of the table, spilling some of the tea. I presume that is my tray, and I also presume I'm not supposed to eat from the buffet, seeing as the single tray is full and set at the end of the table, away from everyone.

I contemplate sitting at the end and eating where the king wants me to, or if I'll taste the lovely smelling breakfast soup with rice and fresh boiled eggs. On my tray, I spot a croissant, a Summer Court specialty. It's served with pickled peaches.

I love croissants, but I've also never had the traditional Unseelie breakfast or brunch he's serving for the people working here.

"Eat something," he orders.

I opt to ask him to help me choose. "Something, anything?"

"Anything, though I prefer if you wouldn't eat my croissant or the peach. Especially not the peach."

The way he says peach conjures images of last night. He sure knows how to eat peaches. *All* the peaches. I clear my dirty thoughts and ask, "That breakfast is yours?"

He licks his lips. "A taste of summer."

Whaaaa... Is he flirting? Reminding me of last night, referencing how I taste? Like summer? A peach? When he slides his gaze toward me and a tiny silver star lights up in his eye, I have my answer. The king *is* flirting with me.

For all my bravado, he makes me blush, and the twins giggle. They knew the Unseelie king ate me out, and now they know he liked it. Still, I wonder if he's putting on a show for the benefit of our bridal story or if he liked it for real.

25

AAMAKO

The span I'm spending with people in my house is progressing better than I expected. I have not killed anyone.

And judging by the way Augusta woke up this fine span and announced her excitement over last night, my killing spree will have to wait so I can see what happens in my court tonight.

I would've wished for more time to prepare for presenting my bride and announcing my engagement to the Winter Court, but that would mean giving my enemies time to prepare as well. Not that I believe any of them stand a chance of killing me, and while I hope they try, I have recently discovered that I can't stand any harm befalling the seer while she's under my protection.

This means I must ensure her safety as well as her enjoyment while we attend court. We might also have to hold court, meaning we'll have official dealings and conduct court business such as governing the lands. That's something I normally enjoy, but I resigned those duties to my nephew when I retreated to Dakkuyasu. I'm returning now, and Augusta must be ready to assume her bridal duties.

Judging by how she deals with these village folk, Augusta isn't ready. She's kind, chatty, and warm like the summer. Her kindness has corrupted my staff. They brought food to the table. Tsk, tsk, tsk. Awful indeed.

In my court, we're less warm or welcoming of strangers, and we tend not to want them to feel at home in our house. We want them to leave as quickly as they came.

Or maybe that's just me.

I barely suppressed my anger at Augusta accepting not one, but two bridal maidens who will serve her until our wedding. And since we're not getting married, but rather will have a prolonged engagement, the two females will practically live in my house now.

They giggle and smile all the time. Annoying.

Truly, the suffering I shall endure for a bit of Seelie seer pussy might earn me a medal.

"All done, Your Majesty," Emio, the finest tailor in the three villages, says. "Everything will be ready no later than late afternoon. I'll deliver it personally."

"No need. Hang it outside your shop's door." I step off the fitting platform and head for my end of the table, far from where the females are congregating. Sitting down, I stare at the bitten-off croissant. Augusta bit a piece of my croissant. Nobody else would dare eat from my plate, but I can't believe she bit into it, then put it back.

I pick up a fork and knife and slice off a piece of warm croissant. Melted sharp cheese carrying chunks of bacon flows from the middle of the pastry. My mouth waters. I stab the portion and go to put it in my mouth when Augusta appears next to me.

I drop the fork.

She wears only little white underpants, with her long hair covering her breasts.

"Croissant with bacon is blasphemous. It should be stuffed with ham." She picks up the fork and offers to feed me. I grab her wrist, guide the food to my mouth, and snap my teeth at it.

Augusta jumps away, then laughs.

Her laughter pleases me, though I don't show it. I continue eating my blasphemous croissant. Maybe I'll try ham next time, though I don't care if it's bacon or ham or chicken. I eat because I want to live. That is all.

I hope the other male in the room wants to live as well. We'll find out soon enough.

I keep my gaze on him as Augusta steps onto the platform and spreads her arms. "I've never had a professional fitting before," she announces, then presses her lips together, knowing she overshared.

"Do they not have fittings in the Summer Court?" one of her bridal maidens asks.

Their father shakes his head. "Silly girl. Of course they have fittings." The male seems unfazed by the sight of the nearly nude seer and starts taking her measurements in a mechanical manner that tells me he wants to live. Not that I should care if a male looks or touches her. I have not a care in the world about that.

"In the Summer Court," Augusta tells the girls, "the designers hold promenades of new and fashionable items each span before lavish suppers."

The twins seem enchanted. "Tell us more."

"And the queen wears something different for all three meals of the span."

The girls get dreamy looks about them. "What's their queen like?"

Augusta pauses before answering, turning her head toward the horizon. "She's the best."

"Augusta is speaking of the future Summer queen, not the queen mother," I inform the people. "For the king is yet to marry his chosen."

Augusta smiles. "Thank you, King Aamako. I often live in the future, where things have already happened."

I note she called me King Aamako and not "my king," which grates, but that's what I get for bringing a summerling I can't keep into my life.

The girl standing behind Augusta and helping her father with waist measurements clears her throat. "And what's the Summer king like?"

Augusta giggles. "He's like the sun. So handsome, it's hard to even gaze upon him."

"Milady," the tailor says. "Is there a particular dress style you would like to wear?"

I'm glad for the interruption, because I don't want to hear about how handsome Et'enne is. I've seen him and the way females gaze upon him. Fucking sunshine boy.

Augusta shakes her head. "I'm afraid I'm out my depth here." She eyes me warily, probably wondering if I secured a dress for her.

"The seer looks great in any style," I supply.

The tailor bows. "Of course. I wasn't suggesting—"

"I know you weren't. And I made your job easier when I picked out the dress for my bride."

The females in the room ooh and aah, as does Augusta. The mood will change when they see the dress.

"Where is it?" the seer asks and looks up at the staircase.

In my chambers, my magic grips the sword the dress hangs from and arranges it to hold up the dress by the sleeves as if the sword were a hanger. It carries the dress out and over the first floor, stopping at the top of the stairs.

The first person to see it is Augusta. I can tell by the way she reacts to it, namely how her hands come together at her chest and she squeals in excitement, that she has no idea of the history of this dress. But my people do. Even the common folk in this remote village. They do because this dress is a symbol of the Unseelie soothsayer's power. The seers of my bloodline have passed it down for many generations.

It is a black dress made by layering silk, fur, leather, and at least three other materials I'm unfamiliar with over the bottom half of the gown. The materials seem randomly cut and pieced together to create a sprawling gown held up by a tight leather corset. Intricate metal-and-leather designs form rose petals over the corset and parts of the bottom half of the gown.

When worn to battle, the dress comes with matching shoulder armor, which I shall provide for Augusta later tonight instead of now. This way, she won't reject the idea. Although she referred to dresses as armor, actual armor on a dress might scare her, and I wish for her to want to wear this gown.

The summerlings wear lighter items of clothing, so I'm a little shocked she likes it. Shocked, but pleased, nonetheless.

The sword brings the dress down the steps, and the twin girls start moving away from it while their father looks like he might urinate on himself.

None the wiser, Augusta hops up and down. "It's so pretty! Thank you so much. I can't wait to wear it."

As the dress makes its way to the platform, Augusta rips it off the sword, eliciting a collective gasp from the people.

She presses it against her body and starts fussing with the fabric.

"Yes?" I prompt.

"Oh, that's right. There is a mirror in my room." She turns as if to move away, but I tsk and she stops, gazing at me like a puppy who got caught hovering over the food on the kitchen island.

I supply the mirror from her chamber. "The mirror will make its way to you. If I'm not around, ask for it, and it will be brought. You no longer fetch things."

Augusta nods. "That's right. I forget sometimes."

She forgets oftentimes, but we shall speak about her authority (or lack thereof) when we're alone.

Augusta positions herself in front of the mirror while I keep my gaze on her and away from the dress that carries painful memories of my dear sister. It also carries a strong message and will indeed serve as armor against my foes.

"Do you think you can alter my dress and the king's outfit by tonight?" she asks the tailor.

He opens and closes his mouth like a fish.

"He can." If he can't, he will anyway. "Put it on, my seer."

In the upper corner of the first floor, Tima's face flashes from the shadows. She's here with information I'll want to hear before I enter my court. Standing, I begin to walk upstairs, but while my brain is heading there, my legs, as if led by my erection, carry me toward the podium. I climb it and grab the seer and kiss her until the room drowns in her mating scent. After I leave, she needs help holding herself upright.

Everyone must believe she is to be my bride. That's why I kiss her the way I do. Mmhm.

26

AUGUSTA

One would think that after the king leaves, the awkwardness in the room would subside and that people would relax, especially the tailor, who appeared comfortable and confident of his craft. But now that King Aamako has left, while some of the tension has lessened, the tailor, along with the ladies sitting at the table, aren't at ease yet, and the twins, who were so friendly to me only moments ago, seem skittish now.

I try lessening the tension by smiling more, and while they return my smiles, they're wary. It's almost as if they're afraid of me. Which isn't only weird, it's absurd. They ought to be more afraid of Aamako than me, yet they didn't seem so troubled when he was around.

"Is there something wrong?" I finally ask.

"No, milady," one of the twins answers.

"What are your names?"

The twin who wears her hair in a braid that falls over her left shoulder answers. "I'm Rin, and this is Nami."

Nami steps up to the podium with her father. "Would you try the dress, milady?" he asks.

After struggling with the layers, I find the hole in the middle of the dress and fit through it rather easily. Too easily. The dress proves too big and slides right down my body. The tailor stares at it crumpled around my feet. I pick it up and try adjusting it, but it just slides back down.

I pick it up again. "Good sir, are you going to help me fit into the dress or not?"

He goes to touch it, but then pauses, his hands awkwardly hovering in midair.

"Shall we start with the hair before the dress?" a male voice asks while a female approaches me. She's tall and might've been a male at some point in her long life.

"Milady." She curtseys. "If I may touch you?"

"Sure."

Her heavy boots slam on the platform as she climbs. I have to crane my head to look up at her. Immediately, I notice the bump in the middle of her throat that only males carry. She smells like blossoms and evergreen, neither a male nor a female scent.

Pursing her glossy, pink-painted lips, she says, "I suggest a trim." Long, elegant fingers with pink-painted claws thread through my hair. "You have lovely curls. I want to show them off by letting your hair down, and yet your collarbone is pronounced." She taps said bone. "That's seductive. If your hair is down, it will draw more attention than the bones." She sniffs visibly. "Also, you smell like a thousand aroused summerlings, and when I'm done with you, every male in the Court will be a drooling fool over you."

The other female, seemingly middle-aged, with short dark hair and a large frame, approaches the mirror. Magic colors her eyes purple, and the room dims a bit. "I'm Dahlia, milady," she says, her voice evoking images of my mother for some reason, perhaps because of her age, perhaps because of the worn-out face telling me her life hasn't been easy. "I'm a *pictorra*."

"She's a shoemaker," the male spits.

A little animosity there, I sense. The twin girls exchange glances while Dahlia ignores the comment.

"And a shoemaker. But more importantly, a *pictorra* who happens to work best with mirrors. I can draw anything Your Royal Highness wishes. Shoes, dresses, hair clips, bedding. Visions."

"How dare you offer to draw visions for the seer," the tailor grumbles again. He puts away the needlework and fists his hands. "Keep your mouth and your magic in check, or you'll get us all killed."

"Mind your business, old fart."

"You wretched imposter!" He stomps toward her.

The blade from the sword that held the dress unsheathes and flies at the tailor's throat.

"Papa, Papa!" the girls scream, and my hairdresser steps behind me.

Dahlia stares at the sword, her eyes wide, her magic completely dissipated.

The mirror shakes and then gains the eyes of the Unseelie king, who returns the sword to its sheath. Everyone falls on the ground, their foreheads on the floor, begging forgiveness for bickering around his bride. The mirror doesn't speak, but I don't think it needs to. This is a warning.

Once the mirror loses its eyes, I say, "Rise."

Ordering people around feels strange. If they only knew I had no magic and that "seer" is just a title that's been bestowed upon me by a wishful Summer king blinded by his love for my sister. Still, the Unseelie, like all the other fae in the world, value power above all else. Thus if I am to be the Unseelie king's bride, I have to appear powerful.

He can't keep rescuing me out of these minor situations. Two people who dislike each other almost fought in my presence. "One does not raise one's voice in the presence of royalty," I say. "Let us get back to our duties. You were saying, Dahlia?"

Dahlia reaches into the deep pocket of her red cardigan and pulls out a piece of what I think is white chalk. Or perhaps it's a pen with paint? Her magic flares again, and she kneels beside the mirror and starts drawing, her eyes never leaving me or the dress. It takes her only moments to paint a pair of white boots that magically reflect in the mirror as if I'm already wearing them. They rise past my knees and fold at the top. The color of the top fold is blood red.

"Thigh-high boots with pointy toes over a sensible heel." Dahlia says.

I skip to the left.

In the mirror, the shoes she drew follow along with my legs.

"Oh, this is delightful. Some sort of designer magic, I presume?" I ask.

Dahlia frowns. "In a way, milady."

"Boy, they would love you over where I come from."

The tailor snorts, but doesn't comment.

I sense the same tension as before, but I want them to focus on the attire and not their differences. "I wish to cut the dress down the middle to show off the boots."

The tailor looks like he swallowed a live bird that's poking him in the throat with its beak.

"Is it a problem?" I ask.

He swallows harder.

The king descends the steps. "Cut the dress."

"Yes, my king," the tailor says.

Finally, we're getting somewhere. The male starts measuring again, asking me questions about the dress while Dahlia is drawing the final look on the mirror, showing me exactly what I'll look like. I love seeing it. It's a vision of something that will happen in the future made real in the now, and the thing about visions is that one can tweak them now so that they turn out perfect in the future.

The king snatches an apple from the table and comes to stand behind me. Etiquette says that one must not turn one's back to the king, and I'm feeling all sorts of uncomfortable as he watches the mirror while Dahlia draws the style the hairdresser, Rist, is creating with my hair.

When the tailor asks, I turn to the side, toward the windows. My gaze falls on the white landscape, the snow-covered mountaintop, the place where the mountain touches the sky, and then I peer over the horizon.

A vision comes. I know I'm opening my mouth and closing it, but I can't hear if I'm talking or not (probably I am). It's over as quickly as it comes. After I have one of my visions, I always feel out of place. It takes me a moment to adjust to the present. I used to get headaches, but then my sister Julie suggested grounding.

I wiggle my toes and look for no fewer than three familiar objects or people around me.

The first thing I see is the mirror where Dahlia finished a painting of me.

A white veil covers my pregnant, nude body.

What in the world?

Dahlia drops the chalk and steps away. "I don't know why I drew you that way, milady."

The room is silent. I look to the king behind me, whose face seems drained of all blood. My visions are random at best.

"The image is a symbol of fertility and good fortune for you, Dahlia," I say.

"Is that what you saw?" she asks, all excited now.

I nod. "Mmhm. You have lots of business coming your way." I'll ask her to return to the Summer Court with me. Prince El'jah might marry her when he sees what her magic can do.

Unblinking, the king keeps staring at the mirror. "Erase it," he hisses.

Dahlia looks to me as if to confirm she heard him correctly before the king shouts, "Erase it!"

Tremors shake the whole house, and everyone grabs something safe to hold on to. I grab the hand of the Unseelie king while his magic lashes out, making the mirror beg for its life, an anomaly since it's dead in the first place. The begging is hard to listen to, even if I know it's just a stupid mirror.

I wonder if the king will show mercy.

The mirror loses its footing. It falls flat on its "face" and shatters into tiny pieces that scatter all over the floor.

The shaking stops. The house staff, the brooms and mops, make their way into the main space and instantly start cleaning up the mess.

The king squeezes my hand. "It happens when I have to repeat myself." He bites into his apple, chews, and swallows. "See that I don't. You all have until Solomar serves supper to have my bride ready for court."

"Who's Solomar?" I ask.

"The tavern owner in our village," Rin supplies.

A large leather-bound book appears in front of my face. I rear back as it opens to a marked page. An image of a female wearing the very dress I'm going to wear to court standing next to my king takes up most of the left page. The female looks like a courtier, graceful, proud, and she's so pretty that my shoulders deflate instantly. She wears the gown with confidence and pride. I can tell. Her chin is slightly raised. Her nose, adorned with a tiny diamond stud, is turned up too.

And the way her breasts fill the corset... Well, her breasts are as big as June's, and June is busty. I'm not sure why the king wants me to look at this image of another female with him or why he's throwing it in my face, but whatever his reason, I find it impolite. An Unseelie-like play of cruelty. He brought me a dress his lover wore already. People will gossip. As if I needed more insecurities and fears over going to the Unseelie court.

I take the book and slam it closed. "I'm happy I didn't read this yesterday."

"Are you now?" the king asks.

"I am," I answer back.

"Augusta, you will read the marked pages by the time we ascend to the court. I am not asking you. I'm ordering you as your king."

"You're not my king."

Gasping, I clap a hand over my mouth. Even if it's true, I can't say it, and I can't disobey him in front of other people, for people talk and our ruse must hold. I'm his bride. We're supposed to be merry and, most importantly, *believably* merry. If I don't hold up my end of the deal, he could take my life, not to mention that Et'enne would be placed in an impossible situation, perhaps even forced into war.

Just when I think he'll order me lashed for the outburst, he cups my cheeks gently. "Believe me, I know I'm not your king. If I were your king, you would have been prepared for my court and you wouldn't dare disobey my orders, for fear I would cut out your tongue." A silver storm brews in his eyes. His magic suffocates me.

"I'm sorry."

The curtains are coming to life, hissing like snakes and twisting over the windows.

I continue, "The picture of the female wearing the same dress made me angry. It's rude to show me I'm wearing the hand-me-downs of one of your previous lovers. It makes me feel awful. It's not polite."

His magic dissipates, and he steps away. "You misunderstand. The dress has been worn by females in my bloodline for generations. It is a symbol of power, and that is my sister, Princess Emishi, the most powerful soothsayer in existence. Of course, if you read the assigned readings, you would know that. Solomar's supper, Augusta." The king marches out of the house.

I bite my lip, then look around, finding solemn, uncomfortable faces. They're going to hate me. Even though I am within my rights to not call the Unseelie king my king, I offended him, and his people seem to like him even when they fear him.

Dahlia smiles politely. "Milady, shall we continue?"

I nod, feeling bad and utterly alone.

My hairdresser claps her hands. "If we're done with shoes and clothing, I will take you to bathe and start on your hair. I served at court once, and although the courtiers change over the turns, the people you'll converse most with are permanent fixtures. We shall bring the books with us, and I'll tell you all I know about the prince regent. The queen regent. Lady Oswalt." She pauses. "She's a cunt. Duchess..."

27

AAMAKO

The bite of winter never ceases to surprise me, even though I've lived in the Winter Court all my life. Standing in front of the door to my home, I breathe hot air into my hands and rub them before slipping on my gloves. The brutal wind blows straight through my bones. And that's saying something since I'm wearing my uniform, a jacket, and a thick velvet coat lined with bear fur.

I sure hope one of the people I brought for my bride dressed her well, for the time for my bride to enter a court full of vipers has come. She is kind, and lacks a mouth filter and therefore ill prepared, and that puts me on edge even more than I already am, given the fact my enemies want to kill me and take my throne. Now that I've decided to reenter the court with a bride, support for their treason should subside.

The queen regent or my nephew might also attempt to turn my bride against me. They'll find her naive and gullible, easily manipulated, and they will use it to their advantage, which is why I assigned readings to Augusta. I hope the information she gathers from those books gives her some leverage.

At least she will familiarize herself with the power and history of my family members. Lots can be learned about people from their past, mine especially.

Thinking she's not ready, since she hasn't come outside yet, I walk back into the house. As I make my way toward the fireplace, I'm thinking I'll get warmed up, maybe have a bite to eat before leaving, but the lady standing at the top of the stairs makes me stop.

Quickly, I change my path and walk toward the stairs, never taking my eyes off her.

Or those thigh-high boots.

The dress, now short in the front and long in the back, appears to be flaring out to show the boots and her pretty thighs. It's cut very short, ending just beneath her mound, barely covering her pussy, and as she descends, she flashes me with her white underpants. They're made of lace.

I recall her summer taste and swallow as the memory of it accumulates at the back of my throat.

She stops on the last step, almost eye level with me. Her pretty gray eyes, almost silver this evening, contrast against the black dress. Naturally curly, her hair is pulled up into an elaborate hairstyle with several strands of carefully placed curls touching her slender shoulders, drawing my gaze toward her collarbone.

A drawing of a single golden butterfly glitters behind her ear. It's a tribute to her court, so I lick my thumb and erase it.

"Your idea, I presume?"

She nods. "It was a tiny mark."

"Nothing is too small to notice. You cannot wear gold in my court. Others can. Not you. Clear?"

Augusta nods and peruses my body with the boldness of a hundred males on the battlefield. "You look...handsome."

"Is that so?"

She nods. "Big and kingly."

"Kingliest," I correct playfully.

The team of people who dressed her are all lined up along the first-floor railing. They deserve praise, so I dip my head, a form of a bow and a thank-you. They were instructed to prepare the bride for court, which included feeding her information, so I presume they read to her or otherwise told her what I needed her to know. Needless to say, my bride looks stunning.

I offer her an elbow. "None of my family members ever looked the way you do in this dress."

"How so?" Augusta tucks her hand under mine, then curses and corrects herself by placing her hand on the top of my forearm. Gently, not as if I'm her hanger.

My gaze lands on her raised breasts, and for a moment, I recall the image she had somehow projected in the mirror earlier this span when her vision took her. In the projection, her breasts were large, as they would be on a female whose body is preparing to feed an infant. I'm repulsed by how sexy I find the thought of Augusta feeding a baby, for the baby cannot be mine.

If Augusta sees herself pregnant in the future, then I haven't done a very good job as a husband, even a temporary one, of educating her about the life of a seer.

I'm sure the Summer king would have bred her for her seer bloodline.

Not me, though.

I need no power or bloodlines to carry on anything of mine. On the contrary, some of the powers and bloodlines should cease to exist, starting with mine. Our court would be better for it. Our people safer too.

Before I open the door, one of the twins rushes toward us and covers Augusta with an undercoat, an overcoat, and a fox-fur scarf. She hands Augusta gloves.

"I can barely see my bride."

"Your Majesty." The girl curtseys. "Your betrothed is a summerling. I'm afraid she might freeze."

"She already froze once. Hopefully learned her lesson."

Augusta scoffs. "I didn't know your cellar was a maze, or that I couldn't find my way back."

"It's not a maze."

Augusta points to the front door. "The cellar door was there, and then it wasn't. That's a maze."

"It's not a maze. Just a cellar you got lost in." I escort her toward the door she pointed at.

My magic opens it, and the moment the winds whoosh in, Augusta snatches the handles and pulls it shut.

I give her a side-eye.

She stares at the exit.

"Is everything okay, milady?" the girl asks.

"I didn't expect the wind to be this cold."

"You are in the Winter Court," I deadpan.

"I know, I know. It's still colder than I thought." She hops from one leg to another. "I presumed we would use the shadows to travel to the palace."

"Contrary to Seelie folktales and imaginings, my people don't always travel via shadows."

"Horses can't possibly scale these mountains. How are we getting to the court?"

"You have to go outside and see." She'll like our ride. I only hope the ride likes her, or we'll have to find another, because I'm not skulking in the shadows of my own palace.

My magic opens the doors again, and I slide on my gloves, then take Augusta's hand and almost drag her outside. The winds beat at us brutally, lifting the fallen snow, which makes it hard to see. I think a storm might be coming, which means we better leave while we still can.

"Oh my fates, my pussy lips froze and fell off like petals."

I laugh. I should remind her she's to be presented to the Unseelie court as their future queen, but reserve the chastisement. The image Augusta evokes is funny. The summerling is fun.

The sound of huffs stomping over poured concrete precedes the animal that rounds the corner of the house. When Augusta spots the creature, she stays in place with her eyes wide as he makes his way toward us. Without any ado, he walks up to her, his head held high, majestic antlers almost as tall as Augusta rising above his head.

Once near her, he flares out his nostrils and sniffs.

Augusta whispers as if she's afraid she'll scare him off, "Do you see the silver stag?"

"Mmhm."

"So it is real?"

"It is a he. And he is real." I take her hand and guide it to the stag to see if he'll let her pet him.

Not only does he let her pet him, but he nudges her shoulder, moving even closer to her. The lashes of his dark Unseelie eyes flutter as he inhales her scent. Flecks of silver magic flake off the tips of his antlers, and the wind blows them onto her skin.

Mmhm. No golden butterflies to be found here.

Some flecks start landing on me, and I try to dust them off to no avail, so now I'm annoyed while Augusta is delighted.

"That's enough, boy." He's not a boy. He's older than I

am, from the time unicorns and stags ran over our world. After the fae wars, stags and unicorns could only be found at the Well frequented mainly by powerful Seelie folk. This silver stag, however, comes when I need him. He always has appeared when I needed him. Perhaps he has foresight too.

Augusta squeals, thrusting her hands up toward me like a child. I scoop her up, and as I'm trying to get her up on the stag, she cups my face and kisses me the way a girl kisses a boy. The way a female would kiss a male. She makes it no secret that she likes me, and that she celebrates the things I find ordinary. There's some sort of joy about her, I admit, that is addictive.

28

AUGUSTA

A s a seer, even a weak one, I dream wildly, yet never in my wildest dreams did I ever even imagine a living, breathing silver stag. Hence, the silver stag I'm sitting on now, with black horns and black eyes, an animal considered the equivalent of the unicorn in the Seelie court, is beyond a dream come true for me.

Stags come from another plane, a magical place called the Well. Only a powerful few are allowed inside the Well, for the magic that lives there is secret and guarded in its purest form.

Under my coats, the stag's body warms my bottom half, and behind me, the Unseelie king practically surrounds my entire upper half. And yet he's fussing with my fox fur, arranging it so only my eyes are peeking out as the stag snorts and digs into the earth with his hoofs.

The tailor comes outside and hands the king a large brown leather sack.

The king takes it and clicks his tongue.

We take off at a gallop down the mountain. Straight

down the mountain. The stag picks up lots of speed. I barely make out the white setting around me, but I sure make out the trees in front of me.

"The trees," I cry.

The stag sprints for a row of thick evergreens that mark the boundary of the forest.

"The trees," I shout.

"Trust me," the king says and covers my hands with both of his. I clutch his words and hands for dear life as the stag speeds up even more. A ribbon of silver magic pours out of his antlers and, like a magical river, flows right under his galloping hoofs, and we lift off the ground like a bird.

My brain isn't catching on. "What is happening?" I ask. The silver magic pouring out of the stag's antlers is creating a path under his legs so he's still galloping. In the air. "I had no idea stags could fly," I shout over the wind.

"Not all do," the king says.

"Do unicorns fly?"

"Some of them."

Under me is a thick, dark forest and then the villages in the valley. The king starts making strange noises at the back of his throat. The stag answers him and drops down just above the village, where people are starting to come out. No, not people. Children. In their pajamas and slippers. They're bursting out of their homes and shouting at us.

The king turns up the sack and colorful items fall out of it. I can't make out what they are, but I think it might be candy because the kids are squealing delightedly and pushing each other around to snatch them off the ground.

I can hardly believe what I'm seeing. I would never have expected the reclusive and oftentimes grumpy Unseelie king to shower kids with joy. Because it's not just about the candy.

Most of those kids down there have worked all span long, because when you are poor, everyone contributes or you don't eat. Especially out here in the Winter Court, where the ground is often frozen and one can't just go to the garden in the back to pick whatever vegetable is in season to put in the stew and on the table.

The king brought them joy.

Turning my head so I can see him, I trace the slight curve of his nose, wishing I had the courage to trace a finger over his lips and his sharp chin, down lower and over the male bump on his throat that I find terribly sexy. He must know I'm staring, because he looks down his nose at me. "What?" he barks.

"Nothing."

"It's something," he mumbles.

I think he's right. It is something. I think I'm falling for the Unseelie king.

～

The stag gallop-flies for what feels like forever.

I can't feel my bottom or my legs, and I'm a bit nauseated. Whenever I'd go into the lower towns from my village in the upper mountain range, which was all of three times in my life, my belly would get queasy from the bumpy carriage ride down the winding mountain roads.

This feels something like that, albeit a bit worse given the height. The pressure in my ears makes me deaf, the winds blowing in my face make me blind, and therefore I don't realize we're in descent until my belly rises.

Through my eyelashes, I make out lights. Bright twinkling lights in the middle of the darkness.

"Can we slow down?" I ask.

The king speaks with the stag, who obeys. As the gallop turns into a trot, I dab my eyes with the gloves and blink a few times to clear away the wind-induced tears.

The Winter Court is an entire city built as a part of the mountain, with most of its structures ending in sharp points. In the middle of the city, there's one massive tower that rises above all the rest. That's the Winter Beauty. Next to it is a smaller tower identical to the bigger one. The two towers and the surrounding structures give an impression of a pair of elegant females wearing lavish gowns made entirely of ice. The towers reflect all the lights around them, making the entire court twinkle. It is breathtaking.

I point at the smaller of the two towers. "That is your family's tower, called the Ice Princess."

The king grunts. "At least you read some of the marked pages."

"It was an annotated drawing," I tease.

When he doesn't reply, I turn in my seat and bump against the hilt of his weapon. I wiggle, then go to stick my hand between us to move the weapon, but the king catches my wrist and puts it back into my lap, trapping both my hands in one of his. It reminds me of how he tied my wrists last night.

I try to move away, but it's not helping. "The hilt of your weapon is poking my back."

"That's not my weapon."

And just like that, my body heats up again. "Um, the top floor of the tower is the king's residence, isn't it?"

"Mmhm," the king purrs.

"Why not call it the King's Tower?"

"Because of the prophecy."

"Oh, I love those. What was it?"

"I'm starting to think I'll have to teach you how to read."

"I aim to shock you with how well versed I am in your court dealings tonight. Besides, none of the marked pages said anything about the prophecy."

"It's unimportant."

"Oh, ye of little faith in the fates. I happen to believe in prophecies especially when they come from seers as powerful as your sister." I turn and crane my neck, catch him looking down at me.

"You look very beautiful tonight," he says.

"As do you."

"Other males will look at you."

"I sure hope so. For all they know, I'll be their queen, and the queen should make a great first impression."

King Aamako pinches his lips.

"What is it?" I ask.

"I'm having violent thoughts."

"Aren't you always having those?" The fire poker in all the rooms is constantly arranging the wood by stabbing it, whacking it, and arguing with it. The king uses the objects as an expression of his thoughts.

He looks down at me and whispers, as if anyone can hear us. "Not over a female."

"I don't know what to make of that."

"I do. Are you ready?"

"No."

He sighs. "There has to be a way you can call your magic at will."

"There is, but I don't have much magic, so it's really not as helpful—"

"You will need all the help you can get in there."

"You're scaring me."

"And that's the issue. Fear. They will sense it, and they will descend on it like vultures."

"You'll be there with me."

"Hence my violent thoughts," he says. "Don't fear them. Fear what I might do if they try to harm you."

"It's looking at the horizon. The view sometimes ignites my magic."

29

AAMAKO

A snow-covered fae court should be a common sight for me and a novelty for Augusta, but I haven't seen the Winter Beauty in many spans. Thus we spend more time than we should hovering in the air.

Like the Golden Palace of the Summer Court, the main palace in the Winter Court has a name. It's called the Winter Beauty. Located at the front of the court before the family tower, it is the most stunning structure in all the Winter Court, with residences sprawling over an entire mountain range and converging densely around the tallest tower in the fae lands.

The Princess tower is the residence of the king. My sister predicted that the Winter Court shall have a queen with blue eyes and blue blood running through her veins. She would have no heartbeat, but she would be alive, marking the rebirth of a necromancy bloodline, the same bloodline that originally created notturnos.

Since the nature of her magic would be rare and terrifying, hearing of it, my parents decided they would name the tower in which she would presumably be conceived the Ice Princess, reminding our enemies (foreign and domestic) that we fear no death. We welcome it since the dead comprise our terrifying princess's army.

But because I know how prophecies work, namely that there are several futures at any given time and even the slightest shifts in occurrence or someone's behavior change the outcome, thereby changing the future, one can never quite know if the prophecy will come true or not.

I hope this one does. The Ice Princess sounds like a fearsome creature, and fearsome creatures belong on the throne of my court. Which is why my poor little seer needs to act fearsome tonight, or I'll have to become the feared creature everyone except her knows me to be.

The stag lands on the large metal plate designed for dragon landing, and I help Augusta down while the guards roll out the bridge that connects the landing with the palace. Sadly, as the Unseelie king who's not shown face in here for decades, no guards are loyal to me. Even if most people fear me, I can't guarantee they won't try to drop us into the abyss below.

Thus, my magic takes hold of the bridge, and it grumbles like an old male as it connects the two palaces, making the platform shake. Augusta grips my arm and the guards exchange terrified looks. Once I cross the bridge, I release it from the magic, and we walk toward the high metal doors.

"Wait," Augusta says and starts removing her coats.

"What are you doing?"

"Getting rid of my layers."

"Whatever for?"

"I recognize this entrance from the drawing in one of the books. It's not like the Summer Court where there's an entrance before the entrance and before that, a square and a million other mini entrances one must pass through before the throne room. Here, we enter the throne room and before accessing the rest of the court. Is that not so?"

"It is so."

"Then I can't enter covered in fur like a bear." Augusta removes the layers and looks around for a place to put them. The pair of males guarding the door attempt to stare straight ahead, but try as they might, they fail. They fail because here's this pretty Summer fairy taking off her clothes and revealing a dress worn by Unseelie seers.

One of the guards swallows hard when Augusta walks toward him.

"Excuse me, sir," she says. The formal address makes me smile since the guard and Augusta are about the same age.

The poor male blinks as if unsure she's addressing him. He looks at me for confirmation, and I'm not sure what kind of expression he sees on my face, but he looks away instantly.

"Sir?" Augusta repeats.

"The Winter guards don't speak with royalty," I say.

"One of the many things I should know and don't."

"It's not a written rule.'

"Can you help me, then?"

"I can, my love." I kiss her cheek and linger a bit, hoping my little lamb won't get slaughtered in there, because if anyone so much as offends her, I might destroy them and their entire lot. I would hate to have to lay waste to another Unseelie court.

"Here is how we address guards. Are you paying attention?"

Augusta nods, a little more flushed than before.

I take the coats and hand them over to the guard, who

takes them with his dark eyes pleading for instruction on how to handle this very unusual thing he's experiencing. Guards guard. They're not here to talk or become coat hangers or keepers of anything, least of all coats.

"Take the coats to your commanding officer and tell him to set up a coat check outside the palace so that the seer can use it whenever she arrives. Which, tell the officer, will be frequent since I intend to marry her."

The guard runs off to execute my order. I wait to see how long it will take for another guard to replace him. My count is up to seven when another guard arrives. Ah, not a guard. He's a commanding officer, judging by the number of stripes on the collar of his uniform.

"My king, I will have the coat check assembled by the end of this evening."

"Excellent."

"Welcome back to court."

Huh. "We'll see if I really am welcome or not."

The male nods at the guard across from him, and I offer Augusta my arm. Her hand lands on it with the grace of a butterfly. I notice her chin is raised and her eyes are sparkling gray turning white as the excitement is stirring the little magic she has. Her smile is radiant, her attitude exceptional, and she is fearless. Fucking fearless. I smell nothing but excitement, and I find myself pausing to ogle her some more.

The guards have left the doors wide open, and the warmth of the fires raging inside sweep over us.

Still, I don't move.

Augusta's head tilts back as she takes in the high ceiling of the throne room. I can tell the moment she spots the throne because her eyes widen. The throne sits on the right shoulder of a statue of a giant. Made of dark gray clay, the top of his head holds up the ceiling. Carefully arranged gargoyle statues guard the throne. They've just been decorations for decades, but they're about to come alive.

The gargoyles are some of the first objects I commanded as a boy. I remember naming them, and when my parents realized I was collecting statues around the palace for my army, they commissioned the clay giant and more gargoyles to be added to the back wall of the throne room so that it's the first sight visitors see when they walk in.

But that's not all. There should be an army of one hundred gargoyles stationed on the ground against the walls and at my disposal.

There isn't.

One of the gargoyle statues near the giant's foot awakens. It stretches with a loud yawn as if waking from deep sleep, then hops down with a thud, causing many couriers to scream and widen the already wide path I'll walk to my throne. It spreads its wings and fluffs them up, dust falling on the raised dais my family stands upon, looking offended that a bit of dust landed on their outfits.

The gargoyle cracks his neck. If the room didn't reek of fear when I arrived, it reeks of fear now. The stench pleases me. Most of these couriers arrived after my departure, and I would be shocked to find a single ally. Unfortunately, I will need allies if I want to stay in power now that my nephew will make an attempt on my life.

He and his mother glare at me from the raised dais between the giant's feet. I'm certain my nephew destroyed all of the one hundred gargoyles my parents placed in the room, which makes me think the silent army of many other sculpted creatures I used to play with in the palace have been destroyed as well. They've been replaced with guards and military personnel, who are in attendance, my court seemingly on high alert. As they ought to be. Traitors.

The gargoyle's heavy footsteps ring in the room as it makes its way toward me, and more than a few ladies yelp. When it reaches us, it turns and announces in a deep voice, "Your king."

30

AUGUSTA

When I was a little girl, I always thought the first snow of the turn was more magical than all the others, and I would get out of bed at the same time that June would wake up to feed the animals. Instead of doing my chores, I would sneak into the kitchen and steal bread and cheese for my secret trip up the mountain, where the snow was thickest.

There, I would build a snow castle and pretend it was mine.

My parents wouldn't even notice I'd been gone all morning, so I never got in trouble. On the way down from the mountain, I'd pass some houses with snow figures outside and steal the carrots stuck in their "heads" as their noses and apples as the eyes. I'd eat them because supper was always a little less in the winter than in the summer.

Standing at the entrance of the Unseelie Winter palace feels surreal, as if it's happening to someone else and not me. Surely, I'm dreaming again. Surely, I haven't really arrived here on a silver stag. And I'm about to walk into the palace with its king.

"Your king," a gargoyle statue announces and fluffs up its wings, calling me into the present and telling me I'm really here.

King Aamako moves, and I walk with him into the Winter palace, surrounded by people who want him dead because they fear him. The stench of their fear is intrusive, and I wiggle my nose. I can't see their faces since everyone is bowing or holding a curtsey with their heads down, but I note the colors favored in the court.

The current fashion is mainly boots and black dresses made of heavy material to keep people warm in the winter. Ladies wear their hair high, stacked in a towerlike fashion, which explains why my hairdresser insisted my hairstyle should rise higher than I think is pretty.

Also, the collars are exaggerated and rise even higher than the hairdos.

Pristine white walls make the space seem larger than life. Statues of various mythical creatures give the walls texture and an ominous, dangerous feeling since most of the statues are painted white with a few red birdlike creatures made of stone and gargoyles made of dark gray marble.

The couple waiting for us on the dais is clearly the Winter prince and his mother, the queen regent. I recognize him from the pictures my hairdresser showed me, but the images don't do him justice. While I saw him in the Summer Court, King Aamako overshadowed him, so I didn't pay the prince much attention.

If one is into a clean-cut and severe-looking male who is also cruel, then one would find him handsome. He's got sharp features, an elegant nose, large, seductive, dark eyes, and long, straight, jet-black hair that he wears in a high ponytail that reminds me of our Summer king, Et'enne. Except when Et'enne looks at one of his subjects, it feels as if one stands with their feet in the sea and face turned up toward the warm sun.

This male makes me feel like I'm standing in a puddle of blood.

I glance at the floors.

They're not red.

On his right stands his mother, dressed in a white dress with black sleeves draping all the way to the floor. Her makeup is dark, her lipstick even darker, and her hair is made into the tallest tower in the room. It's held together with red snake pins. She stands as regally as any queen might, although she's never been a queen.

I learned she always wanted the throne, that rumors surrounding her and King Aamako's involvement in her husband's death plague the court still. Many believe she and King Aamako killed her husband so that she would be free to marry the king she's always coveted. Some rumors say the prince is Aamako's offspring, seeing as how his magic is associated with moving objects. *Achitektus* magic means the prince designs the spaces people frequent. For example, he could swap the left wall for the right wall, his magic rearranging spaces like pieces of a puzzle.

Because King Aamako never claimed his brother's wife as queen and the boy as his, but has instead retreated to Dakkuyasu, some say that he did so out of shame and regret for the murder of his brother. I've no way of knowing if any of these rumors are true, and even if they were, my role in this engagement pact is to act as if the king everyone fears wants to marry me.

Thus, my plan at the Winter Court is simple. Say not what you mean, mean not what you say, for this is the Unseelie court and the viper bites kill. The moment we climb onto the dais where the pair of vipers who are ready to kill my king stand, defiantly not bowing or curtseying before Aamako, I move my hand from gently resting on his forearm to the top of his hand.

Unexpectedly, the king takes my hand and interlaces our fingers. I think he likes doing that. I think he doesn't care much for protocol or the decorum of his court. I guess when you're king, you're the one who makes up the protocol.

The queen regent's gaze slides to our hands before she grabs her lavish black dress and lifts it. Her curtsey is elegant and deep, and her ample breasts are in a prime position for Aamako's gaze should he care to look. Since we're being watched, I don't side-eye the king to see if he's noticed her posture while she stays in her downward position.

I observe the brazen way the prince stares at his uncle. I'm unsure why I expected the prince to greet us with a smile, even a fake one. Perhaps because that's how it would've been done in the Summer Court. The royal family of the Summer Court is not without problems, but when they're in public, they pretend everything is perfectly fine.

King Aamako waits.

Will the prince not bow?

The king is standing before him. He must bow. What if he doesn't? I've no idea what happens to fools who disrespect the Unseelie royal family, but I'm not one of them. Unlacing my fingers from the king's, I lower my gaze and curtsey, hoping my gesture will remind the prince we're soon to be family for all he knows.

The queen regent clears her throat while still holding her curtsey. As am I.

"Neguan," the king says, amusement lacing his voice. "Have you met my seer?"

Since the king is introducing us, I straighten back up, feeling bad for the queen regent, along with the entire court who are still holding their bent positions. I can hear the pained whining of the people behind me. What they say about the Unseelies enjoying inflicting pain on others might prove to be true after all.

The prince steps toward Aamako. With their height being about the same, he can look the king square in the eyes. "Welcome back, Uncle. I see you've brought a souvenir from the Summer Court."

The king faces the courtier, effectively turning his back on the younger male, telling everyone he's unafraid of back-stabbing or having the prince behind him. I'm certain that's not the case, but I recognize the power move.

The prince refused to bow.

King Aamako must save face or show force. I think he's opting for the former, which makes me more comfortable, for I never wish to witness this male showing force. A male who single-handedly conquered an entire fae court isn't someone anyone would want to piss off. Hence the reason our King Et'enne agreed to the engagement scam. Hence, the prince is likely very stupid.

"I heard you've grown into an arrogant dumbass, but to challenge me in such a petty way shows me how little time you've spent listening to your mother. Surely she's taught you better than that. Isn't that right, Larho?"

Oh my fates. He called him a dumbass and addressed this awkward family reunion in front of the entire court.

Having been addressed, the queen regent rises on unsteady feet, yet manages to smile prettily. A mature fae lady, Larho is gorgeous, her wrinkles few and only adding to her overall beauty. A cold kind of dark-eyed beauty, but a beauty nonetheless, with smooth skin and carefully arranged diamond studs all around her earlobes. Her diamond necklace is in the shape of a snake and wraps three times around her neck, closing as a head that bites the tail. The eyes of the snake are red rubies.

Something about this piece of jewelry seems familiar. "That's a lovely necklace," I say.

She doesn't even look at me when she says, "Aamako, I wish you had consulted with us before you brought a peasant with nothing but a sliver of soothsayer magic to the court."

Some people whisper, others snort, suppressing laughter, and some even giggle.

The king glances aside at me. I'm unsure what he wants me to do. Talk back to the Unseelie queen regent? I'd rather not, but I must do something or say something, or they'll think I'm a weakling. When it comes to magical power, I *am* a weakling, but my tongue can be sharp when I want it to be.

"Your necklace feels oddly familiar," I say. It does. Truly.

"She is talking to me again." The queen sighs as if annoyed.

"It's oddly familiar because, it will be mine after your death."

That catches her attention, and her dark eyes flash silver. "Is this what you see in the future?"

"I don't see it, no. I rarely ever actually see. I know it as if it's already happened."

The queen regent slides up to me, her face distorting as if she's holding back her shapeshifting magic. "You don't actually see because you're not a powerful seer, and everyone knows it because we can sense the magic you carry, so whatever you and your sister have done to our poor mad king will be uncovered by me, and when I do uncover it, I will string you up by your legs and cut into you slowly so that you take spans to die, and just before you die, I will take you down and feed you so I can do it all over again for all eternity!" she spits.

I wipe her saliva from my face.

"A threat to my queen is treason," King Aamako says matter-of-factly.

"She's not your queen!" the female shouts, her hands balled into fists.

"Neguan," the king says in a voice I recognize as formal. Et'enne has a similar voice when he's addressing his subjects, when he's issuing orders he wants executed immediately. "You and your mother will retire for the night. The family, whatever is left of it, shall enjoy a private meal tomorrow." Aamako's people, who are no longer able to hold their positions, are on their knees on the floor, with their heads touching the marble.

The pristine white floor reflects the lights almost like a mirror. It captures my attention, a vision pulling me into the future.

Oh no, I don't want to *leave* the present for fear of what will come out of my mouth, but the visions aren't something I can control. The lady wearing a white dress and running over red floors appears again. I can see the pristine white walls of this castle surrounding her and her hair is down, curls bouncing. It's me. I'm running away.

From what?

From who?

31

AUGUSTA

"That went well, I thought." King Aamako's voice drifts into my consciousness, along with a vision-induced headache. Lying down, I cross my arms over my eyes and groan.

"What went well?" I ask.

"The court visit."

"You really are wild, my king."

The silence that ensues allows me time to rethink what I'd said. I called him my king again. That's twice now. I recall telling the queen regent she'll die, effectively threatening her. It doesn't help with my headache.

I wet my lips with my tongue. "My mouth is parched." Sitting up, I rub my face and groan again. "My head is pounding. I passed out, didn't I?"

A teacup appears before me, and I peek inside before sipping some sort of pale pink alcoholic drink. It tastes sweet, and it's served with a large ice cube melting in the middle. I drink the entire thing, and the liquid settles gently in my empty belly.

"Aamako," I call out and look around the dimly lit room.

My nose detects burning herbs, but I don't see any smoke until I look up. Dozens of rectangular candleholders hover in the air, their small fires burning herbs whose pleasant scent wafts into the room.

"Aamako?" I call again, only now realizing I've called him by his first name. I blame it on the headache.

"Here," he says from behind the wall partition on my right. It's got a thick gray texture with rosebuds woven throughout. The design is so pretty that I roll over the thin mattress (if one can even call it that) to stand and touch the texture of the rose. Under my fingertip, the fabric feels coarse. I think it's wool and that someone made this by hand.

"Whose quarters are these?"

"The royal family's."

"And my room?"

"My mother's."

"I'm staying in royal quarters and wearing your sister's dresses, and feeling awkward about it all."

"It's for your protection. My sister's things remind everyone you are a seer, and she was a terrifyingly powerful seer. However, after your debut in the court, I doubt I'll have to remind them of it much longer. Things went so well that I don't believe I'll have to kill anyone for trying to offend you."

Before putting me in bed, he undressed me, leaving me in my undergarments. I take them off as I walk the length of the partition, my fingertips gliding over the textured wall.

"Did your mother make this wall?"

"Yes."

"It's very pretty." I find the end of the wall and pause to gather my wits about me. It takes me no time to know what I want. I do want it. Him.

I want him, and I know that if I round this corner and

appear inside his chamber, there is no going back. Aamako wants to repel people, but nature designed him as an attractive male. He's tall, broad-shouldered, handsome, powerful, reclusive, mysterious, and familiar. It's that familiarity that makes me bolder and unafraid of his rejection.

I turn the corner and stand there while he takes in my nude body. He lets me gaze upon him as well. He's resting on a large, thin mattress on the floor. A fluffy white comforter covers his middle while he leans back on the pillows, hands tucked beneath his head.

"I take it the tea you drank cured all your ills," he says, gaze darting between my legs.

"That was not tea, and you know it."

His chuckle sounds like a purr, so very intimate that it feels like a caress of a tongue over my clit. I release my mating scent, feeling pain in the middle of my back, a sign that my wings will emerge and I'll go into heat. Excited and nervous, I pad toward the king, then kneel at the edge of his bed and reach up to release my hair.

It takes me a beat to remove all the pins holding my hair up, but the king gets an eyeful of my breasts, so he doesn't seem to mind waiting. Once my hair is down, I let it fall over my breasts and crawl between his legs. I pull back the sheet to reveal his beautiful cock, which stands up proud, like the king himself.

Between his legs, I kneel and reach for his cock with both hands. Once I have my hands on him, I sigh with pleasure. It feels silky and smooth, yet so hard, and it makes the heat in my belly churn more. My mating scent blooms fully. I don't even care to pull it back. It's not as if the male has no idea I'm attracted to him.

"That's right, little seer. Grip it tightly and pump your hands."

There he goes, talking again. It makes me uncomfortable, but it's also arousing. I wish I could talk back, but I'm at a loss for words.

The king commands a small glass vial to hover in the air. The cork pops, and the vial turns over, dripping hot oil on my fingers.

"It smells like crushed rose petals and sea," I say.

"Like your mating scent." The king sits up and grabs the back of my head. He pulls me toward him and closes his other hand over my throat. I can smell his masculine scent, and I can tell he's turned on. I can also hear his breathing pick up, his heart beating faster. It's confirmation that I excite this male, so I pump my hands faster.

"That's a good girl," he praises me. "You're going to make your king come, and he wants to come in your mouth. What's a good girl say?"

"Yes, my king, please come in my mouth."

Gently, he squeezes my throat and holds it long enough for me to feel the heat crawl up my face as the air is obstructed. He pecks my lips. "You're a good girl, Augusta, and I will enjoy, perhaps too much, spoiling you. Now, suck me well and make sure you swallow all the seed. We don't want any mess ruining these nice sheets, do we now?"

I shake my head, and the king fists my hair with both hands. As his hold tightens, the rough way he handles me makes my heat gather. The fireball in my belly drops and starts coating my virginal channel, some of the liquid heat escaping onto my thighs. Frightened I'll expose my lust and stain his sheets, I go to close my legs, but the king's hand cups between my legs.

I gasp as his finger touches my clit.

The hand in my hair tightens more. "Don't hold back on me now." He slaps my entrance.

I yelp and try to close my legs, but he slaps it again. "Keep them open, or I'll put a bar between your knees."

Oh my fates.

He slaps my wetness again and starts stroking me, edging out my heat. It takes me no time at all to respond to him. My body is his pianoforte, playing any tune the king strokes out. My channel pulses, expelling liquid heat all over his fingers. He cups his hand, collecting it all in there. And then he smears it on my cheek, letting it drip over my breasts, which he then squeezes while licking my face in one fast swipe of his long, rough tongue.

I've no idea how other people do this, but I swear this king does some of the filthiest things I couldn't even dream of.

Once done licking, he lifts an eyebrow. "What are you waiting for?"

I scoot back and bend, my mouth open and accepting his large cockhead, which I barely fit inside, my lips stretching painfully around it. The king groans and takes my head and starts moving it up and down his length while I pump with my hands near the base.

"You're doing well, Augusta. Your mouth feels like it's made for sucking me. Is it? Hm? Why, yes, I think it was made for pleasuring me."

Tears start streaming down my face. He's choking me, shoving himself into the back of my throat. I moan because the way he's using my mouth excites me, and I wish to have sex with him. The thought comes just as the king ejaculates, pumping copious amounts of seed I can't possibly keep up with swallowing. I start coughing, and the king lets go of my hair.

Moving back and bending over, I cough a bit more and

then wipe my mouth as I sit back on my heels, looking at him through my messy hair.

The king's reclining on the pillows, his long penis twitching on his belly, still releasing the cum I couldn't swallow.

The comforter scoots away from him as if it's a living thing, and it's replaced by another comforter, this one dark gray, so likely from the room I'm staying in.

"You made a mess." There's magic in his eyes. He's smiling, so I crawl forward and over him to rest my head on his chest. The moment I settle, I close my eyes, and a strange peace comes over me. This, the Unseelie king and I, also feels familiar.

32

AAMAKO

Footsteps outside wake me out of my stupor, and the first thing I do is snatch my little Summer fairy from where she's sleeping beside me and bring her closer to my side. Then I listen for the intruders. As silent as Tima and Kense are, I still hear them, for I've lived alone for far too long not to notice even the slightest of changes in my vicinity.

My magic grabs the sword and meets them outside.

The sword's handle grows my lips and whispers in my voice, "You two walk like the Unseelie army marching over Summer fae graveyards." It's a joke. The crawlers are as silent as the night. They are assassins, after all.

The footsteps pause.

"What do you want?" the sword asks.

Tima speaks, her voice also low. "The queen regent is requesting your presence for breakfast."

Oh, it's morning. "I promised her breakfast?"

"We don't know if you did, but she sent the guards to deliver a message that she and your nephew are expecting you."

The queen regent's message ignites the rage I've tamped down during my absence from court. I left so I wouldn't kill my brother's widow or their son and my only heir. But her attitude, her treatment of me, namely the way she thinks she can speak to me as if she's my queen, makes me murderous.

"Tell her Augusta and I will arrive when we arrive."

I await acknowledgment, and when I hear none, I ask, "Is there something else?"

"The queen won't take it well."

"That's her problem. Carry the message as I spoke it or I shall carry it with this sword and, who knows, maybe sever her head. Do we want that?" I'm not sure who I'm asking, but my old friends wisely don't answer. They leave, and the sword returns to its place on the recliner, my magic retreating from it.

I sniff Augusta's hair and, feeling a peace I haven't found in decades, I drift off to sleep again.

A noise in the hallway wakes me again. I hear hushed voices, then the same quiet footsteps. Again, I use the sword to communicate, although this time, I unsheathe it, a clear sign that I'm annoyed.

"What?" the sword whisper-hisses, not that I need to be quiet. Augusta sleeps like a dragon in hibernation. I can even hear soft snoring. It must be nice to be this worry-free. Or perhaps she's worry-free because she feels safe with me.

I wish that were the case. I'm crazy and volatile, and if the queen regent doesn't stop sending her guards, I'll show everyone just how crazy I really am.

"The queen insists on your presence," Kense says.

"The Unseelie court has no queen."

Tima elbows her husband. "He's sorry, Your Majesty. A slip of the tongue. The queen regent is angry and is requesting an audience with you."

Hm. She wants an audience with me.

Augusta's back is to my front, and I trace a claw over the protrusions on her back. Under the skin are the wings the female fae sprout during their heats. "Tell the queen regent I'll grant her an audience." As before, the sword returns to the chair, and I withdraw my magic.

I trace my palm down Augusta's back and over her bottom, then slip my hand between her legs. Even in sleep, she's wet, though not as wet as she gets when I'm touching her. With a finger, I gently push inside her virginal hole and feel the intact hymen. I leave it that way, for I truly do not wish Augusta to lose her sight, and a seer's foresight is tied to the maidenhead. Not sure why foresight magic behaves in such way, but it does. Seers are to remain chaste or lose their sight.

I rub her entrance gently so I can entice her heat and watch the bones of her wings shift under her skin, ready to push out and spring at me like flowers. Stirring her heat stirs my own, and I spray my seed on her ass cheeks. Smearing the seed over her butt, I sneak a finger between her ass cheeks and touch her back hole. Since my finger is wet, it slips inside her hole, which opens like a rose bud now that Augusta is going into heat.

"You know what they say about Summer fae?" I can sense she's wide awake now, but remains quiet, letting me touch her in any way I please.

She doesn't answer. Maybe she wants to pretend she's sleeping. That's fine with me. I know she's alert.

"They say that when a Summer fairy goes into her heat,

no hole is to be left unattended. I wonder if that's true about this back hole?" I push my finger inside it some more and elicit a moan. When she tries to turn, I roll on top of her back.

"Good morning, Augusta."

"Top of the morning to you, my king."

I chuckle, and Augusta finally opens her eyes. Specks of white in her gray eyes tell me she's in full heat. I peck her cheek and whisper. "Did you sleep well?" I work her back hole with my finger, stretching it and adding another. Augusta is moaning, not hearing me talk at all, it seems.

"I asked if you slept well?"

"Mmhm."

"*Yes, my king,* is an appropriate answer." I gather up her wrists, then press them at the small of her back. "Keep your hands fisted and arms crossed at the wrists right here. Do not move them."

I grab my pillow and slide it under her belly to lift her bottom a bit, and then I spread her ass cheeks. The vial of oil drips onto her hole, lubing it nicely. Then I gather more oil on my left hand and rub it on Augusta's back, between her shoulder blades, over the skin under which the wings are almost ready to come out.

"Oh my fates, this feels so good," she mutters.

Stroking a fairy's wings heightens her arousal, and some fae females can even come just from having their wings stroked. It's the same with fae male horns, which are starting to protrude out of my head.

Augusta's small hole prepared, I take my cock and pump it a few times so the seed spurts on her hole before I position the head and start pushing it inside. I still massage between her shoulder blades to ease her pain and get her as aroused as possible.

She's moaning, but I detect some pain in her voice. Her fists are clenched tightly. I tap them. "Relax and take a deep breath. When I start pushing inside, you exhale slowly."

I move my hips forward, and her hole tightens around my cock like a belt. Seated halfway in and not planning on going farther, I move inside her, slowly, at leisure, while I rub the lines where the wings will jut out.

"Your wings are starting to come out, Augusta. Can you feel that?" I tap my claws over the wing bone under the skin.

"I think so," she mumbles.

"Have you never had wings?"

"No, my king."

"I'm curious what color they'll be."

"Red, my king. They're red."

"How do you know if you've never seen them?"

Augusta doesn't answer.

She knows because she's the seer, and it reminds me just how careful I must be with her sight. It's a gift, and I don't wish to take it from her, even if it's only a little bit of magic that I never needed from her in the first place. I just needed a female in a position of power as a fiancée during my reclaiming of the Unseelie court, for I don't want to have to kill the last few members of my family. I want them to retreat from court or bend to my rule as they should. And an engagement would take care of the courtier on the side of my nephew. Once he loses power, meaning once I choose a bride, they'll cross over to my side, shifting the power in the court in my favor.

As the fates would have it, Augusta kissed me on the bench that one night I'll never forget, and here I am, enjoying her body. She's bold and fun and fuckable, and she means more to me than I care to admit.

I stroke between her shoulders and hear the footsteps enter the hallway.

I pick up my pace and fuck my little Summer fairy in earnest, though not too roughly so I don't damage her, but rough enough to get her worked up. With one hand, I hold her hip, and with the other, I massage her, her wings now living things writhing under her skin, fighting for their freedom.

"Show me those pretty Summer wings."

"Oh, Aamako, I'm close."

"I know, seer. Show me your wings." Her back bends, her body bucking as she comes hard. I slice the skin on both sides of her spine and Augusta screams as her wings sprout, showering us with fairy glitter.

Footsteps that have stopped at the door behind me now retreat outside.

The wings are, indeed, red.

Everything about Augusta is made to entice me into mating her, and now even her wings are the color of my court. They signal danger. They signal I must back off from her before I destroy her life. Yet, I can't part from her, and not because I need her to act as my bride.

33

AUGUSTA

As far as perfect mornings go, this one ranks at number one. The king is inside me, unmoving now because I sprouted wings that tell him I've entered heat, and he's my chosen.

I glance behind me. Red wings tipped in black rise from my back. Summer fairies grow blue or maybe yellow, even coral wings. Okay, maybe not coral, because coral wings are more common in the Spring Seelie fae, but certainly not red and black. Those colors represent the Winter Court.

Aamako's large hand closes over the top of my left wing, and he runs his palm over it, petting me in a way. I shudder, my clitoris pulsing with need. Using the wings as leverage, he's moving in and out of my butthole and telling me what a good little seer I am for him and how he loves fucking my small hole. I get up on all fours and push back against him, letting him know I'm so crazed for his body and the way he fucks that I'm no longer in pain from penetration.

It's all perfect, more perfect than I ever imagined it could be, especially with how he's holding my wings and grunting, and how now, when he's losing control, he gets up off his knees and crouches instead, pistoning deeper inside me.

My eyes roll to the back of my head, and I open my mouth in a silent scream when he comes, shouting, "*Mine, mine, mine,*" at the ceiling, making the walls shake. The swords slip off the hooks, the wardrobe screams, teacups, oil vials, and a tray all scatter.

"Come again," he orders me and flicks my clit. It's so swollen and sensitive that I buck under him and spray the sheets again with liquid heat.

Exhausted, my body a puddle of used flesh, I almost melt into the soft sheets.

The king withdraws from me with a groan and lies on his back beside me. Long black horns start retreating, magic dimming from his eyes, his strong jaw and the lines of his face start softening back to normal.

He swipes a finger over his cheek, and it comes back red.

He's covered in red glitter from my wings.

My face burns. When a female in heat showers a male with glitter from her wings, she is displaying great affection for him. I am fond of the king. He is my first.

Technically, we didn't do it the way most folks would, but nothing about this king surprises me. He's not like most people, so why should he have sex like one? As for me, I've never shied away from anything new and different. An adventure, especially a safe and pleasurable one, under the guidance of a king who I know won't hurt me is a grand experience. One I wouldn't miss out on.

The Unseelie king stares at the ceiling as the wardrobe starts whispering with the other wardrobe in my bedroom. They're giggling, and I listen in, trying to make out the language they (the king) is using, but can't.

"What language is that?" I ask quietly, then regret

speaking at all. I think I'm disturbing his thoughts. Maybe the king processes out loud via his magic and objects instead of inside his head. If that's the case, I'd hate to interrupt even though I just did. Bad Augusta.

I think I should be punished.

Perhaps he'll spank me again.

Inwardly, I laugh.

Outwardly, I clear my throat, and since the king doesn't answer me but continues to stare at the ceiling, I scoot closer and lay my head on his chest. His arm comes around me and squeezes my shoulders.

"Your wings are the colors of my court."

"Curious that, no?"

"No."

I look up to see him smirking. "You don't think my wings are trying to please your tastes, do you?"

"I'm thinking all sorts of things."

"Like what?"

"Nothing I wish to share."

"I'm shocked you don't wish to share." Sarcasm is one of my favorite forms of humor. The king doesn't respond, so I continue, "I think a lot too. I like talking about the good things I see are happening in the future, as if I can make them happen just by thinking them."

The king tilts his head. "So when you visualized yourself pregnant, you counted that as a good thing you wish to happen to you?"

"Um." My face must match the color of my wings. I press my cheek to his chest again, hiding the blush. "It felt good to see that I might have babies in the future."

"You realize that you can't have babies and preserve your sight."

"I don't have much sight."

"The fates never do."

I sit up, my hair draping over my right shoulder. "What?" The wings feel awkward on my back and erect behind me, stiffly at attention as if projecting my sudden shock. "What do you mean?"

The king strokes his jaw where the hairs are growing now. It's so sexy and makes me want to bend over and bite. I rest my hands on his chest and lean in to do just that. Bite his jaw.

At the last moment, I pull back with a headshake. "Where were we?" I touch my flaming cheeks. Biting is considered marking, and males bite or mark females they mate with in ways that show their affection. My sister came out of her heat bruised and bitten as if she'd gone to battle and back. The Summer king showed his court that he loved her hard.

I want that for myself, but I can't be the one biting a male. A male ought to be the one biting me.

"The fates are born with little magic, so they're often-times disregarded and shamed in the courts."

"The fates are the most powerful fae in existence."

"Yes, but there are timelines associated with the magic of the fates. Did your sister have magic before she became a fate?"

"Not at all. Oh my fates, you're right!" My wings flutter in excitement. "June barely had any magic, and it was blood related. Like she'd have to bleed or someone nearby would have to bleed for her magic to ignite. And it was never a guaranteed thing. It came and went randomly. Then one span, she was a fate. I wish I knew how it worked for sure, but June is so tight-lipped about the fate business. June is tight-lipped about everything. Unlike me." I purse my lips. "How do you know about the fate magic?"

"I read," he deadpans.

I trace the red viper tattoo under his rib cage. "Despite what you might believe, I can read."

"I'm so happy to hear you *can* read, Augusta."

I punch him in the ribs.

He chuckles, so I punch him again, and when he starts laughing at my very serious attempt to hurt him, I bite him near his nipple. As I move to release the bite, the king holds my head there.

"Harder," he orders.

My small fangs pierce his skin, and the copper taste of blood makes me pull back. The marks aren't bleeding much, but they're there nonetheless. I look up into the eyes and see they're pure silver. Every object in the room levitates around us. The king growls, his upper lip lifting.

Some would fear him, for he looks deadly.

I kiss the space above his nipple and bite again.

The king flips us over, and I yelp at the sudden movement. Hovering above me, he traps my wrists above my head and lets his body lie atop mine. Between my legs, he is hard, and our position is one that lovers assume before and during sex. I think the king might do it with me. I think I'm about to have sex.

The actual common way people all around the world do it.

I lift my hips slightly, but he growls, making me retreat a bit.

"I cannot be the reason you lose your magic."

He's talking about my virginity being tied to my foresight. "I don't have enough foresight to hold on to it." *I would rather hold on to you.* I don't say that. It leaves me open and vulnerable, a gaping wound inviting more damage, and the Unseelie king could hurt me.

"Even that sliver of foresight is worth holding on to."

"Says the king."

"What do you mean?"

"Foresight in a king's possession is power, and power is everything. You were born with abundance and wealth in a palace, a place of outmost comfort. It makes sense you speak from that place. If you didn't, then you'd know that there are other things in life people value more than magic and wealth."

"Magic and wealth are power," he answers. "There's nothing more important than power."

"There's love." I swallow. "There's finding that one person with whom even the hardest challenges of life are easy. That one soul among millions that makes yours sing. And I'm not even talking about fae-ted mates, but love between two people in general." When the paths of two fae-ted fae merge, they form a new path called the heart line, and the male fairy gets his wings. These pairings are rare, coveted, and I've yet to meet one such pair, even though I had a vision of King Et'enne wearing wings.

I await Aamako's comment, but he just stares.

It's official. I'm the dumbest, poor Seelie in the world for sleeping with the Unseelie king and dreaming he would one span be hers. But hey, I never claimed to be smart, and if I am to dream, then my dreams ought to be king sized.

And the king is size extralarge, my weeping pussy supplies.

Too bad he's also emotionally unavailable.

And all of this is fake.

Since he's simply gazing at me, magic retreating from his eyes, objects returning to normal, I take it I doused the heat of our moment with bringing up the dreadful L word. Might as well have poured ice over the male and then asked him to service me in heat.

Oh fates. I *am* in heat. Crap. If he won't have sex with me while I'm in heat, I will suffer through it.

"My king," someone hisses from outside.

"Tima, this better be urgent," Aamako growls.

"The queen regent is threatening suicide."

"Did she send you here to retrieve the weapon? Take any of them and tell her to hurry up."

I suck in a breath.

Aamako kisses the tip of my nose. "Don't worry, kind Augusta. Larho is a narcissist who would never hurt herself." To the person outside, he says, "Tell her *we* will receive her for brunch in our breakfast nook. Be sure you use plural nouns when referencing my future queen and me."

"Aamako!" a female shouts from far away. I think it might be the queen regent.

"Let her in."

What?!

34

AAMAKO

Approving an audience with the queen regent who has a sick obsession with me is the second best thing I've done this morning, first being the obvious sex with my little seer, whose submission couldn't have been more pleasing to me than if I controlled all the magic in the world.

Hence, I almost buried myself inside her pussy, thereby destroying her life because eventually, according to our deal, I must return her to the Summer Court. She would arrive there deflowered and stripped of what little magic she possessed, rendered useless to the Summer king and making her unlikely to ever find a powerful match.

Not to mention, she could be the next fate, and I like the little seer far too much to destroy her. I wish her good fortune.

Allowing the queen regent to witness our coupling will serve everyone well.

"What is going on?" Augusta whispers under me, her hands resting on my chest, poised to push me away.

"Nothing. I'll deal with this."

At first, Augusta frowns, but then her eyes widen, and I can tell she heard the queen regent lingering outside our door. Since the walls inside are but thin partitions, Augusta blushes some more. She blushes easily and often, more often than I would've thought possible for a girl who isn't typically shy.

"Larho," I say, "you really are a glutton for punishment."

"I got what I came here for," the queen regent says, making Augusta push at my chest.

Standing, I cover Augusta with a comforter, then wrap the sheet around my middle. For a moment, I stare at Augusta on the mattress with her hair splayed over the pillow even though the queen regent is talking, her voice rising. I don't care if the queen regent is upset.

Augusta sits up, her pale gray eyes wide, her lips swollen and pouty, her skin shimmering, her beautiful fairy wings spread out behind her in a way that makes me think she ought to be a queen. There's something majestic about them, something Unseelie, something dreadfully *mine*.

Or maybe I'm just aroused and a female in heat inside my chambers is a healing sight for my eyes, which have seen more death and destruction than any living fae king in existence. The fae kings that have seen what I've seen are now dead because I ended them.

Including the Fall Court's king.

Which reminds me of the person talking outside. "Larho, you're losing grace. The shouting is unbecoming of a lady of your station."

"You're the one who decided to act like a peasant and call me in here to witness your debauchery!"

I open the door and try to leave, but she blocks the exit, attempting to get inside. I don't think so. "Tell the staff to start preparing the brunch, and have it served in the breakfast nook. The family has much to discuss."

"Your summerling whore is not family."

A pair of blades cross over the queen regent's neck and slice. Blood gushes out, and she covers the wounds with her hands. She can't stop the bleeding. The blood spurts between her fingers, and yet she's not getting help or leaving. She just stands there, her gaze on the bites Augusta left on my chest. Good.

"Larho, you will heal and clean up, return to the breakfast nook rejuvenated and clear minded, ready to serve your king, or the king shall have your head. Dismissed."

The queen regent turns on her heel and runs outside, my shadow crawlers bowing their heads as she storms out. Tima closes the doors with a big grin on her face.

I rest my hands on my hips. "Join me for brunch."

The wardrobe supplies a robe, and a towel slings over my shoulder as I turn to see that Augusta has left my bed. I round the partition to find her in her bed, comforter over her head and only her wings peeking out from under it.

"Augusta, join me for brunch."

"I heard you."

"Then why are you not getting ready?"

"Because I don't want to go." The comforter flies off, and Augusta sits up, her eyes red as if she'll start shooting flames out of them. Clearly, she's upset, and the good thing about Augusta is that she verbalizes well, so she let me know right away.

"You invited her in after you fucked me."

"Don't curse."

"Fuck."

"Augusta," I warn.

"Oh, you have some balls on you to correct me on

cursing while inviting the queen to watch you fuck another female."

"The Unseelie court has no queen."

"That's not the point." Her voice is rising, and I allow it.

"Larho witnessed me enjoy my future queen."

"But why would you need her to witness that?"

I grit my jaw. Augusta and I have grown far more attached than we should have. It's time we face the painful truths of our arrangement. It seems both of us forgot. "Because she needed convincing, and if she is convinced that I mean to marry you, everyone else will be too."

"Is it that hard to believe?"

"Yes."

Augusta winces.

"I have lived in solitude for a long time. During that time, I have rejected all attempts from nearly every Unseelie and some Seelie families to push their daughters and a few sisters into my bed. Before I went into seclusion, I swore I would never...mate. I swore off heirs. Larho started rumors, saying I rejected everyone because I love her, saying the prince regent is mine. He is not."

"But did you love her?"

I shake my head. "Never. And I never will."

"You can't say never. You don't know what the future holds."

Just when I think Augusta will come with me, she flops back onto the bed. "Maybe I'll bathe later. I really am tired."

It sounds like a dismissal. Crossing my arms over my chest, I stay.

Augusta peeks above the comforter. "Did you say something?"

"You practically dismissed me."

"I don't feel like getting up now."

"What do you feel like doing?" The moment it comes out of my mouth, I know the answer.

"Fucking." She smiles.

"Again, the queen doesn't curse."

"I'm not a queen."

"But you could be." The moment I say the words, I know them to be true. I want Augusta to be my queen. I want it more than anything but I cannot ruin her life either. I like her too much to destroy her.

Augusta gets up and walks up to me, her wings spread, her breasts hard with pointy nipples begging to be sucked.

"I'm trying not to interpret your words to mean what I wish them to mean."

I press a palm against the small of her back and bring her closer to me. When our bodies touch and the heat of her skin seeps through my skin, my seed leaks out of the tip of my cock. I want to breed her.

Fuck.

I want to breed her.

I step away. "Rest and find me later. Tima will escort you."

35

AAMAKO

Back in my chambers, I walk toward the corner where the darkness collects and let the shadows take me into the shared quarters of the family tower. There, I pause by the vase on the right side of the nook by the door.

I crouch beside the vase and search for the crack my brother and I mended after we broke the vase. Mother kept warning us not to run around the lounge and near the ancient vases her family gifted her when she married my father, but my brother and I misbehaved. I kicked out at him, and he skipped away, causing my foot to hit the vase.

The giant hole in the vase made my mother furious, and she ordered us to patch it up by hand, without our magic. Of course, we didn't know how, so she suggested we visit the royal library and read about the vase and how to repair it. It was then I learned I liked researching.

There. I trace my claw over the glued-together pieces near the middle of the vase on the side that's turned toward the wall. The staff hides the flaw from people the same way most of us hide the broken pieces of us that we never mended. Those are our flaws, things we don't wish people to know.

And those of us born with magic that destroys others must protect the people we care about from ourselves. My brother's death taught me that. The destruction of the Fall Court reaffirmed it.

I wish I could have repaired my relationship with my brother by reading some books and putting glue on the cracks. Try as I might, once he realized his wife coveted the throne and, by default, me, he grew bitter and angry with me and the queen regent.

He started whoring, even bringing concubines into the palace. One night, he brought a female into the queen regent's chambers, at which point I believe his wife decided to end him. A few spans after the incident with the concubine, my brother was found dead by a sword.

Rumors have it he wanted my crown, and I killed him.

Rumors have it his wife wanted me and she killed him.

I could've found out who killed him, but then I'd have to punish the person who did it, and I would rather not, since I suspect my nephew to have done it. I think the queen regent played a long game with my brother to get to me. To get to my throne. My brother never wanted the throne, but with him gone, and with my growing fondness for retreating to Dakkuyasu, she figured she could rule.

And she was right. She ruled in my absence quite well, but she cannot have the throne. Not while I'm alive. And neither can my nephew, who sits at the head of the family dining table as I walk in.

I do not ask him to move.

I need not sit at the head of the table, for I am king, and

wherever my royal ass sits is called the throne. It's not the chair that makes the king. The king makes an ordinary chair into a throne once his ass sits on it.

My nephew doesn't seem to understand that. Perhaps that's another sign that I should breed Augusta, despite the price she'll pay in her foresight. Unfortunately, it's not only about her foresight. My children would carry my bloodline of magic that causes chaos and destruction. This magic must cease with me. I shudder to think what the world might look like if more than one *armatuno* sat on an Unseelie throne.

We would conquer all the courts by laying waste to everything and everyone until we were the only people left standing, and then we would turn on each other.

At the table, I'm about to tell him we shall have brunch in the breakfast nook instead of here when a low whistle sounds, a long-drawn-out tune calling for me. I recognize it immediately and excuse myself, leaving my nephew simmering in fury over the way I bloodied his mother. He's lucky she's still alive, and his fury is starting to stir mine.

"You've kept us waiting long enough already. Where are you going?" he asks.

Without giving him an answer, I retreat into the shadows.

The whistle I'm certain nobody else can hear leads me toward the family baths, where a female dressed as a widow with a transparent black veil covering her face waits by the window.

"Emishi." I greet my older sister, the Unseelie princess and the fae fate who sees all that will come to pass.

"Brother," she says, sounding cold and impartial, her body still turned away from me.

We stand at the window overlooking the storm whipping through the Winter Court. Everyone is indoors, waiting for the blizzard to pass. It could be a span, could be seven spans, nobody knows except for the female standing next to me.

"How long—"

"Four spans."

I chuckle. "I should reschedule the engagement dinner."

"There will be no engagement dinner," Emishi says, making the tiny hairs on the back of my neck stand, for her voice is that of a fate, echoing in the silent baths.

"Is that why you came here?"

"It is." A seer sees the events that will happen in the future. A future fate can influence the coming events. The fates can influence what happens in the future, can change what has happened in past, and can alter the events occurring in the present. Therefore, their will is our reality. It is why fates are feared by all the fae. Including kings.

"The Seelie seer is lovely," my sister says.

Emishi hates the queen regent and wants my nephew exiled. Since Emishi knows I don't wish the burden of my madness or magic on my offspring, at one point of our lives, she threatened to give up her sight so she could bear children of her own and put them on the throne.

Emeshi's magic raises my hackles as she peers into the future. "Ah yes, the seer is of good heart and humor. You could use both."

"I'm plenty funny."

"But you can be heartless."

"Kings often are. If you came here to talk me into having heirs, you're wasting your time. I won't seed Augusta. Our engagement is fake, and once I announce it, I will return her to the Summer Court." Where she will find her happily ever after in a coven of virgins forever dedicated to serving the fates.

"Mmhm," my sister comments.

"Once the storm passes, I will return her."

"Which storm are you referring to? The one inside you or this one?" She taps her claw on the window.

In answer, I snort.

"I thought you promised her a turn or two," Emishi says.

That was before I wanted to breed her. "I changed my mind."

"She is in heat."

"I'm aware," I deadpan.

"Will you not service her?"

"I will."

My sister chuckles evilly. "How will you do that without breeding her?"

"I have ways."

"The womb seeks seed. Any seed will do, and you will deliver her to the commander of the Summer fae armies."

I smile. "The male is chaste. Besides, the Summer king forbade anyone from touching Augusta. I will reinforce that rule, and she will forever remain the royal seer."

"And you will forever remain the royal asshole." Emishi grabs the collars of my robe, and her magic flares. She opens her mouth to speak my fate, but I press a hand over her lips to muffle her, for I know whatever comes out of her mouth will come true.

"If you bend my future to your will, I will never forgive you," I hiss, then yank off the veil so I can see my sister's face.

The white of seer magic leaves her eyes, and Emishi blinks as if she had enchanted herself. "Fine, I'll stay quiet."

Emishi takes after our mother, with narrow, black eyes

and a small, perky nose, as well as narrow lips she paints white.

"The turns have been kind to you," I compliment her.

The corners of her eyes crinkle. "As they have to you, brother, but I fear you are at a crossroads, and I want to help you. If I cannot help you and the Unseelie throne I was born into, then my life and all this magic is in vain. Ask me!"

The magic of the fate strikes. My knees wobble, threatening to fold, but the king kneels only before his queen, so I grit my teeth and ask the fate to tell me my future, "Will I have children?"

"You will."

"Will my son have my powers?"

"She will not."

"I will have a daughter?"

My sister nods. "A daughter born without a breath," Emishi whispers as if she's speaking a secret. It is a secret. She is telling me I will father the Ice Princess, who will not carry my magic, but the deadliest magic of my peoples.

"And the mother. What of the mother?"

"Ah," my sister says and puts a palm over my heart. "The mother will be fine."

"Will she lose her sight?"

"Her sight? Do you mean to tell me you think the mother shall be a seer?"

I flush with need, my heart starting to race. "Yes."

Emishi taps my chest. "You're getting excited now, hm?"

I slap her hand away.

She laughs, reminding me of spans when we were kids, before she became the fate, before I became the monster she always knew I would become.

"How come she gets to keep her sight and virginity?"

"The mother is not a seer."

My chest constricts painfully, my heart stops beating, and I suddenly cannot breathe.

"There you are, brother." The magic of the fate stirs. "I gave you the vision of a life without your seer. Welcome, for now you have arrived at that moment when you find out you are in love with her. What will you do?"

36

AUGUSTA

The floor under my bare feet feels cold as I pad to the wardrobe to grab a fluffy, white robe and slip it over my wings, hoping it doesn't damage them. At the bottom of the closet, I find a pair of furry, white slippers with antlers, reminding me of the stag.

There are no fireplaces in the chamber, but I can hear fire crackling somewhere, warming up the indoors and adding heat to my already hot body. I step into a narrow hallway. I look both ways and find walls at both ends of the hallway. Seemingly, there's no way out.

In search of Tima, who will show me how to regulate the heat in the chambers, I go left, and the path in front of me changes as if by magic. Walls merge into one another. I walk a little uneasily, unsure where I'm going.

"Hello?" I call out, and when nobody answers, I keep moving, carefully watching my step.

While I don't see the floors shifting, it feels like they are, and before I know it, I find myself padding over smooth, wet rocks. I slip and catch myself on the wall, then remove my slippers and continue barefooted. The voice of the king sounds, and I follow it toward a light. I'm starting to make out steaming, blue waters. I must've found the baths on my own.

I was looking for the fireplace to regulate the heat in our chambers. The king will service me during my heat, and I want to nest and create a welcoming place for him. With some blankets and candles, and the right temperature in the chambers, I think we will enjoy our time.

Perhaps Tima would help me gather nesting supplies. The tunnel I'm following is dark and slippery, and I'm more than a little uneasy, but the king's voice guides me until I walk past my slippers.

Stopping, I double-check if it's really them, and it is.

Am I walking in a circle? Just as I'm about to call out, Aamako's voice sounds as clear as if he's close by. I rush toward it, the light from the baths I saw before brighter since I'm almost there.

"The Seelie seer is lovely," a female says.

I halt right as I'm about to round the corner to the baths. Is he here with someone else?

"Ah yes, the seer is of a good heart and humor. You could use both."

"I'm plenty funny," the king says, his voice low, almost a whisper, as if he doesn't want me or anyone to hear. My heart's pounding in my ears as I imagine the queen regent and the king bathing together. Sometimes, the ability to visualize everything sucks.

"But you can be heartless," she says.

I suppress a snort.

"Kings often are. If you came here to talk me into having heirs, you're wasting your time. I won't seed Augusta. Our engagement is fake, and once I announce it, I will return her to the Summer Court."

Oh my fates. I cover my mouth to muffle a gasp as my heart starts breaking inside my chest. I knew it was fake. I agreed. I entered the fake engagement with him. He was open and honest about not wanting a queen, but to hear him say this right after he said I could become queen hurts.

"Once the storm passes, I will return her."

"Which storm are you referring to? The one inside you, or this one?"

The king says nothing.

"I thought you promised her a turn or two," the lady says.

"I changed my mind."

Pain makes my chin quiver.

"She is in heat."

"I'm aware."

"Will you not service her?"

"I will."

I don't think so! I spin on my heel and sprint down the hall, trying to find the exit, but run into the Unseelie prince. He steadies me as I nearly fall and then steps away respectfully. I blink my tear-filled eyes to clear them and curtsey. "Prince Neguan."

"Seer." He greets me with a voice on the verge of a purr as he takes in my wings. "Those are the prettiest Unseelie wings I've ever seen."

"They're not Unseelie wings."

"Everything inside this court is Unseelie. Including you."

I lift my quivering chin, but I can't cry before this male. I won't. "You're misinformed. I'm under the protection of the Summer king."

The prince offers me his elbow. "The king has summoned us for brunch. I will escort you to the breakfast nook."

His uncle, the king, is bathing with the prince's mother. Does the prince know that? I hesitate to accept his elbow, but the ground tilts under me, and I fall into his arms. He catches me effortlessly and, much to my dismay, releases his mating scent. It's potent, masculine, and, since he's related to the king, similar to Aamako's. Like coaxing a mouse into a snake's mouth, he's luring me in.

My head pounds. I'm sad and angry and confused, but most of all, I'm in heat and shouldn't wander the palace on my own. How did I even get here?

Where *is* here?

Disoriented, I hold out my hand. The prince takes it and leads me away.

37

AAMAKO

Most of us don't wish for the presence of a fate because their presence generally means they're exercising their magic, the magic of willing events upon the people. It is a form of manipulation of both the mind and the time so that the visions the fate favor will unfold, whether we like it or not.

One such event happened over seven decades ago, when the then king of the Fall Court found a centuries-old parchment bearing the signature of my father and his. It was a marriage agreement promising my sister to the Fall Court's king.

The king invited my sister for a visit, and she and I went, thinking nothing of the invitation, until he cornered us with a deal made many centuries ago that our father likely forgot about. Our father, toward the end of his reign, had forgotten many things, including our faces.

A deal made with the Unseelie is a deal that must be honored. A horrible fate awaits those who don't honor such an agreement, and once presented with the signatures, and after verifying their authenticity, we started negotiating with the king.

Since the Fall king was already married, we thought he would nullify the pact. For a price we were happy to pay. Unfortunately, the king still wanted Emishi's hand in a marriage, primarily because Emishi was a powerful seer. At the time, nobody besides me knew she was one of the three fates. He wanted her for her power and beauty and the ties to my court.

Emishi refused to honor the agreement and vowed to have it changed, but the fate who sees all that's come to pass didn't agree and wouldn't change the past. Thus, Emishi decided she would change the future. She agreed to marry the Fall king on a beautiful sunny span over in the Fall Court. It was one of the only spans not overcast with clouds, and I remember the Fall fae remarking on the unusual weather.

Little did they know Emishi had picked that span because she wanted as many people as possible to gather. And they gathered, all right. And while they all came to watch the wedding, the Fall king murdered his queen.

He arrived at his wedding covered in the blood of his queen. In the Fall Court's hall, full of the fae's highest nobles and most powerful people, Emishi waited for him in the robes of a widow. She laughed at him, telling him she was a fate and would never give up her sight for the likes of a male who murdered for power.

The king flung a blade at my sister. Midflight, I spun the blade and aimed it at the king.

Once the Fall king fell under the blade of the Winter king, his guards responded. The Winter guards got involved too, and by the time twilight fell, Emishi and I were eating cake surrounded by the corpses of the Fall fae.

Before we left the Fall Court, seven of their own fire dragons burned it all to ash.

There were no survivors.

Emishi showed force. I was her puppet, and the creator of the Fallen Kingdom.

While I regretted the carnage, I don't regret defending my sister. Moreover, I would defend Augusta in the same way. Perhaps with even more vigor. If anyone so much as looked at Augusta wrong, I would deal the same fate upon their entire court, including my own. Which is why, now that I have realized I love her and I wish her to be mine, I must remove my nephew and his mother from the premises. I would hate to have to show the kind of force that would make Emishi's wedding look like child's play.

Since Augusta and I are meeting with my nephew and his mother for brunch, I will deliver the news then. Removal from court will come as a surprise for the pair. As it stands, with the courtiers at their backs, they believe they have the upper hand. Having the support of many gives them the false hope they can defeat me. They forget that some of us are our own pillars, and that when you are your own pillar, you will prop yourself up even when the world around you is crumbling down.

Augusta will handle our engagement party and the wedding. Those two maidens she accepted will help her, and I will bring the entire damn village to the court if I must and if it means she'll get the celebration she deserves.

"The mother is not a seer," a torch on the wall says as I pass.

"Nonsense," I tell it.

"You will ruin her," says the door handle.

"Be quiet."

"Take her back," the picture of my father says in his voice.

I hiss and change the route for one with bare walls.

If it were up to me, there would be no engagement party. The flyers announcing that the king is engaged and getting married would be sent out with baskets of food so people could celebrate my engagement in their homes if they wish. Unfortunately, I can only marry a Seelie seer once in my lifetime and the people expect a celebration. The Summer king has been celebrating his engagement for three cycles now, and the wedding span is going to be one of the most attended events of our time.

Augusta can decide on the wedding span and the length and, well, everything.

I only want her.

38

AUGUSTA

The prince and I stand at the threshold of a small space surrounded on one side by books and the other by windows overlooking what I believe is the back of the Winter Court. It must be the breakfast nook where the brunch will take place.

Since his mother and Aamako are in the baths, I find myself sharing a space with only the prince. Uncomfortable, I remove my hand from his.

Smirking, he walks past the round table that seats only six. Drinks and appetizers are already set.

The prince faces the window, his hands folded at his back. My instincts scream at me to run, but I have nowhere to go. I can't very well return to Aamako's chambers, not after what I overheard in the baths.

I can't confirm he was with the queen regent, but I presume it's her by voice and context. She's not here either, and neither is the king. I'm trying and failing not to visualize what they're doing, and because the images in my head make me sad, my wings fold. They droop as if told to bend the knee. I glance behind me and see they're draped over my back like used linens.

"The Winter Court is more beautiful in the summer than any other time of the turn. Did you know that?" the prince asks.

"It's my first time visiting."

"The summer makes the winter more beautiful. Wouldn't you agree?"

Unsure where the prince is taking the conversation, I nod in agreement. Is he drawing parallels between Ammako and me, or what exactly is going on? I'm still reeling from practically walking in on Aamako and the queen regent's conversation, grateful I haven't walked in on them in the act as well. I think such a sight would ruin me forever.

The prince turns his profile to me. "Augusta?"

I take pleasure at how my name rolls off his tongue. My heat is making everything he says sound seductive.

"The summer heat melts the snow," I say, not knowing what else to say.

The prince smiles, his perfect nose lifting. "Exactly. It melts the snow. The ice too, depending on who or what we're talking about, because surely even a girl of your station knows I didn't call you here to talk about the weather."

"What did you want to talk about?"

He takes the largest chair at the head of the table. "Have a seat." The square piece of marble under the chair he points to slides out, taking the chair away from the table.

I remain standing.

The marble under my feet tips, and I stumble forward, landing on the floor. Quickly, I scramble up and take the offered seat.

"There you go." The prince tosses me a napkin. With his

left hand, he places his napkin over his lap, then tilts his head at me. "Shall I come over and arrange the napkin on your lap?"

I shake my head and do as instructed.

Across from me, with his hair pulled back, his high cheeks riding on his face, the prince inhales deeply. "Your summer scent is enjoyable. It's no wonder our king is taken by you."

Taken by me. Ha! I stab the breakfast steak with a single lashi and bring the entire piece to my mouth. I rip into it with my teeth.

The prince smiles, showing fang. "Savage, are we?"

"We are."

"Good. As am I, since your arrival has complicated the matters of my crown."

I chew the delicious beefsteak. My dear father would love the bloody beefsteak with poached eggs. I pour myself a green-looking tea and chase the steak down with it.

The prince blinks at my lack of etiquette. At the moment, I care about nothing. My life is ruined. Perhaps I'm even at the end of the road, for the prince might end me.

"My uncle was supposed to emerge from solitude and transfer the throne to me."

I almost choke on the steak. "I don't think you know your uncle well."

The prince narrows his eyes. "You've known Aamako for a handful of nights, most of which you spent on your back, and I've known him my entire life, most of which I spent at the throne, ruling in his stead. What makes you think I don't know him?"

"You've lived away from your uncle. Your mother counseled you. What I was trying to say"—I pause for another bite—"is that if you knew your uncle, you would know he would never transfer the crown. That's the rub, isn't it? If he takes a wife, the crown goes to his offspring. You're plotting against your king."

"Not I. My mother is plotting against him."

"I doubt it."

"How so?"

"They're together in the baths as we speak."

The prince drops his lashi. "Impossible. My mother would never."

I laugh, a little hysterical. "You've been played like I've been played. Your mother plots to marry Aamako, give him heirs, and rule the court. That's what's happening, and you're just a tool in the same way I am."

"I assure you we're nothing alike. You are an object my uncle is using, and I am offering you a way out before you're rusty and old."

Huh. "Well, it just so happens that I wish I had a way out of here."

"Excellent." He brings his chair closer and leans in, his eyelashes fluttering, his silver magic dancing in his eyes. It's my heat and the mating scent that's in bloom that's making him frisky.

"The way out?" I prompt.

The prince flicks two fingers. "Come now."

From behind the bookcases, shadows slide out and converge into the shape of a female I recognize.

"Ah, the beautiful scent of a Summer fairy never fails to arouse," the queen mother of the Summer Court, an Unseelie fae wanted by her son and my king Et'enne, materializes in the breakfast nook. She is wearing black on black and looks as striking as ever, with sharp, narrow, dark eyes and lips painted in dark purple. She is a powerful emotion-reading fae who abducted June from Et'enne. Now her son is hunting her all over the world.

The Queen Mother sits down, and the Unseelie prince continues. "The deal between Et'enne and Aamako was that my king will hand over the queen mother of the Summer Court in exchange for you."

"But I'm not going anywhere," the queen mother says.

"The deal has to be honored or amended," I remind them.

"You will return to the Summer Court," she answers.

This is easier than I thought. "When do we leave?" I ask.

The pair of them look at me in confusion.

I elaborate. "I never want to see the Unseelie king again."

"Is that so?" Aamako walks inside the room.

39

AUGUSTA

They say the Unseelie court is difficult to navigate because of the scheming plots that courtiers and royals occupy their time with during the long winters. I have a feeling I'm about to witness one such scheme invented by none other than the male they call the king.

At the threshold, Aamako takes in the room. "What's this?" he asks.

"Augusta and I are getting better acquainted," the prince says, then leans into me, sniffing my hair.

The king sprouts horns, and his body starts expanding into his battle form. "Touch my bride and die."

Prince Neguan smirks and moves his chair away. "Have a seat, Uncle. You remember Demina, the Summer Court's queen mother?"

Still in battle form, with muscles almost twice their normal size, long sharp fangs, and obsidian horns erected at the top of his head, Aamako approaches me and sniffs my hair, a purr rising from the back of his throat. If I could purr, I would too, for he smells enticing and, in his battle form, like something I'd want to ride for the rest of my life and not just in my heat. It's too bad he's playing a terrible Unseelie game with the queen regent and her son. A game where I'm one of the pieces he's manipulating.

I'm not going to fall for his *touch my bride and die* act. I am not.

Aamako sits on my left and flares out his napkin, his battle form slowly retreating. Once he's completely recovered, the food starts arriving on trays instead of being delivered by the staff. I've gotten used to the king's ways, but the other two people stare wide-eyed at the arriving objects. It's been over half a century since they've witnessed their king's magic, and I was right to call the prince out on it. He doesn't know his uncle well at all.

"Where is your mother?" the king asks the prince.

"As if you don't know," I mutter.

Aamako frowns just as his magic picks up my plate. "What would you like?"

I shake my head. "Nothing. I would like nothing from you."

His frown deepens. "You must eat before another wave of heat takes you." The king puts a piece of roast beef and some mashed potatoes on my plate. He covers the potatoes with gravy. I love gravy, and the food smells delicious. I'm hungry too, but I can't let him feed me. It's a form of courting. When he serves me the plate, I push it away.

"If there's something you wish to say to me, future queen of my court, first dismiss the audience and then we will talk."

I fist my hands. Fine! "I got lost and ended up at the baths by accident. I heard you and the queen regent talking."

The king has the audacity to look surprised. I guess he is surprised that I uncovered his plot.

"The queen regent?"

As if called, the queen regent enters. She's wearing a dark gray jacket over a layered black dress. There's a freshly picked rose in her hair, and I immediately wonder if Aamako gave it to her. The recently healed scars on her neck rise from the skin. They appear like red welts. It makes me wonder what role the scars have in the whatever plot they're creating.

A chair flies in after her and lands next to the queen mother, who takes one look at the scars the female sitting down next to her wears and pales immediately.

The king says, "I arrived at court in one of the finest moods I've had in decades, and—"

I interrupt. "I bet."

Aamako gives me a death stare. "As I was saying, I arrived at court in fine spirits, eager to present my new bride who recently went into heat and whom I intend to serve, only to find my nephew flirting with her while the elder lady of the Summer Court witnesses the act so she can take the gossip all around the world, no doubt in an attempt to infest everyone's hearts and minds until people turn against the marriage of me and Augusta so no courtier will support it, and we shall have no choice but to retreat into Dakkuyasu and hand the throne over to my nephew. Or his mother. Did I miss anything?"

The king is accusing the people at the table of treason. The temperature in the room rises, and the atmosphere becomes more dangerous. My heart thuds in my chest. But because I'm in heat and around a dominant male, his authority, voice, and scent turn me on.

The two females reek of fear.

The prince shakes his head as the king continues eating as if he's talking about the weather rather than treason punishable by death.

"I would never take the seer," the prince says in a way that sounds dismissive of me.

"The seer would never have you," the king retorts. "Because she is mine."

"Not quite." I hold the king's glare. "I want love and sex, and above all, honesty."

"You will have it all," the king answers.

The queen regent smiles broadly. "The seer loses her sight if she loses her virginity." A newly healed wound on her neck rips and starts bleeding. She ignores it. "Which means she must remain pure in order to serve the Unseelie crown, for the crown is best served by her magic not by her womb. Her womb would produce a weak heir."

"In which case," Aamako says, "your son remains my only heir. One would think you would approve of my bride, welcome her, treat her like your own. Instead, you're conspiring against both her and me."

"My mother schemed against you alone," the prince says hastily. "Uncle, I swear to you I will honor your reign upon your death and rule with honor over our family. If you've heard anything else, it's all her doing." He points a finger at his mother.

"You little prick," she hisses. "I sacrificed everything for you."

"Your reign won't be necessary anymore." Aamako butters his piece of bread and offers it to me. I turn my head away. "I will breed my seer."

"The hell you will," I tell him.

The queen regent laughs. "Breed the seer? The offspring of a magical weakling will leave us open for invasion."

"Does someone want to invade us?" Aamako, who's the only person eating at the table, now puts down his buttered toast. He looks excited.

The queen mother answers. "If given an opportunity, Et'enne would move on the Unseelie court."

"Oh dear fates." King Aamako closes his eyes in a prayer. "Did you hear that? From her lips to your ears, dear fates, let him come and try to invade my court." When he opens his eyes, his *armatuno* magic sweeps the room. Spoons coil in on themselves, knives lift, poised to cut, forks wiggle, ready to stab. "The Unseelie court is ready."

"Et'enne would make a formidable enemy," King Et'enne's mother says, her chin proudly raised.

"Because he is a *voca*?" Aamako prompts, then leans in, awaiting her answer.

"Yes."

"Yes!" The king slams his fist on the table, making everything rattle. "Yes! What do I have to do to provoke him?" A knife flies and stops at her throat.

I scream and hold out my hands. "No. No, please. I need her." She's my getaway carriage.

"If I killed you, would your son come after me?" Aamako asks the Summer Court's queen mother, his magic rattling the pictures on the walls. One by one, his magic unhooks the pictures from the walls, tearing the frames apart and using the knives to sharpen the wooden frame pieces into points, effectively crafting stakes.

This is getting out of hand.

Dread joins the heat churning in my belly. Oh no. I dislike it when I have these feelings. Usually, I'm right about the dreadful stuff. My visions often predict someone's end, but rarely ever nice beginnings, like babies being born or stags farting silver bubbles.

"If you killed me, he would come after you," the queen mother says. "Only because you took the pleasure away from him."

The knife nicks her skin, and I gasp.

Demina holds her throat, blood seeping through her fingers.

"Healer!" I shout, and press a napkin on her neck. "Healer!" I'm compressing her wound, and she holds it with her hand, putting pressure on it as well while the king finishes his meal as if nothing is happening at the table.

"My engagement party will be held after the storm passes in four spans and after I have bred the seer."

"No," I say.

"Yes."

"I won't do it."

"We have a deal," he says through clenched teeth. His eyes are cold, his magic lashing out elsewhere in the castle. People are starting to shout. Footsteps are running toward us. If I were them, I would be running away.

"We're not engaged," I say. "It's fake."

"Augusta," Aamako warns.

"It's okay, girl, go on," the queen mother says. She removes the cloth from the wound. The cut is deep, but the wound has already closed. Powerful fae heal quickly.

"The engagement is fake," I announce.

"Not anymore. I will marry you."

"But I will not marry you."

The objects moving around us all halt. The sudden stillness makes me swallow a lump in my throat.

Aamako blinks and slides his gaze to the prince. "You and your mother will attend the engagement party, and you will return all the riches to the royal treasury from which you stole them. Once the engagement party ends, you will take your mother and any courtiers you wish and depart for the Fallen Kingdom. You can assume the throne there for as long as you understand that I lord over all the Unseelie."

"You're exiling me?" the prince asks.

"The throne of another Unseelie court is hardly an exile."

"There's nobody there!" the queen regent screeches.

"There're dragons. You're fond of dragons."

"I'm fonder of you." She starts begging. "Please, Aamako, in your brother's name, marry me and let us rule together."

These royals really know how to cut you. She's behaving as if I'm not here, as if what she says doesn't affect me. Not that she should care. She doesn't know me. She knows our engagement is fake, and I have no claim on the king.

The king looks at me. I don't know what he sees, but he says, "Augusta, don't listen to her."

There's something wet on my cheek. I wipe it off, thinking it's tears, but I'm not sad, so I rise from the chair and stand there confused, just now realizing that everything the queen mother ever said to my sister June was true. We weren't raised in the court, and we weren't raised to be vicious or mean or cunning. As a result, neither June nor I know how to deal with these fae who fight for power and would trade even their husbands and children for it.

"I'm not listening to her, but I heard her all the same."

"Mother? What are you saying?" The prince rises slowly. The walls around us start cracking. Aamako's magic is already controlling every object in the room, and now the table lifts and the legs start unscrewing from under it.

The queen regent smirks at me. "Did you really think I would let you steal my crown?"

"Mother," the prince warns.

"I don't care about your crown or your king," I say. "You can have them."

"You don't mean that," the king says.

"I do!" I scream and stomp my foot, my wounded fury the only power I have. Tears gush out of my eyes and words flow with them. "I heard you at the baths talking with the queen regent. You told her our agreement is fake and you would return me to the Summer Court right after my heat."

"I did not share a bath with this female."

I pick up an apple and throw it at him. "Liar."

Aamako catches it, then bites into it. He swallows a bite, then bares his fangs. "You want a prophecy, my seer? Hm? I will speak it as it was told to me by a fate. You and I," he says, "are not meant to be, but I am fighting for us, and I would die for us. Yet, here you are, not even giving me an ear so I can speak my truth. At the baths, a fate visited me. Knowing her, you were meant to hear us, and her voice was meant to sound like another's voice. It is a test of our paths. Of us. You are ready to run. To leave. To abandon us. I'm not. I'm ready to destroy for us."

"Awww," the queen mother says. "Another poor village girl stole the king. It's a trend, my dear Larho. First my son fell, now your lover is falling."

The prince slams his palms on the table. "He's not her lover."

And then, everything happens at once.

Aamako's magic strikes and folds the table, breaking it in half, then four quarters, then eighths, until a small army of tall wooden sticks starts circling around him like a windmill. A dagger appears behind the king, and the army of wooden sticks line up to be sharpened.

At the same time, the ground under us is shaking, the walls are rearranging along with the books in the library.

The prince's magic makes me feel displaced and disoriented as it's changing the layout of the room and possibly the entire court. This is why Aamako was studying the court layout on the maps.

Demina stands slowly and starts moving back. "Both of you should consider walking away before you destroy the palace."

"Uncle, the seer has blinded you. I tried to get rid of her and prevent all this, but you brought her here anyway."

"What do you mean you tried to get rid of her?" Aamako's magic suffocates the room. I can smell the carnage it will leave in its wake as if it's already happened. He will destroy more than the palace. He will go after every enemy in his court. Oh my fates, I have to flee.

"The cellar," the prince says. "I tried to help you."

Aamako stills the objects again. It's disturbing, like being inside the eye of the storm where it's quiet, right before it ravages you and everything you claim as yours. The walls twist as if made of clay. That's the prince's magic.

I'm reeling from what Neguan is saying. "You..." I stutter. "You made me think I was incapable to find the damn door out of the cellar. And now, you made me walk to the baths and then into you when I was returning. I... I was heading toward the nook, but you practically walked me to the baths."

"Fool, I guided you there because he was speaking with the future fate."

Aamako assumes his full battle form, with long obsidian horns, bulky muscles, and extended claws. In a voice that sounds like the bottom of a deep well, he says, "Careful how you address my queen."

"She's not your queen!" the queen regent screams, her

face taking on the shape of several different faces at once. I look away from the gruesome sight.

The queen mother retreats slowly toward the shadows. If I were smart, I would go with her, but I have to know the truth. I have to know so that my heart can break completely, for if it's not completely broken, I will still have something to love the Unseelie king with.

"What did the fate say?" There's a ringing in my ears, and my heart's beating so fast that I'm gasping for air. I heard Aamako tell me the fate said we're not meant to be, but I want to hear the words as the fate spoke them. I need to receive the prophecy as it was said by the female. For the first time ever, I fear the future. I fear what her vision told her.

The prince replies, "The mother is not a—"

A spear pierces Neguan's mouth. The force and speed of the weapon make his body fly at the wall. He hits it, and stays pinned there, his limbs flailing until they twitch and cease moving at all.

Time pauses. Everything freezes, even the people.

My sister June appears next to the dead prince. She is wearing a dark dress, and her veil is longer than she normally wears it. It whips around her as if the wind is lashing at it. She looks frightening, every bit a fate feared by all. She doesn't speak to me, but only extends her hand.

I stare at the offering of escape. I want to take it, but I can't help feeling as if I'm standing at the forked road of my life. If I leave with June, Aamako's and my paths will not merge again. I will never see him again. And that's fine, because I was prepared to leave anyway.

If it were any other time, if it were any other male, I would take my sister's hand and run away with her, trusting that she would take care of me. Not this time. I choose to stay in the moment, in the present as it unfolds.

June disappears as suddenly as she came.

The momentum continues, and the queen regent screams. An army of guards rush into the room, swords drawn and directed at their king. Meanwhile, Larho watches me, her body taking on a red tint as it grows. Scales appear on her neck, her chest pushes out, her legs extend, and her eyes take on a reptilian shape.

"Augusta," King Aamako calls as he fights the guards. Shouting comes from all around the palace. This is the coup. Larho is making her move for the throne, and Aamako is likely engaging everyone all around the court. "Leave!"

"I cannot," I whisper, my feet unmoving either from fear of the queen regent, who is shape-shifting into some sort of reptile, or from the feeling I'm supposed to linger here at this moment of time.

The queen regent's animal form bursts through the ceiling at the same time that she spouts dragon wings. Her red fire dragon form rears back, and she opens her mouth, showing me the flames collecting in the back of her throat.

"Get out!" Aamako shouts.

I'm frozen. My legs won't move.

A ball of flame flies at me.

40

AAMAKO

Another carafe tips in the air and pours wine into my chalice. I drink the entire contents, then use the dagger to carve the face of my seer on the cup. It's taking over four spans to carve Augusta's portrait on the metal chalice, but time is all I have left. I destroyed everything else.

The mother is not a seer.

My nephew trying to repeat what the fate had said in front of my seer undid me. I destroyed what was left of my small family, my palace, and more than half my court, along with the future I could've had with the seer.

When I engage an enemy of substantial size such as the Winter Court's guard and the Unseelie army of several hundreds who mobilized outside the palace, I'm forced to release the full power of my magic. The details of the battle become a blur of blood and the cries of fallen fae, courts, kingdoms, the entire world. I'm unaware of how long it takes me to conquer a court or my enemies in general, but by the time I come to my senses, I emerge a victor.

Every time.

Nobody can defeat an army of one, the only one left standing after a conflict. Or perhaps it's left sitting, since I'm sitting on the throne at the only wall that's left of the Winter Beauty.

The storm has passed. The weather, this span, is more pleasant then I remember it ever being. As if the destruction of the palace signals a new beginning of time where the sun shines over the Winter Court, melting the snow, creating waters that make rivers with currents that wash away the blood running down the streets.

The bodies of courtiers, guards, even foreign mercenaries litter the streets. The court is in ashes after my sister-in-law's fury burned whatever she could reach before she fled for her life.

The carafe pours more wine into my chalice. Again, I drink it all.

The underground tunnels remained intact, so the wine and the nearly empty treasury survived.

The gargoyles are dragging away body parts as they clean up.

I never should've brought Augusta with me. Should've left her on that bench where I found her.

"You should've known," her face that's carved into my chalice says.

"I'm not the seer! I couldn't have known," I shout at the chalice, then fling it down the mountain, where the survivors are coming out of hiding to survey the carnage.

I growl at them.

"There, there, my king," the carafe says, and another chalice appears in my hand. The carafe fills it. "Drink more."

"When I went to the Summer Court seeking a bride, I had no intention of finding a female I actually desired. Hells, I wanted to breed my seer, believing I had a future where I would live a normal life. Whatever normal life looks like for me. But no. It is not to be. Just as Emishi said. The seer is not fated for me. "Sister!" I shout into the bright blue sky as if my sister lives there. "Come here, you wretched wench." I stand and spread my arms. "Are you happy now? I have served your will yet again. I'm the king who lords over nothing!"

41

AUGUSTA

Demina, queen mother of the Summer Court, snatched me right out from under the queen regent's ball of fire and dumped me in the kitchen of my parental home, where my sister Julie found me sitting at the table, apparently catatonic. She moved me into our old shared bedroom and has been holding vigil over me, standing with her back leaning against the wall near the window while I lie on the bed.

Julie worries her bottom lip a lot.

I'm staring out at some point in the forest outside the window while Floki barks at the chickens that won't come out of the coop. Julie says all the animals have been behaving weirdly ever since I arrived. They're hiding, she says.

They're hiding because the future is a blank canvas. I wish to tell her that, but I can't seem to speak. I can't seem to eat, sleep, or do anything besides stare at the forest, never once looking at the place where the tree line meets the sky. There's nothing over the horizon.

I cannot peer over the horizon. I no longer think the horizon exists. I am without magic.

Finally, I am no longer a seer.

"Julie?"

My sister rushes to kneel beside my bed, her beautiful feline-shaped eyes reflecting worry and kindness. "I'm here, Augusta. I'm here."

"Is June well?"

Julie nods. "She visited once, but you started sobbing, so we thought it best you recover before she returns."

"Recover from what?"

Julie swallows. "The...um... events at the Unseelie court."

"Oh, those. I'm fine. Just fine." I sit up. "Better than ever. You see, I am not a seer anymore. I can get back on track with a new life."

Julie fixes my hair. "You say that as if you went off track with your life while you were a seer."

"My life wasn't mine. The Summer king stole it and gave it to the Unseelie king." I hitch a breath at the mention of Aamako, but force myself to continue, "Now that I'm of no use to the Summer king and the Unseelie king..." I don't know what happened to Aamako. A scorned fire dragon might've burned him. "I can have my life back. Where should I start?"

"Start what?"

"My new life path."

"Do you want to eat something before you start living your great, new life?"

"I'm fine. Better than ever." I stand, and the world goes dark.

≈

Julie made chicken soup. The circles of fat accumulated at the top remind me of the spans when our parents farmed this piece of land that's now left abandoned. After June's engagement, my parents moved to the city, and Cecile's mother next door took over caring for the chickens. She sold the eggs, but now, with her taking ill and Cecile farming, not to mention the animals staying indoors, Father will likely sell the property. It should fetch a fine price, if only because it is of historical importance. The court's future queen and fate grew up here.

"I didn't know you can cook," I tell Julie.

"Me either. Soup any good?"

Suddenly starving, I slurp up some more. "Excellent." An image of the Unseelie king sleeping in his chair by the fireplace flashes. He's cradling a bundle in his arms.

I swallow. "What baby are you talking about?"

"I didn't mention a baby."

"Of course." I eat the soup. That wasn't a vision of the king. It wasn't. My magic is completely gone. I'm grieving and seeing things in my head. Why are my cheeks wet again?

"Oh, Augusta." Julie sits on my bed and kicks off her boots, then gets comfortable next to me. She takes the soup from my hands, then hugs me, and I listen to her breathing, center on the steady beats of her heart. Julie's magic is tied to the present moment, and she can ground me unlike anyone else.

I owe Demina for saving my life, but moreover for dropping me off with Julie and not with June at the palace. I love June. But I needed to grieve whatever I lost (my heart or future or both), away from the prying eyes of the Summer Court. I wonder if Demina, being in tune with the emotions of other people, somehow did me a favor by bringing me here. It's possible she'll bargain with me for a favor at some point in time but for now, I am grateful for her being in that room at that time.

Julie smells like she's tended the farm all morning, and the scent makes me think of the stag, and the stag makes me think of magic, and the magic is lost to me.

"I miss it," I tell her as I wipe away the tear.

"Miss what?"

"The magic."

"But you get to live your new life now."

"I do."

After a while, Julie asks, "Was it worth it?"

"Was what worth it?"

"Having sex with the Unseelie king and losing your magic over it?"

"We didn't have sex."

"Huh. So how did you lose your magic?"

"I don't know. I miss it, but I don't want it back either, for if I had it, I would foresee the future without Aamako, and I would rather remain blind to that. And now I make no sense at all."

"No need to make sense. Emotions are senseless. If they made sense, they'd be called logic, and logic is boring."

I chuckle. "What are you doing back home, Julie?"

"Same thing as you. Living my new life."

She looks down at her hands playing with my hair. She blows on her bangs that fall over her light brown eyes. "The parties are exhausting."

"Huh. I thought you loved them."

"I tire of the same thing quickly."

"That's the reason El'jah exists. He keeps things interesting at the court. Never a dull moment."

Julie blushes and drops her gaze to her lap, where she starts picking on her nails.

"Holy crap, you slept with El'jah."

"Nobody *sleeps* with the prince."

I put my head on her lap so she'll look at me and not at her hands. There's a glint in Julie's eyes.

"You have to spill."

She shakes her head. "There's nothing to spill."

"It's just me, and I won't tell nobody. I'm dying for a story with a sad ending that's not mine. Your misery will marry my misery, and the two can walk into the sunset together, leaving us to live out our great, new lives."

Julie plays with my hair. "You may have lost your magic, Augusta, but you've not lost your spirit."

"You think so?"

"I know so."

"How do you know so?"

"Because I can tell what's happening now, and now, all hope is not lost, for you and I are still here. The moment is ours for the taking. What do you want to do?"

"With our great, new life?"

"No, silly, right now."

I purse my lips. "I want to get out of bed."

"And bathe."

I flick her pinky finger. "I don't smell."

"You think you don't."

"You smell like the chicken coop, mother hen."

Chuckling, I sit up on the bed and plant my soles on the cold ground. I wiggle my toes and remember how Aamako would have the slippers ready for my feet. He even made the slippers follow me around the castle so my feet wouldn't get cold.

I miss Dakkuyasu.

"I wish we never went to court," I whisper.

It would have saved me the heartache. In the end, Aamako used me as a prop, and like most props he commands, I was one of the tools he brought into his court to use for power. In the breakfast nook, he showed me he really was the monster everyone feared yet I never did, because I'm the gullible clown who believed in redemption and love. That's what I get for believing in the bright future.

As I stand, my knees weaken, but to keep me upright, my wings flutter. The moment they do, I remember how they sprouted for the male I chose to mate with.

"I am so over him!" I shout. "I do not wish to think about him! Is he dead?"

Julie doesn't respond.

"Is he?"

Her eyes soften. "I don't know. Truly, I do not."

Someone knocks on our bedroom door. Strange. I slide my hand into my sister's, and we step back. The door opens slowly, creaking in that very creepy way things do when they're opening on their own. Nobody steps inside or calls from the outside. Nobody is there.

"Fates, is *he* here?" I mumble.

"Hello?" Julie calls out, fear making her voice shake. Both of us are frozen in place, the same way I froze under the dragon fire.

A fate walks in.

42

AUGUSTA

The fate wears a stylish black gown and holds a silver walking stick in one hand. With the other, she removes her veil. Julie gasps and, oddly, turns away, giving the fate her back.

I stare at the elegant Unseelie female, who I recognize from images in the books as Aamako's sister, Emishi. I had no idea his sister was the fate who sees all that will come to pass. I don't believe this is common knowledge. Even if I went to school, I wouldn't have learned about Emishi, the same way I didn't know about the Seelie fate who came before June. Before June, Et'enne's grandmother was the fate who sees all that's come to pass, and I didn't know that either.

I curtsey deeply, my knees wobbling. I catch myself on the bed. "Excuse me, oh fate who sees all that will come to pass. I'm unwell and should sit down."

"Come sit with me, then. The future will wait." White membranes cover her eyes, and while her magic glows white and can make her lose her sight while seeing the future, Emishi does not appear sighted and uses the walking stick as we walk through the hallway.

"You must be wondering why a fate who sees all things ahead of her can't see a few steps in front of her when she is walking."

"It has been said that the seer who lost her virginity loses her sight."

"What do you think?"

"It sounds untrue for a fate."

Emishi pauses and levels me with a stare. "It sounds untrue because you know that a fate is too powerful to lose her sight once her hymen is punctured. I made that shit up when I didn't want to marry anyone." Emishi winks.

Behind me, Julie gasps. "The people believe it to be true."

"As they should." The fate seems amused.

"I'm not amused," I dare to say.

She giggles. "I cockblocked you, I know. But trust me, this is how your story is meant to unfold."

And there it is. The power of the future fate. She can tell any story she wishes. "May I know how you lost your sight?" In the pictures and stories I've heard, Emishi was sighted.

"In good time, you will find out." The fate leads me a few steps down the hall and into our kitchen, where June stands facing the sink. She wears black on black, but her veil is off as well, her light brown hair pulled up into a messy bun.

The third fate is in the room as well. A red-haired female with a pleasant smile and the emerald-green eyes often indicative of a Spring fairy. She is knitting at the head of the table in my father's chair. When I walk in, she stands to greet me. Quickly, I curtsey, but I'm weak and barely able to hold myself upright. The short walk here exhausted me.

Julie and Emishi prevent my fall and find me a chair to sit on.

It's on Father's right. "Oh, this isn't my spot."

"It's okay," June says, speaking for the first time. "We can break the house rules for once." June sets a pumpkin pie on the table and takes a seat across from me. Her eyes are red, a telltale sign she's been crying.

"I baked your favorite," she says.

"Because you're June's favorite," Julie pitches in, then sits next to June, who is sitting in my spot across from me. Julie's eyes are bright and cheerful as she tries to lift the mood in the space, but I'm not sure she can. I'm sure I'm the only person who can do that, and I have done it when I decided to move on and live my great life with no foresight. Mmhm.

I stare at the pie. "June, don't cry."

"I keep replaying the events at the Unseelie court. They're hard to watch." She glares at Aamako's sister, but Emishi can't see it, or if she does, she appears unfazed.

"They're all part of life," I say, "and sometimes life is hard, right, June? It's why you three exist. To toy with folk, especially young, inexperienced fae." Like me.

"That's not—" June starts, but I jab her pie with a knife and start carving.

"Since the Unseelie king needed a bride to secure his throne, and also threatened the peace of the Summer Court, I entered into a fake engagement with him. It's not your fault I fell for the king." My breath hitches, and everything I've held back comes rushing out. "Or maybe it is your fault, June. You could've warned me he had a thing with the queen regent and that she would almost cost me my life."

"He has never had a relationship with Larho," June says.

Emishi butts in. "It is true. He has not. You cannot blame

him for her obsession with the Unseelie court's throne. My brother loves you."

I throw a piece of pie at her chest. It splatters all over her dark clothing. "You lie! I heard you at the baths with him. He said he would return me to the Summer Court like I was a borrowed shoe." I'm sobbing now, great, big, ugly tears.

"You weren't meant to hear that," the fate says.

"You shouldn't have been there," June says to Emishi.

My emotions are erratic, rolling down like an avalanche of tears, rapid heartbeats, and sweaty palms. "He treated me like a princess," I mumble between sniffs. "He promised me nothing and gave me everything and made me feel special. For once, I was heard and spoken to and I mattered and I felt I had a purpose. I was faking an engagement with the king of two fae courts. I was going to save the world." I lean toward June, who's also crying, but with more grace than me. No snot is running from her nose, and she's definitely not wiping it with the back of her pajama sleeve.

"Do you want to hear the worst part?" I ask.

The red-haired fate nods. "Definitely."

"Secretly, I was looking forward to a future with him." I clear my throat and wipe my nose with the back of my sleeve again. "Meanwhile, the Unseelie king played by the rules of his fake-arrangement game, and since he disclosed the fake arrangement to me from the beginning, I can't even fault him. I'm placing blame on you, dear fates, and on me for being the naive idiot all the way until the bitter end. Which is why I'm glad to have lost the stupid seer magic. I can start my new, great life now. Isn't that right, Julie?" I look over at my sister, who's nodding vehemently.

June and I have always been closer than Julie and me, but ever since June became the fate and also the future queen of the Summer Court, she's been busy. Before I left for the Unseelie court, we barely ate breakfast together anymore.

Emishi passes me a tissue. "Is the pity party over?"

June whips her head toward the future fate. "And what if it isn't?"

June's magic rises in the room, creating pressure in my ears. Time slows down somehow as June grows red in the face. My sister is the kindest person I know, and when her face grows red like that, she's really mad. June doesn't do mad often. Outbursts of temper are more my thing, so seeing her express her anger frightens both me and Julie, who says, "Holy fates, Augusta, I think the fates are about to have at it."

"I think we should leave," I suggest, since the last time I stayed for the show, I almost died under a ball of dragon fire.

"What if I want to join my sister's pity party?" June says to Emishi.

Emishi shrugs and serves herself a piece of butchered pie. She tastes it and nods in approval, not that my June needs her damn approval.

"You can do what you like, for you are one of the fates," Emishi says.

"Fates cannot always do what they like," June says. "They cannot intervene in the matters of other fates. What if I intervened?"

Emishi shrugs. "Even if you rewound the events and the people chose different paths, the outcome would have been the same. I've seen more than a dozen versions of the same future."

"June," the red-haired fate says, "Emishi hid the intervention from me. How did she interfere?"

"She visited the Unseelie king and told him his future. My sister overheard a part of it."

The red-haired fate gasps. "Oh no, Emishi, why would you do that?"

"Because my brother is a male who would've protected the seer fiercely, even from himself. Especially from himself. This means he wouldn't have agreed to breed Augusta had I not assured him of a future where she wouldn't lose her sight."

"Ha!" I start laughing hysterically. "I lost my sight anyway. I can't see anything. I have no magic. It was all for nothing. But hey, I still have my hymen."

"This is why you went blind," the Spring fate concludes. "You sacrificed your sight during the intervention, or you couldn't have hidden it from me. You knew if I saw you speaking with Aamako, I would try to stop you."

"It's not too late to stop her," June says in a voice not her own. This one is the voice of the fate that's about to change the past. I don't know how I know this, but I can feel it.

"You can't change the past either," Emishi says. "For I have traded both my sight and foresight. I gave it all up. Everything."

"You almost cost my sister her life." June's voice is as deep as the bottom of the well.

"But she is alive and well, isn't she?"

"She lost her king!" June shouts, then snaps out of fate mode, her magic leaving as quickly as it came. Everyone takes a deep breath. Time starts moving again. Birds are singing outside, Floki's barking, and under the table, Julie's picking at her nails. "She lost her king, and the female shape-shifter who can turn into a fire-breathing dragon is still alive, lying in wait for a chance to strike again. When will that be, Emishi? Hm? Since you've been so gracious with your visions."

Emishi stuffs her mouth with the pie.

"What do you mean when you say you've traded your foresight?" Julie asks.

"I can no longer see the future."

"That's absurd," I say. "You're the fate who sees all that will come to pass."

"No." Emishi shakes her head and looks at me with her blind eyes. "You are."

43

AAMAKO

The violin and the cello are the only two instruments brave enough to play for me. Even the grand piano has hidden away in the attic somewhere, afraid I'll destroy it in a fit of rage. The fire pokers are serving breakfast while the spoons strike the fire. The rest of the kitchen staff has formed a marching band, and they're stomping down the village streets, singing random songs about females, wine, and a comb. Not sure what's with the comb.

Since I returned to Dakkuyasu with marginally acceptable control of my vast magical faculties, the people in the village have been hiding in their homes.

One of the chalices arrives from the cellar and lodges itself between my eager fingers.

I drink with my gaze on the sun's position above the mountain, telling me it's a little past noon. I am drunker than I was at this time two spans ago, and, fates willing, I will be drunker tomorrow than I am right now. Must make progress.

"The plan is to drink until the cellar is empty," I say when I sense an intruder.

"Why stop at one cellar?" a male says from the door. I recognize his voice, but my brain is too busy and too drunk to identify him. Sniffing, I scent Vane the vampire before he strides into my line of view smelling of sandalwood and cedar with a dash of citrus mixed with a drop of vanilla. A complex scent designed to attract his prey, who are often the fae peoples, our magic making us a delicious meal for the notturno.

Notturno are undead and belong under the cover of the night, and even the old and powerful master vampires like Vane require magic to move under the sun. He once told me the sun slows them down, which is a weakness a male like Vane despises.

"What are you doing here in broad spanlight?" I ask.

He snatches a candleholder floating in the air and puts it above the fireplace. "What is going on here?"

"Most of us are having us a pity party," the candleholder says. "The arrows are standing around the pillar conspiring against the blades that are guarding the house."

Vane stares at me, refusing to speak with my objects.

"Join me for a drink?" I offer him my wrist, wishing he would come closer and bite so I could rip his head from his shoulders for no reason whatsoever.

Vane is smarter than that and remains at a safe distance. "You must gather your wits. The people are starting to pack and leave their homes in fear you will destroy the villages."

"My people are so smart. I'm proud of them."

Vane shakes his head and sits across from me in the chair in which I sat with Augusta in my lap. I can almost feel her perfect curls draping over my arm. Again, my chest contracts, and I lose my breath. Gasping, I inhale loudly and let the wine from the chalice heal me, make me forget.

"You can't go around destroying everything."

"I can. I really can."

"But you won't, because deep down inside, you're not the monster everyone thinks you are. You can regain control of your magic. This is not the first time—"

"Shut up, Vane. You sound like my conscience."

Leaning forward, he rests his elbows on his knees, his eyes sparkling red with either thirst or fury. "You can't afford the pity party while your enemies gather."

"Let them gather. Let them try. The army of one fears no one."

Vane takes a moment to process this and then asks. "Where is your nephew?"

I shrug. "Somewhere in the afterlife. I destroyed him along with my court. Me. It was me. I destroyed the court and buried my enemies under the rubble."

"You have no heir, then?"

"No heir. No bride. Nobody. Well, except for my sister, which isn't saying much since she's the fate."

"Your seer is the new fate."

The arrows start weeping. Swords fall to the ground in dramatic fashion as if stabbed. I roll my eyes. "You can't talk about her. You're upsetting my staff." I drink more. I'm happy for her. Truly. It just goes to show I was right when I abstained from breeding her. My Augusta, a fate. Something expands in my chest. I think it might be pride.

I have no right to be proud of her, but I am all the same. To be chosen as a fae fate means the old magic believes her to be pure of heart. I guess Emishi will now retire somewhere.

"When I drank from her, she showed me all this," the

vampire continues. "You in the chair on this span. Me talking to you. I saw it as a part of my own future."

"And?"

"This is going to sound insane..." he says, but when I give him a pointed look, he continues. "Okay, maybe not to you, but it sure is surreal to me. The seer gave me a message for you. No wait, when she delivered me a vision, the future Augusta gave me a message for you."

"What the fuck are you? Fate's messenger?"

He smirks. "I have an interest in all this, don't worry."

Moments stretch. I don't ask about the message. I fear what future Augusta has to say to me. And there it is. Fear. The army of one does fear something after all.

Vane stands and makes his way toward the door, where he stops and says, "Grow a pair."

I snort. "Is that what she said?"

"Yes."

I laugh. "That's my girl."

44

AUGUSTA

I spent a few more spans at the farm, and then June brought me back to court to help with her wedding. She doesn't need me, but June wants to keeps an eye on me. I've been...under the weather a bit.

June's wedding span approaches swiftly, and the excitement in the air for the big event is palpable. Tonight, we're receiving the vampire houses. Since notturno bites are extremely pleasurable, and we love pleasure here at the Summer Court, nobody wants to miss tonight's party the king is throwing in the main ballroom.

Even El'jah is present. He walks up with a flute and a smile that brightens the dark hallway I'm hiding in. Even though Emishi told me I'm the fate who sees all that will come to pass, I was too weak to accept the magic of the fate, and it seems the future is waiting for me indeed. Emishi promised that when I'm ready, I will know, and I'll receive the magic.

While the future is in limbo, I've followed my internal knowing, which told me I should attend tonight's party.

Getting dressed for tonight still proved rather difficult. I'm still mourning the future I won't have with my king.

I accept the offered flute and give El'jah a once-over. He's wearing leather pants and a thin silk shirt under a leather jacket that has metal spikes on the shoulders and the collar. Streaked with natural highlights from the sun, his golden hair drapes over his shoulders and contrasts against his tan. His blue eyes are like the sea, and if I keep looking at them, I might drown in their beauty.

"I'm not a male who wishes to tempt fate, but if you start looking this attractive every night, I'll touch you in ways that'll make your sister fate forget your hymen ever existed."

This male finds all the right things to say. Shyly, I smile.

"How long have you been in heat?" he asks.

"I don't know. Keeping track of time has been a challenge." Due to the disturbance in the power of the fates. But I don't say that.

Emishi and June aren't on speaking terms. June thinks the future fate interfered with time, meaning she time traveled into the future, which caused a disturbance in the present because she hid what she was doing. When June looks back into the past, there are gaps she can't explain. Last time a fate interfered this way, the ripples caused devastating events.

The gaps bother June, and she won't let them rest. She'll find a way to fix the time gaps and patch up the magic as well as the paths again. I'll help. As soon as I can. As soon as I'm mentally prepared for seeing the future where the Unseelie king and I aren't together.

El'jah sips his drink. "I presume you've held on to your hymen during that difficult time?"

I chuckle. "I have."

He offers me his elbow. "Allow me to present you to the court."

I take his offered elbow, and we walk downstairs toward the railing of the upper floor where the bright lights shine and the people converge in their little gossiping cliques. I chew my lip, fully expecting the gossip will run along the vein of *the Unseelie king returned the young seer to the Summer Court untouched and in heat.*

The rumor mill is running with all sorts of speculations. June is mitigating some of them, but the tongues wag and wag. It appears as if the Unseelie king dumped me, and while some people feel sorry for me, most of them think I got what I deserved after I flirted with him during dinner in the first place. They think I'm a traitor.

"If I asked you what the future holds, would you tell me?" El'jah says.

"The future is blind right now." Emishi lost her foresight, and I haven't gotten it yet, so we're in this odd limbo...a transition of sorts.

"Then we have to live in the moment." El'jah guides me out of the darkness onto the terrace, where the bright lights feel like strobe lights directed at me.

I blink a few times and allow my eyes to adjust to the many chandeliers hanging low from the high ceilings. Trapped inside a huge reflective glass ball, light bugs have multiplied and are thriving, making the room even brighter.

Downstairs, dressed in sunny, bright fabrics in all the colors of the rainbow, people speak and laugh over the live music playing on the stage right under us. Once they see me, the fae lingering on the balcony wrapping around the first floor quiet down and murmur under their breaths. More than one person turns.

At the railing, I grip the metal with both hands, for if I don't, I think I might leave.

"She looks sad," I hear them whisper.

"I wonder what she's thinking, coming here."

"Nobody will touch her now."

"Fraud. No seer who sees the future would choose this willingly."

Cursing my excellent hearing, I turn, wanting to flee, but something inside me makes me stop in my tracks.

"What is it?" El'jah asks.

"Something is coming," I say.

"Shall I alert the commander?"

"It won't help."

"Is there something I can do?"

Just as I'm about to answer him, the king and future queen walk in through the main entrance, and naturally, the people forget all about me. June is wearing a short, white dress, teasing everyone with the wedding. Rumor has it the king commissioned a thousand-diamond dress, which explains why nobody has seen Taliant. He's been missing from court, and they think he's holed up somewhere working on June's wedding gown.

At the palace entrance, June looks up, and I give her a wave. She waves back, and the couple enter the ballroom. A male standing in for Taliant this evening announces the first vampire house, and a vampire master walks in. A tall, handsome male, dressed in charcoal-gray, he wears a single dark red handkerchief peeking out of the pocket of his jacket that signals an alliance with the Unseelie court. His brooding gaze roams over the crowd as if searching for someone. When he sees me, recognition passes over his face, and he bows deeply as one would bow before my sister June.

"You've met Vane in the Unseelie court, I presume?" El'jah asks.

I dip my chin, acknowledging the notturno's greeting. "He feels familiar." As if I met him sometime in the future. I don't have time to ponder because people outside start screaming.

The guards rush out, the crowds in the palace start moving away from the entrance, and the commander steps in front of our king, grabbing the hilt of his sword.

The vampire lifts his hands and moves away from the entrance. "Not one of mine, I assure you."

The king remains calm, his gaze on El'jah whose blue eyes take on a magical glow. I've never seen El'jah display magic like this before, and since I'm near him, I feel it the most. It makes me wish for my heart's desire, which is that Aamako comes for me.

Every girl wants to be chased.

It hurts when you're the girl who isn't.

It hurts when you're separated, and he never even tries to get you back.

This must be why I imagine the Unseelie king walking into the Summer Court wearing an unbuttoned burgundy uniform top and black leather pants. His long and unkempt beard matches the messy hair that's covering most of his face.

Wings rise from behind him. His wings. They're black tipped in red and match mine, which I've tucked away and hidden under my dress. Unlike the vampire, Aamako doesn't need to search the crowds for me. He looks up instantly, his eyes dark pits of despair.

The guards surround him, swords drawn, sharp ends pointing at his chest, but the Unseelie king doesn't seem ruffled.

"El'jah," I whisper.

"Oh my," El'jah says breathlessly. He steps away from me. The people on the balcony start moving away as well.

"Am I having a vision?" I ask, but there's nobody around me anymore.

The Unseelie king walks a few steps, then his wings flutter, making everyone gasp and step back farther. They line up along the walls of the ballroom, giving Aamako the floor. Wings flapping, he lifts and meets me at the terrace. There, he hovers in my line of sight, smelling like the cellar and looking like the wounded crow Floki once chased inside the house. Secretly, I take pleasure in seeing he's had a rough time.

Instead of a bouquet of flowers, he pulls out a dagger.

Spears, swords, and arrows fly at him, but when he lifts his other hand, they stop in midair. Hundreds of guards pour into the room and run up the stairs to engage him physically, but the king pays them no mind. I love that about him. The confidence in his abilities, his magic, his might.

"You look well, Augusta," he says.

"You look like you drowned in your cellar."

He smiles, eyes crinkling in the corners. "I have."

I swallow. "What are you doing here?"

"I came to tell you something."

"I'm listening."

Never taking his eyes off me, the Unseelie king takes me by the wrist and lays the dagger in my palm. He forces my fingers to close over the hilt and then cups my face. He tilts it the way a male does when he wants to kiss a female. I've seen it so many times when our king is kissing June, and I've coveted it, and so I close my eyes and let the love of my life kiss me.

Aamako's lips close over mine. They're soft and, more importantly, familiar. I know these lips as if I've kissed them till the end of time. He is mine. The Unseelie king and I are fae-ted.

"Marry me or end me," he says.

45

AUGUSTA

When I told Julie my loss of magic means I get a new start on life, I was thinking the two of us could sell the farm and move to the Spring Court. Or even farther away, to Kilseleia now that the hordes rule it. During the Summer season opening, we met the ladies who ride with the hordes. They are sisters, and we liked them. We could get to know them better while building a new life in their city.

And since the future is out of my reach for now, I didn't foresee Aamako walking into the Summer Court and asking (demanding) that I either marry him or end him. So publicly.

I'm so glad I didn't see it coming.

For if I did, I might not have shown up tonight, convinced my future casting was just girlish hope that the male I love would chase after me and profess his undying (or dying) devotion to me.

But I didn't see it.

I didn't imagine it.

And I can't deny it.

The Unseelie King and I 265

The Unseelie king and I are fae-ted, his glorious wings matching mine, the ones that I can't seem to shed, likely for this reason. Somehow, at some point in the fates' timeline, our paths have merged into a single line we call a heart line. I'd love to ask June when this happened, and perhaps I will sometime, but now the king awaits an answer, and one must not keep the king waiting.

I drop the dagger and hug him, whispering in his ear, "Take me home."

Aamako tackles me and propels us back into the shadows of the stairways from which I came. The darkness spins around us and sucks us in. My belly rises and my head spins, and the violent way the shadows take us makes me want to scream, but since I'm in the company of a fearless male, I pinch my lips, squint my eyes, and pray for it to be over soon.

The shadows spit us out on the floor of the Dakkuyasu living space. The king and I stumble forward, almost hitting the chair by the fireplace.

"Pardon the landing," the king says, and tightens his hold, pulling me closer.

I shiver from the cold. "Pardoned."

On my left, the fireplace is unlit, the fire poker still on duty poking and prodding the ashes, repeating the same phrase over and over again: "Breed with me or end me. Breed with me or end me."

Winter is seeping into my bones, and since I'm barely covered by my little red dress, a light overcoat covering my wings, I press tighter against the Unseelie king. My sandals hardly count as shoes.

"We're coming!" someone shouts, and several coats pile upon me, topping me off with a fur hat way too big for my head. It covers my eyes. Warm now, I tip the hat so I can see around me.

Chalices, trays, and pitchers litter the floor, most of them accumulated beside the chair on the right side of the fireplace. He's always sat on the chair to the left of the fireplace. The new chair is white and piled with many blankets, I presume to keep Aamako warm while the fireplace is not in use.

The staff in the kitchen are arguing. The coat hangers are spinning over the table.

Aamako runs a hand through his hair. "The staff... I can't believe you're here."

I tilt my head. "Did you think I would say no?"

He runs a hand though his hair again. Is he nervous? This is so unlike him.

"Did you?" I press.

He nods. "Yes. I couldn't be sure. I'm not a seer."

But he asked me anyway, and in front of all the royals and courtiers of a rival court. Had I said no, he would have been shamed or even killed. "I'm not a seer anymore either."

Aamako scrubs his beard and suddenly goes still. He levels me with a heated look. "The mother is not a seer."

"Excuse me?"

"The mother is not a seer," he repeats. "Oh." He laughs in a deranged way. "Oh, Emishi, you royal bitch."

"Hm?"

Words start pouring out of Aamako's mouth: "At the baths. Those dreadful baths where you overhead all the wrong things, Emishi also told me that the mother of my child will not be a seer. I thought she was giving me a vision of a life without you, but she spoke my future true. This future. This... What of your foresight? Would you give up all the power of the fate for a life with me?"

"It's a lie. The future fate doesn't have to be a virgin. Emishi made it up so nobody would ever ask her to marry them."

He makes an angry face and sticks out his hands as if imagining wringing someone's neck. "She's evil. Pure evil."

The Unseelie often enjoy toying with others, but what Emishi has done, namely have every seer believe they are to remain chaste or else lose their magic, is very wrong. "I think she did right by you." Emishi lost her magic, sight, and foresight. I don't believe he knows that or the reason why she did it.

With Aamako worked up, the house is louder too. I can barely hear him over the clamor of the objects.

"I'm a fucking mess without you." He tilts his head back and exhales as if tired.

He says this so matter-of-factly, but it means everything to me. I was a mess without him too. I lay in bed and cried, while he sat in the chair and drank. We shouldn't be parted. We will never part again, for our paths are intertwined, our hearts mated.

"Fuck, don't look up," he says.

I look up and gasp. Swords that should line the middle pillar supporting the house are hovering above us, sharp tips facing down. If the king loses control, even for a moment, they'll rain down upon us, and we're done.

"Get your shit together, everyone," the Unseelie king shouts, startling me. He comes toward me and throws me over his shoulder. I yelp as he lands a slap on my butt. "Augusta is back, and you all need to clean up your mess."

"*Our* mess?" comes from the kitchen. "You did it."

"I'm the king, and I can do no wrong," he shouts back, arguing with himself as he climbs the steps to the first floor.

At the top of the stairs, my fluffy red slippers await, like dutiful soldiers.

They march behind the king as he takes a left, away from my chambers and toward his. I'm giddy with excitement, for I shall finally lose my virginity. And that's not all. I will lose my virginity to my king, my very dangerous king, who destroyed more courts than any other king, but who loves me with the whole of his violent heart.

I'm excited, that is, until he throws me onto his bed, and rips off his clothes. It's nothing I haven't seen before, and yet it's as if I'm seeing him for the first time. Aamako rests one knee on the bed between my legs and picks up my left leg by the ankle. He touches his lips to my calf, then drags his beard over the inside of my leg.

Liquid heat from my channel soaks my underpants at the same time that his seed spurts out. We are really going to do this. Are we?

I'm not sure what the king sees on my face now, but he pauses.

"What is it?" he asks.

"Nothing."

He scrubs his jaw. "I should shave."

"And maybe shower," I suggest.

Aamako nods. "We will bathe together."

"I can't."

"Why not?"

"Because I have a nest to make." I scoot toward the edge of the bed and tuck my feet into the red slippers. I missed the slippers.

I stand, and because the king won't move, our bodies are plastered together. He is as cold as the Winter king ought to be, while I'm feverish and still in heat, releasing my mating scent without reservation.

Aamako's eyes hood, and he takes a lock of my hair and twirls it around his claw. "I'll court you the way a Summer fairy ought to be courted. I'll bring you staff, real staff, I mean. You'll have maidens, cooks, housekeepers, whatever you wish for. I'll secure the finest bedding for your nest, and I'll find luxurious scented candles that can burn for an entire cycle. Sound good?" He slips a hand under my dress and rips off my panties. "Now tell me, my fae-ted, how would you like to be fucked?"

"However it pleases my king."

"That's a good girl. Go make your nest, then."

46

AUGUSTA

True to his word, the king supplies fine scented candles and piles upon piles of furs, blankets, and comforters. He delivers it at the door because tradition says a male can't walk into the nest uninvited even when the female breaks tradition and nests inside his chamber.

First thing I do is change the bedding then move onto arranging the furs and blankets at different places in the vast space. I make a fluffy nest by the fireplace, one at the foot of the bed, one under the window.

In the Summer Court, females are taught to place candles in the corners of the rooms because that position creates an atmosphere and perfectly sensual lighting, but my king uses the corners for gathering shadows. I place my candles on top of the fireplace, near the bottom of the fireplace, and along the window overlooking the mountain peak.

As I'm placing the candles on the windowsill, I catch sight of the king downstairs cutting wood, in preparation for our mating. The mountain of wood already cut and ready is as tall as the king himself, and that tells me, Aamako intends to breed me for spans on end.

Excited, I squeal.

He looks up at the window. Nude, I fluff out my wings and drag my hand from my neck down over my breast, which I squeeze gently.

Aamako's eyes flare silver.

I wink at him and start lighting the candles, the final step in the nesting process. Slowly, teasingly, I unlace my hair and let it fall over the front of my body, covering my breasts. The king drops the ax and walks back inside, chopped logs floating on the air behind him like soldiers. I hear them stopping right outside the door. It occurs to me that Aamako, with his powerful magic, could've done all the preparation like the woodcutting, cooking, and supply gathering while servicing me in heat.

But he chose not to. I want to believe it's because he wants to spend uninterrupted time with me, listening to me ramble about nothing and everything. Maybe he'll read to me, tell me stories of his childhood. Or his conquests.

I light the rest of the candles in the room and turn about to make sure everything is the way I want it to be. Romantic and fine and fluffy and comfortable, and worthy of the powerful king.

When I'm sure it's the best that I know how to make it, I kneel and fluff out my hair, spread my knees, and position my hands on my thighs, palms facing up.

I stare at the door.

Moments pass, and I wait, so hyperfocused on the door, my brain visualizing the moment he'll open it and walk in wearing a robe, or a uniform, or just pajama pants that the wardrobe opening startles me.

A drawer opens, and a single black leather glove rises and travels on the air to me.

"Close your eyes," it says in Aamako's deep, raspy voice, the same one he uses when he rests in his bed with an arm behind his head.

I close my eyes and wait. When nothing happens, I cheat and open one eye. The moment I do, the glove tsks and the door opens, admitting a crop. An actual horse crop. It whips through the air before arriving to stand next to the glove.

I snap my eyes shut. "Message received." Do I want to misbehave and open my eye again? Could be fun. I'm fond of leather. Oh! Does he know about the thing I have for leather? Has he noticed how I'm sniffing around when he wears leather (which is most times) and how I fixate on his gloves? Or maybe he noticed how I shiver every time he touches me while wearing the gloves.

It's a fetish. I'm sure of it. Blushing now that it's occurred to me I have a fetish for the king's gloves and he knows it, I swallow.

The scent of leather grows stronger. It's now laced with the scent of the king, so familiar and arousing that my heat starts stirring. Leather brushes my cheek, trails down my jaw, and I tilt back my head and move my hair out of the way in case the glove wants to touch my breasts. It trails down my neck, stopping at my collarbone and tracing it before moving over my right breast and finally arriving at my nipple. There, it pinches the hard bud and pulls it, then twirls it between the thumb and forefinger, setting my wings into a flurry of movement.

The fireplace flares. I hear it. That's the king. He's not here, but yet he *is* here with me, and even if I had foresight, I couldn't have predicted how he would come at me during

my heat. He's unpredictable and all mine, and I love everything about him.

The glove takes my breast and weighs it as if it's a hand,
and then I feel the crop press against my nipple. It smacks it.
Gently, not painfully, and I find it arousing. I let out a moan
as my wings shake out, making glitter sparkle to the floor.
The glove teases my other nipple, the leather part of the
crop trailing all the way down my belly and between my
thighs.

The glove follows the crop, and as the crop moves away,
the glove starts stroking between my legs. The moment the
leather touches me, the heat in my belly churns faster,
turning into lava, and the liquid heat starts traveling down
my channel, slowly dripping on the floor.

The glove slaps my clit, making my hips jump. It then
strokes my lips faster. Arousal dripping out of me, my wings
flutter, and my legs start shaking. I moan loudly, my head
thrown back, my hips moving over the finger made of
leather. A cold finger tucks my hair behind my ear. I start to
open my eyes when my king slams his lips over mine and
pushes his tongue inside my mouth.

I open like a flower would open to receive rain after a
drought, and my hands fly out to touch him, but he restrains
my wrists by wrapping his fingers around them and forcing
my hands back on top of my thighs. The way Aamako
remains in control at all times makes me crazy about him.

He kisses me as if he's hungry.

Maybe he is. Maybe he's as hungry for me as I am for
him, because he lifts me and carries me to the bed, where he
lies on top of me.

"Open your eyes."

I obey. His gaze is completely silver, his magic is
pounding in the room like a living entity, his mating scent,

that smells of leather and power and winter evergreens, makes me dizzy with lust. Between my legs, I ache.

The king reaches between us and lines up at my entrance. Using his other hand, he takes my wrists and secures them above my head.

His hair falls around his face as he pushes into me, stretching my entrance.

"I was wrong," Aamako says, his voice strained.

"About what?" I hitch a breath as my channel widens, trying to accommodate his girth. Sweat breaks out over my brow.

"About my power."

I remember how he instructed me to breathe out when he enters me and breathe in as he leaves me and that's what I do now.

"How so?" I ask as I exhale through an intensely painful push inside me. Oh, sex is both pleasurable and painful, and I'm confused as to which it should be and aroused and happy and I think Aamako smells like a thousand turns of happiness. I shall cry.

A tear escapes. I hope he doesn't notice. Another tear rolls down, and I pinch my lips because I'm about to let out a waterfall that he will certainly notice. Overwhelmed, I hitch a breath.

"I was wrong about the army of one."

He's talking about his magic.

"What about it?" I barely utter past the lump in my throat.

"The army of one is not undefeated. It fell for a wildling from the Summer Court. It fell when she first kissed him. When you kissed me. I think you knew I was yours before anyone else knew it, and you claimed me before I could find my bearings and before I could erect my defenses. And..."

The king grunts as he seats himself all the way to the hilt. There he pauses and reminds me to breathe before he withdraws, then pushes back in. "The truth is, even if I erected my walls and raised an army that could defeat all the armies of our world, I wouldn't have been able to defeat my feelings for you."

I catch a sob before it comes out. I cry, happy tears flowing freely, while the king fucks me slowly and tells me things I never expected him to say. Not like this. Not all of it. Not so openly.

"You disarm me. The army of one has been slain. Your love conquered it." He releases my hands, and I throw my arms around his neck and bury my face into it where I inhale, and he growls.

A palm lands on my knee and pushes it up so I open more for him. Seated deeply inside me, Aamako starts moving slowly in and out. His arms come around me, hugging me tightly while he pumps his hips, picking up the pace.

He fists my hair, jerks it so that I'm forced to look at him while he fucks me. "Has the pain waned?"

"Yes, my king."

"Your pussy is warm and snuggly and tight, oh so tight. And when I stretch it some more, she will weep for me, begging for seed. How is the heat in your belly?" He wipes away my tears.

"Churning."

He pecks my lips and sucks the bottom one. His wings rise behind him, his horns thrusting their way out. Oh dear fates, he is glorious. I dig my claws into his shoulders.

He snarls and bites my neck, marking me.

The palm holding my knee up moves and slaps my butt cheek, bruising me.

"You will soon take my seed, my sweet girl, my good girl, my queen."

His queen.

I hitch a breath, and the king flicks my clit, making the fireball trapped in my lower belly drop. I scream as I come, my channel undulating, milking him for seed.

Aamako fucks me faster. "That a girl. Demand the seed. Demand your king service you. Conquer me. Take me. I'm yours!" Aamako shoots his seed inside me and keeps pumping while my channel is squeezing, goading him on, wanting to get seeded and end the painful spans of heat that aren't going to be so painful anymore. For my king has come for me, and he will love me as only a fae-ted mate could.

47

AUGUSTA

The rising shutters remind me of eyelids lifting heavily after a good night's slumber. My cheek is pressed against Aamako's chest, and I listen to the steady beating of his heart while syncing my breathing with his. He plays with my hair, and sometimes, his left palm ventures down my back, careful to avoid the sore spots where my wings fell off.

After the heat, a female fae's wings dry up and drop like the petals of a flower, leaving wounds in the back to heal. Fae with lots of magic heal quickly, but since I don't have any magic right now, the wounds will heal more slowly. And that's fine. Well worth the seven spans I spent breeding with my king.

"Your heat is over?" he asks, sounding hopeful. The fae female in heat demands lots and lots of attention and stamina from the male.

I chuckle. "It is."

For the past seven spans, Aamako has serviced me relentlessly with fervor and even fury, expressing decades of pent-up sexual desire I was all too happy to receive. My muscles are mush, my bottom is red, my wrists bruised, and there are tooth marks on my neck, hips, and inside my thighs.

The Unseelie king makes love the hard way, harder than most, I'd say but then again, I know nothing about the others. I have only ever experienced my one. The one. The one whom the fates chose for me.

If I'm to take the magic of the fate, then have I chosen Aamako for myself? Hmmm. Something I shall ponder later.

"Are you pregnant?"

"Um, I don't know."

He sighs. "If you're not, it'll have to happen some other heat time, because you're too sore for more."

"I agree."

Aamako kisses my forehead. "Up we go." His abdominal muscles tense, ready to move his body up, but he groans and stays in bed. "I want to lie here with you forever."

I run a palm over his rock-hard abdominals and lower yet, but he traps my wrist.

"After you heal," he says.

In the past few spans, we have left the bed only to fuck on all fours on the floor near the fireplace and under the window. My knees are sore, so sore, in fact, that Aamako made me cloth pads.

The spans passed in a blur of sweat, lust, and fluids as our bodies expressed love for one another in ways I never thought possible. Aamako is a strong and creative lover, remaining hard for the duration of my heat. I'm sure that's a record.

With a groan, he gets up and walks toward the door. His nude body is so fine, so hard, so muscular and scarred and hairy that it turns me on all over again.

I whistle.

Aamako turns and shows me his front. "Up here, Augusta." He points at his face.

Smiling, I look up.

The king smirks. "Our new staff has arrived." He glances at the fire in the grate, which is dying down, and walks to it. He throws a few logs into it and grabs the fire poker to arrange the stack. He puts the object back then pauses, a small smile playing on his lips.

The king used his body instead of his magic. I think he's happy about that.

Rubbing his hands together, he looks around the chamber at the utter mess we made. Comforters, sheets, and pillows covered in sweat and cum are spread out all over the floor. Those neat nests I made? All history.

"Have you seen my robe?" he asks.

"It's in the wardrobe."

Aamako opens the closet and grabs the robe. Once dressed, he exits the room, and I continue gazing outside, the view of the snow-covered mountain peak and the villages below it the prettiest view I'd ever seen. I find it prettier than the view from June's tower in the Summer Court, and that's saying something since the Summer king commands only the best for my sister.

Hearing the staff downstairs, and identifying the voices of my bride maidens, I sling my feet over the edge of the mattress and into the slippers before getting up with a stretch and a yawn. Wincing as I walk, I open the wardrobe in search of my own robe.

What I find is a black gown with a long transparent black veil.

I run a fingertip over the lace stitched into the hem of the open collar of Emishi's fate gown before I dress and cover my face with the veil. Folding my hands in front of me, I stand at the window and peer over the horizon, opening myself up to visions of all that shall come to pass.

Old, potent magic slams into me, taking my breath away. I gasp as the magic buzzes though my body, cooling it and making me shiver while visions of all that's coming to pass rush into my head.

The visions make me light-headed. I stumble backward to sit on the bed, but when I go to sit down, I fall into the shadows and appear elsewhere, a place where I know I don't belong. It looks...it feels like the future, and I shouldn't be here. But I am, and so I remain in the corner in the shadows, watching myself sitting up on the bed right after labor.

I'm cradling a bundle in my arms when an older lady approaches me. The future me doesn't recognize her because my eyes are covered with the white membranes of a blind female. Emishi, who was a fate, is the older lady. She takes my forefinger and puts it inside my baby's fist. I wince at something the baby does, and when I pull my finger away, it's blue and frozen.

My frostbitten finger.

Emishi walks away, stumbling.

The future me regains her sight, but I don't startle, as if nothing had occurred at all.

The vision ends, and I blink, trying to interpret what just occurred.

I saw what Emishi had done when she was a fate. Emishi knew I was her brother's fae-ted, and when we met, she foresaw Prince Neguan attacking me in the cellar. If I had died down there, Aamako would have lost his fea-ted mate and, with me, also his mind. He would have gone on to conquer all the fae courts, devastating our lands and ending powerful magical bloodlines.

Emishi tried to fix the future by willing it differently, but couldn't, so she took matters into her own hands. She walked into one of her visions and changed my past by altering my future. As a punishment for interfering with the fate of a fate, Emishi lost both her sight and foresight.

I cannot see all that has come to pass, but I will ask June about Emishi. I have a feeling Emishi altered the future for penance. I have a feeling this is her way of asking her brother for forgiveness by gifting him the one thing he wanted but couldn't have.

A fae-ted mate who would love him unconditionally. A queen who would give him a powerful heir.

Inhaling deeply, I leave my king's chambers and close the door softly behind me.

The chattering downstairs dies down before I approach the stairs. Still dizzy from the magic, I grab the railing as I descend the steps one at a time, my maidens and other staff slowly retreating into the kitchen, fear of the fate making them want to run. Not my king, though.

He rushes up the stairs and offers me his elbow.

He's well dressed. Too well for home. "Are we going somewhere?" I ask.

"No. Why?"

"Your attire makes me think we're going somewhere. Or expecting someone." Aamako wears black on black with a red silk scarf wrapped several times around his neck. His silky straight black hair is pulled back and secured at the top of his head. He's even wearing a crown made of granite and white gold, and it occurs to me this is the first time I've seen him wear one.

It has thorns. How fitting.

"I'm dressed to impress someone very important. A fate, perhaps?" He winks.

I love him when he's playful like this.

I love him when he broods.

I love him when he's well dressed or in tattered old clothes that haven't been washed in spans.

I love him all around, and I wish he would tell me all the ways he loves me too, because I know he does. It's in the way he looks at me. It's the same way Et'enne looks at June. It's everything I'd always wanted, and my heart is full.

I accept his elbow and walk slowly toward the table, where our new staff stand at attention. I note they're all females.

They're also terrified, as terrified as I was when I first saw Emishi, as terrified as I would be if June weren't my sister and I hadn't felt her power before. Dressed as a fate and with my veil lifting on a breeze that doesn't exist, I approach them and start drawing back the veil.

They gasp and squeeze their eyes shut, and so I drop the veil back over my face.

"My bride and I will have a traditional breakfast," Aamako says.

The three females wearing chef's aprons and hats curtsey, then scurry away faster than mice, while my bride maidens stand awkwardly against the wall beside the fireplace. I hate that they're afraid of me, but I can't dampen the power coursing through my veins so that they'll be more comfortable around me. Perhaps they wish to leave and fear I would get angry if they withdrew their service.

"Ladies, when you gifted me with your service during the preparation for my marriage, I wasn't a fate, so I understand if you would rather leave now. It's scary being around me. Heck, it's scary *being* me."

They exchange looks.

My king sighs. "Augusta, the reason they're uncomfortable and scared is because you haven't given them anything to do, while I directed the kitchen staff already. Please find your maidens something to do, or they might presume they're no longer needed now that you're a mighty fate."

"Is that true?" I ask them.

They nod in unison, which is sort of cute because they're identical twins.

"I'm relieved you don't fear me."

"Oh, they fear you," my king says just as a red leather box lands in front of him with a thud. "Everyone fears you. As they should." There's pride in his voice. "You are both powerful and kind, a deadly combination for a female." He reaches for the box and opens it. "The only other thing left for you to be is my queen." He flips the box around.

Inside it, on a plush white pillow, rests a crown made entirely of black diamond. It's thorny and matches the crown on his head.

"Dear...me," I whisper. "It's happening."

Aamako rounds the table and picks up the crown. Parting his wings at the bottom so they don't wipe the floor, Aamako kneels before me, not on one knee as if proposing, but on both knees as if begging. Keeping his dark eyes locked with mine, he stretches his arms out, offering me the Unseelie queen's crown.

Seeing this powerful, proud king on his knees is humbling. Visions of us start forming in my head and threaten to make me leave the moment that's happening right now. I push them back, even though I'm tempted to view our future.

Behind me, people sniff.

"Do you love me?" I ask.

"Fiercely." He nudges the crown toward me, and I sense a sliver of fear coming from him. This fearless male fears rejection just like the rest of us. It makes me love him even more.

"You beg so well, my king." I lift the crown from the pillow and set it on my head. It's a good thing I'm wearing a veil. Nobody can see the happy tears gathering in my eyes when the king picks me up and twirls us until his wings lift us and we float in midair, just gazing at each other.

I don't know what he sees in me, but I see all my tomorrows with him.

***

Hello,

I am so happy to have shared this story with you and I hope you were entertained. Aamako has been an interesting presence in my head and I'm so glad he and Augusta got together.

Currently, I'm brainstorming a few stories to write next and I hope one of them turns out to be Julie's. I also think Vane might get a book. He was an unexpected sexy surprise and I think I want to write about him. LoL

You're welcome to stay in this fantasy world and start reading the Savage Horde on the next page now.

SAVAGE IN THE TOUCH TEASER

Seven houses hardly even counts as a village, but since our tavern, which also serves as a bed-and-breakfast, is the last stop before the mountain that travelers must scale on their journey to the capital city, Lyan, we get busy.

The inn is strategically located right at the exit to the valley, and we made sure we put up a sign that says: *No fluffy bed or pillows for another two moons.* Sixty spans is a long time to spend in the forested mountain living in tents. Not to mention, one never knows what kind of criminals lurk in the bushes and what kind of trouble awaits in the mountains.

The road to Lyan is paved with dangers.

Yet that doesn't stop the refugees passing through our little village. They escaped the horde that's been plowing through the south of the kingdom. They say the horde devours everything in its path. They say its hunger can't be tamed.

They say it's coming.

It's all a myth. The "horde" is nothing more than a gang

of rebels, or at most our southern fae neighbors looking for trouble. And trouble they shall find, since half a moon ago, the king's army passed through the village on their way south. This means they must already have reached and defeated the horde and are on their way back now.

"Hey, Mag." I greet my sister as I tap my fingernails on the bar, reminding the drunk in front of me to pay up and call it a night. At thirty-seven, I've spent two decades behind this very bar, and I know when the next pint of ale will topple a man. The man isn't chatty, and the ominous thread-bare black cloak he wears obscures most of his face, which gives me an impression he came in to drown his sorrows undisturbed. Here's to hoping I won't have to carry his ass up the stairs to the third floor.

Although, if I have to, I will. Third-floor room and board runs at eleven silvers, so a little extra legwork for the guy is included in the price.

"Hey," my sister says and dumps a large bag of potatoes at my feet. "Here you go." She wipes her hands on a dirty white apron fastened to our father's old belt around her waist. Her brown pants will need a wash, as will her white shirt.

I wet a bar towel and wipe dirt from her rosy cheek and neck. "Don't tell me Mike called in again."

"It's past twilight, and I haven't seen him, so..." She shrugs. "Guess he's not coming."

I tuck her golden hair behind her ear and wipe away the dirt over her earlobe. Mag takes after her mother, who might've been a fairy because no other creature in all the lands could be this beautiful, with a pixie nose, smooth skin, perfect round eyes with long eyelashes, and shiny hair that never seems to get damaged or dry, not even in the winter winds.

"Rock, paper, scissors?" I ask. I hate peeling potatoes.

"Sure," Mag says, and we play.

I lose and will have to peel the potatoes early tomorrow.

She winks one pretty green eye. "How did we do for the night?" Mag opens the drawer that holds our coins. A few silvers slide over the wood. Not as many as we need to keep the lights on since the southern rebel problem has cut into our business. Most travelers aren't on their way to Lyan for vacation or business. Instead, they're seeking refuge there, and since most of the south is plagued by the same rebellion that's been going on for over a turn now, the king increased the taxes for the rest of us midlanders and northerners. The tavern and the few rooms we offer upstairs that make up our inn aren't covering the extra cost.

I rub her shoulder. "The soldiers will return."

The drunk lifts his head, showing chapped lips in the shadow of his cloak. He snorts. "They did return."

I frown. "What do you mean?"

"I'm it."

Giggling nervously, I hold out my hand. "Pay up and go rest. Breakfast is served early."

He snorts again. "You and I will be breakfast, and the horde serves itself after dusk."

Mag rounds the bar and sits next to the man. She yanks back the hood of his cloak, and it falls open to reveal the tattered red uniform of a soldier. A lieutenant, judging by the stars on his pocket.

"What happened?" I ask, a tingle of fear making my heart beat faster.

The soldier downs the pale ale and wipes his mouth with a sleeve, rests one foot on the floor, and wobbles as he stands. "The question is what *will* happen."

"What will happen?" I lean over the bar, and my sister leans in too, practically touching him.

He kisses her forehead. "The horde will come. They will consume. They will leave."

I lean back. "What do you mean, consume?"

"They're predators."

My sister and I laugh. We've heard the myth a million times, but our father, the king's historian, has been searching for these creatures for over ten turns, well before anyone ever mentioned them. He kept returning empty-handed, and as punishment, a few turns back, the king chopped off his head.

Now, whenever anyone talks about devastated villages, devoured corpses, and ravenous creatures, they say it's the horde. But if our father found nothing, despite the threat to his life, they don't exist.

"There's no such thing as the horde or predators," I say.

"I saw them." He points to his bloodshot blue eye, and I note the crusted blood under his fingernails. "A creature with teeth the size of my fingers, claws, fur, bright red eyes, ripping through my buddy's guts...and eating."

"Gross," Mag says.

The soldier stumbles toward the stairs. "The horde is coming."

"If they're coming, why are you still here?" I ask. He's full of shit.

"Nowhere to run. The king will kill me anyway. I'd rather my family think I died in battle than have them watch my beheading in the square."

The soldier's footsteps echo in the now-silent bar. The last patrons, a family with a small boy, throw silvers on the table and rush out the double doors.

"Hey," Mag shouts as she runs after them. "Hey, come back! He's crazy. Don't listen to him."

"The horde is coming!" the boy yells, and with that, the refugees passing on the road before the inn scramble. Screaming and yelling ensues as people start trampling one another, surging toward the road that leads to the bridge.

Mag waves her arms. "Stop, stop! There is no horde. It's just people like us playing dress-up."

Grabbing the tray, I start clearing the table, knowing Mag can't stop the madness. The word "horde" throws people into a frenzy. That's because they don't know the king like we do. Our father told us of the king's ruthlessness and that the king would protect his land, if not his people. He wouldn't allow the horde to pillage and seize his land, not after he conquered it with blood and magic.

Besides, the king commands medeisars, creatures of magic nobody can defeat. The predatory horde, even if they weren't a myth (and they are) are no match for those creatures or for the king, who is said to be able to kill thousands with a single sweep of his hand. Father has seen it, and so I believe it.

Despite the danger to his life, my father couldn't find the horde.

They don't exist.

"They're a myth," I say out loud into an empty tavern.

Mag returns, grabs a bottle of our cheapest whiskey, and sits at the bar. She pours a pair of shooters.

We down them, then slam the glasses on the bar top. Whiskey burns down my throat, and I chase it with water.

"Let's clean up," Mag says and starts unraveling her messy braid. "You wake up early and peel the potatoes, and I'll cook breakfast."

"For our one guest?"

She smiles. "And us."

I smile back. "And us."

She presses a warm callused palm over my cheek and pecks my nose. "Me and you, sister," she says. "We keep going no matter what. Right?"

"Right."

"The horde is a myth," she says.

"The horde is a myth. The monsters are a myth," I repeat. No, really, they are.

... until they're not. READ MORE...

LYCAN AND THE PRINCESS TEASER

I was born of a traitor and a whore.

Such a birth means I fought for everything I wanted in life. Why should my mating be any different, aye?

First, instead of a lycan female, my mate is of Stenan origin, specifically a former Kilseleian princess who's never worn an apron or picked up a ladle out of a barrel-sized pot to taste the soup she made for supper. While I'm certain that growing up as the princess taught her how to order people around, I doubt she would know how to run a lycan clan alongside me.

The worst thing about my mating?

The princess is eighteen.

Eighteen. I snatch a bottle, pour, and empty the glass down my throat. It's the nastiest bourbon I've ever tasted. In spite of that, I continue drinking it.

I can't remember being eighteen. It feels like a century ago. Almost was a century ago, since I'm closing in on one hundred and one turns this fall. I might look thirty, but as a lycan, I have another hundred turns before any aging shows.

"How old were you when you first shagged?" I ask Rohan, the pirate cousin who brought me to the fairy shores where the king of the Summer Court hid my mate on one of his estates.

"Can't remember." Rohan ponders and presses his lips to a fairy female's ear. He whispers something about her tits. This is one of those times when I curse my excellent hearing.

"Why do you ask?" he says while the female gets up from his lap. He slaps her bottom before she sashays away.

Another fairy comes to stand between his legs. She looks exactly like the one that just left. Twins.

"No reason," I say, watching the other twin return. Now there are two.

"I've known ye forever, mate," Rohan says. "Ye don't yap for no reason." From his pocket, he pulls out a single key and hands it to one lass. They each kiss him on either cheek and leave the upper deck.

"I'm thinking of someone," I say.

More fairies will come soon. They're like flies to honey. It's Summer-fae mating season, and the fae females love the lycan knob. We swell at the base like their fae males, but we're built bigger and smell of forest and rain instead of sea, orchids, and other flowery things I can't name.

"Princess Gloriana, is it?" Rohan asks, a smirk tugging his lips.

I nod. Tall, with long legs and a lean build, I could pin my mate against the wall and not have to bend to enter. She's young and looking for the party, which is why she'll show up tonight instead of staying at home in her estate farther from the court.

Rohan's light blue eyes regard me as I swig from the bottle of dirty bourbon he received from the savages. It goes down rough, much rougher than ale from lycan lands.

I miss the ale. The sooner I can locate the princess, the sooner I can leave the fae court. I'm all sorts of moody over my mate staying in a foreign court. A fae one at that.

Which is why the Summer king promised to deliver her to me. His sister, Fleur, is out with Gloriana tonight, and there's a chance the ladies will attend Rohan's party that's happening below.

I slick back my hair, tuck the slipping strands behind my ears, and wonder what my mate will say when she sees me.

We met only once before, and it was in the aftermath of a horde battle that overthrew her father, who was king at the time. Clearly distressed, Gloriana was skittish and scared when I told her she was mine and that I would protect her. I promised her the loyalty of my clan and my lands, but did not claim her at the time. The next thing I knew, the princess had vanished.

I searched for her everywhere.

I killed a savage male, thinking he'd taken her, and if the savages ever find out I did their male in, they'll plunder the clan lands. All for nothing, since the Summer king took my lass.

Or rather, she went to him and asked him to save her.

Save her. What a sack of shite.

A group of females climbs onto the top deck, and the pixie band perched at the bar turns up the tune. They play something livelier. As if my blood needs more enlivening around the fairies in mating season. My balls are so heavy with seed, I'm surprised they haven't detached and splattered onto the deck.

I grab them and move them around, unsticking them from each other during the summer night's heat.

Five beautiful, scantily dressed fairies of various shapes and sizes start swaying their hips. They smell like the sea and the light oils of the flowers found growing near their shores. Overall, they carry the scents I identify with Summer fairies and not Kilseleians with round ears.

So when I sniff out a Kilseleian female, my heart starts thudding in my ears. I know the scent of my mate. She came here with the group of fae.

She came to the pirate ship seeking the lycan knob, like the other females here tonight.

"She's here," I announce to Rohan, jerking my head toward the group that's eyeballing us like we're candy.

"It's just fairies," he says.

The group of females appears to be all fairies, but the gentle breeze cooling my balls under my kilt also blows the scent of my mate toward me, so I'm sure they're not all fae. Gloriana smells like orange blossom doused in rain. Strong and sexy, and impossible for me not to recognize.

I growl low in my throat. "She's definitely here."

"All right. The Summer king must be disguising her with a glamour. Remember what we talked about."

"I remember."

"I'll remind you anyway. I intend to do business with the Summer king, so we don't want to piss him off. My sources tell me the Kilseleian princess is his pet, so tread with caution."

"She's not his pet."

"You know what I mean by that."

Yeah, I knew, but I hated his choice of words. The Summer king is sheltering Gloriana and providing for her, something I should've done in his place.

Had she fucking let me.

She hid instead.

Well, not for long now.

The scent of orange blossoms grows stronger, and with it, I grow harder, a growl from my chest now a soothing rumble meant to attract a female.

Another fae ascends the steps and joins the group. It's Fleur, the Summer princess, her body sculpted by a divine hand. She exudes beauty and power in her tiny royal dress.

If one can even call it a dress. It covers the female parts and nothing more.

From across the deck, Fleur smiles at me and laces hands with a friend on her right.

"That's the Summer princess," Rohan moans.

"Try not to squirt on her toes."

Rohan snorts. "Won't be easy, but I'll try."

I know what he means. Beautiful fairies in their heat call for a mating.

Fleur tugs her friend toward us, and they walk in our direction hand in hand. Their long, legs capture my attention and hold it until they reach us. The brunette has straight shoulder-length hair and hazel eyes and wears a two-piece outfit. The top wraps around the lass's ample breasts and the bottom wraps around her arse. It's royal blue because that's the color of the season.

Both females approach barefoot, wearing stacks of anklets that will jingle as they're shagged.

Fleur kicks my shin. "Make room on your lap."

I widen my legs, hitting Rohan with my left knee. If I go any wider, my balls will tear off. I love my balls. They'll supply the first heirs of my clan.

Fleur sits on my left thigh. I stiffen. Didn't think she'd sit down. Fucking fairies.

The other female sits on my right thigh. The scent of my mate stuffs my nose, and I adjust my groin before attempting to speak. I open my mouth, but the fae princess presses a finger over my lips.

Blue eyes, a similar color to mine, crinkle at the corners as Fleur says, "It's best if you stay quiet, wolf. You'll ruin the fun with all the mating business."

"Aye, lass. The mating business." I grip Gloriana's hip and squeeze.

My mate giggles as if she likes it, even leans into me, propping an elbow on my shoulder.

Fleur strokes Gloriana's hair. "You have no idea who this lycan is, do you?"

My mate shakes her head and snatches the drink from my hand. She takes a swig and swallows as if the bourbon goes down like water. It does not.

The drink is cheap and nasty.

And the princess should balk at it.

"Nope," Gloriana says, slightly slurring the word, "but he's really hard." She gropes my thigh, her hand squeezing my flesh right near my crotch. If she weren't mine, I'd push her off my lap. But she is mine, and I'm caught off guard.

This is not how I imagined our meeting would go. Not even close.

"What have you done to her?" I bite out.

Fleur stands and stretches her arms high above her head, drawing attention to the scant clothes that lift over her breasts, revealing the curves of the underside. I look away before I start groping my mate.

"I expect her at brunch tomorrow, so be sure she can walk." Fleur winks and leaves us.

Rohan follows the princess.

I snort, surprised he's not crawling after her, tongue out and dragging on the floor.

In a matter of moments, the upper deck clears out, and

my mate and I are alone. The lights dim, and the pixies play something sultry, no doubt music that invites hands to wander.

The female in my lap presses her lips against my cheek.

If I look at her, I can't see through the glamour masking Gloriana's face, so I stare ahead, relying on my scent, something nobody can fool.

"I met a lycan once," she says, her voice sounding ten times more seductive to me than the entire orchestra.

"Yeah?" I squeeze her hip. That lycan better be me. "Tell me about it."

She flips her dark brown hair over her shoulder, but it returns to fall over the side of her face. I'm trying to see through the glamour, but I can't, and I have no idea how long Fleur will keep up this charade. I know this is my mate, and I want to see her face, not the face of this beautiful stranger.

I tuck the soft strands behind her ear.

"Thank you," she says, and locks her pretty eyes with mine. Gloriana's eyes stayed the same color despite the glamour. Hazel, the most common color of eyes for a Stenan female from the tribal lands. Expressive and warm.

"The lycan I met..." Her face moves toward me until our noses are almost touching. I smell bourbon on her breath, along with citrus blossom and feminine arousal that calls to me more than any siren surrounding the boat and singing to the pixie tune.

"He had blue eyes like you."

"Most lycans are blue-eyed."

She nods. "He also had a beard and lots of jewelry." She picks up the hem of my kilt. "And a kilt like this one, but red, not green."

"What was his name?" I ask.

She frowns and chews her lip. The movement makes me leak semen under the kilt. I might come on Rohan's deck.

"You know, I don't recall that he gave me his name."

"Lenox?" I ask.

Her eyes widen as recognition hits her, but still, it's almost as if she remembers me, but not quite. Either it's the booze, or the fairies messed with her somehow. I'll find out later. Right now, she's with me, and I'm going to play along. I've waited a lifetime to hold my mate, and I'm keeping her forever this time around.

Too bad she doesn't know that yet.

"Lenox sounds right." She traces a finger down my jaw. "You're better looking than him."

I shaved my beard, and she likes it better. I'll be shaving for the rest of my life.

"Oh yeah?" I run my nose down her cheek, jaw, and neck, where I inhale loudly. Oh yes, definitely mine. I want to bite her already, mark her slender neck.

A growl rips from my chest.

On my lap, she stiffens, and I take her hand and put it over my torso. I switch from growling to rumbling. I don't purr like a feline, though the rumbling, if done well, sounds as seductive as a feline purr.

My mate leans in closer and runs her hand through my hair.

Mmhm. *Pet me, baby. Pet yer wolf.*

From the corner of my eye, I see her doing something with the left hand that used to rest on my shoulder. I kiss her clavicle and trace my lips to her shoulder and catch the moment she slips a pinch of powder into my bottle. What the f..?

Gloriana bites my earlobe and growls at my ear.

I adjust my groin again, but no position is comfortable.

There's only one way to eliminate the pain. Short of taking her right here, nothing else will do. But I won't take her yet. I'm unsure of what's going on with her. She slipped powder into my drink.

Is she trying to make me sleep or kill me?

On the steps leading below the deck, Rohan clears his throat. I look over.

He shakes his head. "It's a stimulant."

"A what?"

He snorts, suppressing laughter. "A stimulant."

On my lap, Gloriana freezes, and when I look at her, she's blushing.

"You weren't supposed to know that," she says.

Gently, I pinch her chin. "What do you think I need a stimulant for?"

"Intercourse," she whispers.

Rohan laughs.

"Lass, what makes you think I need a stimulant?"

"Fleur said lycans can't get it up if it's not a full moon."

Fleur needs a male with a firm, twitchy palm. Like me. But I'm taken, so I say, "Fleur has no idea what she's talking about, and I'll prove it to you. Let's get out of here."

Rising with my mate in my arms, I head downstairs, then stop. I arrived on this ship full of lycan pirates, and since I didn't think I'd be shagging my mate this evening, I didn't arrange rooms fit for a shag.

"Find Fleur for me, would you?" I ask Rohan.

As if conjured, Fleur arrives. "Do you need assistance?"

The Summer Fae Court's hospitality is something the fairies take seriously, so when the princess asks if I need assistance, she means it. But the truth is, I will come to regret staying at the Summer Court for any length of time, not to mention the time I'll need to secure our transport back to lycan lands. Rohan is staying for the entire summer, so he won't be able to carry my mate and me back.

"I'll need accommodation," I say.

"You will have it."

"Tonight."

Fleur smiles sweetly, showing me a tiny bit of fang. She's up to no good. I just know it. "Gloriana is settled in a large and comfortable end suite. It can accommodate a pack of lycans for the night." She traces a claw over my chest. "A pack of lycans all at the same time. I'm sure you will find it adequate for you and your ego until we can accommodate the pair of you tomorrow."

"Fine." Gloriana's passed out drunk and snoring on my shoulder. "Take me to her rooms."

Fleur snaps her fingers, and a pair of royal guards in yellow coats escort us to the main portal that leads from the boat into the fairy court.

I hate traveling via portals. **Read the story HERE**

ALSO BY MILANA JACKS

Check my website for latest updates and connect with me via email **HERE!**

EXPLORE ALL STORIES IN THIS FANTASY WORLD

The Complete Savage Horde: Savage in the Touch, #1 : Heart, #2 : Need, #3

The Royal Obsession (Summer king)

Lycan Claimed Series:

1. Lycan and the Princess 2. Second Chance for the Lycan 3. A Prize for the Lycan Enemy

MORE BOOKS WITH TAKE-CHARGE POSSESSIVE HEROES

Read the Complete Horde Series:

#1 Alpha Breeds, #2 Alpha Bonds, #3 Alpha Knots, #4 Alpha Collects

The Complete Hordesmen Series:

Hunger #1, Terror #2, Sidone #3, Fever #4, Dreikx #5, The Blind Hordesman #6

Read the complete Tribes Series:

Marked #1, Stolen #2, Lured #3, Captured #4, Consumed #5, Arked #6

Read the complete Beast Mates Series:

#0 Virgin - FREEBIE, #1 Blind, #2 Wild,

#2.5 Goddess, FREE via my Mailing List,

#3 Sent, #3.5 Their, #4 Caught, #5 His, #6 Free.

Read the complete Dragon Brotherhood:

Rise #1, Burn #2, Storm #3, Fight, #4

Short stories in IADB World: Jake 1.5, Eddy #2.5

Read the complete Age of Angels series:

ABOUT THE AUTHOR

Milana Jacks grew up with tales of water fairies that seduced men, vampires that seduced women, and Babaroga who'd come to take her away if she didn't eat her bean soup. She writes sizzling fantasy romance with take charge heroes from her home on Earth she shares with Mate and their three little beasts.

• She entertains readers on her mailing list as they await for books in the series. If you want in, join other readers at http://www.milanajacks.com/newsletter/ •

Meet me at
www.milanajacks.com

.

Made in the USA
Middletown, DE
16 May 2024